Dancing with the Golden Bear

Also by Win Blevins

Stone Song
The Rock Child
RavenShadow
So Wild a Dream
Beauty for Ashes

Dancing with the
Golden Bear

WIN BLEVINS

A Tom Doherty Associates Book

New York

DANCING WITH THE GOLDEN BEAR

Copyright © 2005 by Win Blevins

The author is grateful for permission to reprint excerpts from Jedediah Smith Manuscript, Jennewein Western Library, Layne Library, Dakota Wesleyan University, Mitchell, South Dakota, and from Jedediah Strong Smith Papers, Missouri Historical Society, St. Louis, Missouri.

This book is printed on acid-free paper.

Edited by Dale Walker

Map by Mark Stein Studios

A Forge Book
Published by Tom Doherty Associates, LLC
175 Fifth Avenue
New York, NY 10010

www.tor.com

Forge® is a registered trademark of Tom Doherty Associates, LLC.

ISBN 0-765-30575-5
EAN 978-0-765-30575-6

First Edition: September 2005

Printed in the United States of America

0 9 8 7 6 5 4 3 2 1

To Meredith,
who taught me love

Acknowledgments

Thanks to Laurie Langland of the Layne Library for her help and to the Library for permission to quote from its manuscript of Jedediah Smith's journal. Thanks as well to the Missouri Historical Society, an extraordinary repository of records of the fur trade, for permission to quote from its manuscript of other parts of Jedediah's journal.

I'm grateful to a host of people for expert advice: Pam Blevins, Phil Hawley, Charlotte Hinger, Robert Hudson of the Kansas University Medical School, Dick James, and Craig Stinson.

My companions on this long journey into the past have been the Honorable Clyde Hall of the Fort Hall Reservation, novelist Richard Wheeler, and my editor, Dale Walker. I'm honored to walk with you.

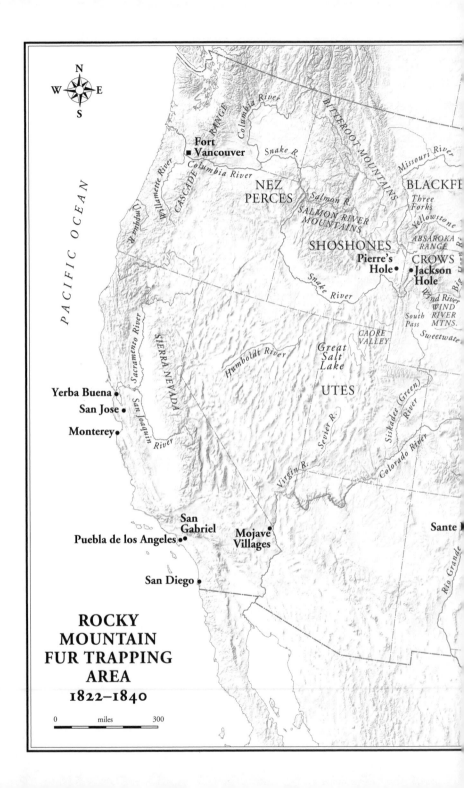

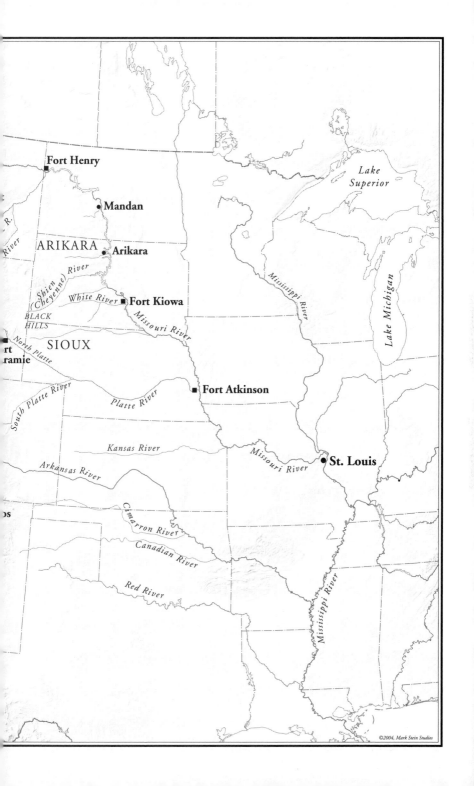

Fort Henry

• Mandan

ARIKARA • Arikara

Shien (Cheyenne) River

White River ■ **Fort Kiowa**

Missouri River

BLACK
HILLS

North Platte

SIOUX

rt
ramie

South Platte River

Platte River

■ **Fort Atkinson**

Kansas River

Missouri River

• **St. Louis**

Arkansas River

os

Cimarron River

Canadian River

Red River

Lake
Superior

Mississippi River

Lake Michigan

Mississippi River

©2004, Mark Stein Studios

Life is a golden bear. It's magnificent, it's beautiful, and it bites.

—*Hannibal McKye*

Life is not a journey to the grave with the intention of arriving safely in a pretty and well-preserved body, but rather to skid in broadside, thoroughly used-up, totally worn-out, and loudly proclaiming, "Wow! What a ride!"

—*Anonymous*

Part One

INTO THE UNKNOWN

One

We Los Dos

Captain Jedediah Smith sniffed the steam rising off his black coffee. Sam and Flat Dog passed the jug back and forth. Though Diah didn't drink, he was accustomed to being the only man who didn't.

Meadowlark touched her twenty-two-year-old husband's white-blond hair. He looked into her face, lit by the last embers of the fire. The eyes of the two honeymooners made promises. "Soon," he murmured. He handed Flat Dog the jug and said, "Kill it."

As though the whiskey had loosened his tongue, Jedediah said, "Sometimes I wonder what it all means."

"What?" Sam tossed back, grinning.

"Life."

"Means?" asked Flat Dog, hoisting the jug, also grinning.

"Yes."

"That's what I thought, Captain," said Sam. "Sometimes you're funny."

Jedediah gave him a peculiar look. "Funny?"

Flat Dog gurgled long on the whiskey. Meadowlark watched it run down her brother's neck. He lifted the jug high, and the last few drops plopped into his mouth. "There!" he said, and slammed the jug down, as though he'd had his say.

After the brigade left camp tomorrow, whiskey and coffee would be only memories until next summer and next rendezvous.

"Isn't it worth asking?" said Jedediah.

"My father taught me," Sam said, "that when a bird is on the wing, all that's on its mind is flying. And he does best to keep it that way."

Flat Dog slapped his brother-in-law on the back. "Coy sees it like that too." Coy was Sam's pet coyote, which lay as always at his feet.

"When we're about to head out," Diah said, "I get thoughtful."

Sam shrugged. "What's on my mind is, there's a new place to go, and my heart is big to see it."

"Where are we going?" asked Flat Dog.

The captain had told all his men that the brigade was headed south and west looking for new beaver country. But he'd told Sam and Meadowlark more.

"I think you know," Diah said.

"California," said Flat Dog.

"Don't spread it around," said Diah.

The Crow nodded. The word "California" hardly meant a thing to him. Adventure meant something. Whiskey did too.

"I want to see the ocean," said Meadowlark.

Sam grinned at her. His bride, who had spent her entire life in the Yellowstone country, was clear about that one thing. She wanted to go to the big-water-everywhere. Sam wondered what was between here, on the shore of a creek in the northern Rocky Mountains, and the Pacific shores. He remembered what Diah had said. When the mapmakers didn't know what was in a big empty space, they sometimes filled in, MONSTERS THERE BE HERE.

"California," said Jedediah.

Sam smiled, stood up, and offered Meadowlark a hand. "Bedtime," he said. Her eyes softened, and she took his hand.

"WE'LL CAMP HERE," said Jedediah.

The place looked good to Sam. It was in a bend of the river, a fair way below the Utah camp. Never a good idea to camp too close to Indians, who thought of horse-stealing as a sport. He would stake Paladin right by the tipi.

"Capitan!" cried Manuel. He was a trapper out of Taos, new to Jedediah's outfit. "This place . . . We go somewhere else. We must no camp here."

A score of men and their several women stopped dismounting and unloading. They gawked at the Mex who dared to tell the captain where to camp.

Jedediah looked at Manuel and around at his men, all waiting for orders. He studied the man's eyes. "What are you scared of?"

"Two years ago on this place, exact this place . . ." Manuel's face was loose with panic. He couldn't go on.

"Set up," the captain told the men.

Manuel's story didn't come out until the men had grouped into cook fires. He told it, at Diah's request, while Sam, Meadowlark, the captain, and others were sharing a supper of fresh deer tenderloin.

Two summers before, in 1824, Manuel had been trapping with Etienne Provost's brigade out of Taos. They held a parley with a village of Shoshones right where the Utah village was now.

The men knew that both Shoshones and Utes, who hated each other and fought at every chance, liked to camp and hunt here on the shores of Utah Lake.

"Bad Left Hand, Shoshone *capitan,* he ask all men, Indio and trapper, they should leave their weapons at a distance from the council lodge. His medicine, he say, it forbid that metal, it come near the sacred pipe."

Manuel watched his companions register this information. Setting down your rifle, your pistol, your butchering knife, even your patch knife, and any hidden knives, that would go hard. Sam thought, *I wouldn't put down my hair knife.* He had a blade disguised as an ornament holding back his long, white hair.

"Provost, he say yes, all right, do this. Trapper and Indio, we watch each other. Slowly. Slowly, we lay down guns, knives, tomahawks, all. Us Taos men, eighteen or nineteen, and maybe twenty-four, twenty-five Indio, we all set down weapons and go into council lodge. Everyone nervous.

"Then pipe is smoked," Manuel went on. "Probably there is a secret signal. Suddenly them Indio, they draw knives and tomahawks from under the blankets and the shirts and attack.

"A knife, it dive at *mi corazón,* my heart. I shoot out hand and knock it away maybe half. The knife, it bites me here." He tapped the point where his shoulder joined the neck. He bore a jagged scar. "Same time the *cuchillo,* knife, it bites me, BLAM, Indio who attacks me is knocked backward big, how you say, ass over teacups.

"*Mi corazón,* it jump. I see that Provost, he is a big man, very powerful and very quick, he toss one Indio straight over my head and onto the fire. Sparks fly. Indio, he scream.

"Provost, he grab tomahawk out of the burning hand. I grab hand of knife that bite me and twist fierce, seize knife—I slash wild, wild everywhere.

"All is, how you say, like whirlwind. Bodies, they spin. Men crash to ground. Screams cut at my ears.

"Provost, he kick one Indio in belly and knock him into two other men, red and white, behind. All go down.

"I leap on the back of Indio and sink knife deep into the belly.

"Provost, he holler, 'Get out! Get out!'

"I ride dead Indio like horse. He fall, I run. Last thing I see is Provo, he throw Indio into mob and sprint one step behind me.

"We two, we *los dos*, charge like bull through darkness, we hack knives at anyone get in the way.

"One hundred yards, maybe, we get to horses. The men we left to hold the horses, they have no idea of trouble.

"The four of us, we ride like hell."

According to the rest of Manuel's story, *los dos* and one more man escaped Bad Left Hand's trap. Fifteen of their comrades died in that council lodge.

"Me too die there for sure, *muerto*, but Provost he save *mi vida*, my life."

"That was then," said Jedediah.

"And those were Shoshones," said Sam. He'd always had bad luck with Shoshones.

Manuel gripped Sam's wrist and spoke urgently. The whites of his eyes flashed in the flickering firelight. "This terrible thing that happen, it still goes on here. Evil deed, it happen over and over, it keep happening always. The evil, it becomes a curse."

Jedediah let the words sit for a minute and said, "I don't put stock in curses."

Two

Parley

SAM'S THROAT BURNED like someone shoved a flaming stick down there. It always did when he was scared.

Nothing to do now but wait and watch.

The Utes and the trappers sat in a circle in the council lodge. The Ute chief, Conmarrowap, sat in the center, the place of the host. Captain Smith sat between the chief and Sam. Now Diah drew deep on the sacred pipe, offered the smoke to the earth and sky, and pretended to think lofty thoughts. Sam knew that Diah, a good Methodist, would offer no prayers he regarded as pagan.

That story Manuel told, Sam couldn't get it out of his mind. *Right on this spot.*

Now Sam looked at Conmarrowap, the chief, and then at the other gathered Utes, without meeting their gaze directly, the way you do with Indians, a sign of respect.

He fingered the ornament weapon in his hair. Its whiteness was a cause of teasing among the trappers, who called him towhead. Sam's friend Hannibal McKye, a Delaware Indian, had given him the ornament knife. It was polished walnut as thick as a finger and a little longer, decorated with circles painted in the colors of the four directions. Aside from keeping his hair back, it also slid apart at one of the circles and exposed a razor-sharp blade. Sam could put his hands on top of his head and surprise a captor with a slit throat.

Diah tapped Sam and handed him the pipe.

He accepted it properly, left hand on the bowl, right hand on the stem. Reverently, he drew the smoke in and offered it to earth and sky. He fanned some of it onto himself, asking its blessing. He smoked again. With each puff he prayed for the success of this parley, the success of the expedition, the well-being of his wife Meadowlark and her brother Flat Dog, and the health of all the men on the expedition.

Then he held the pipe up to the sky, touched the bowl to the earth, and handed it properly to Manuel.

Sam's throat burned again, hotter.

Manuel murmured, "I watch for sign, yell a warning."

Jedediah scowled at the words.

PARLEYING TOOK TIME, time, time, and there was no rushing it.

Diah asked Sam to be here because Sam had a gift for communicating with Indians, either in their own language or with signs.

The captain asked Manuel to be here because the clothing of the Utes showed that they traded with the Spaniards in Taos. But as it turned out, none of the Ute leaders spoke Spanish.

At length the time came for Sam to tell Conmarrowap and his colleagues what Jedediah wanted. Would the Utes please permit the trappers to travel and hunt in Ute country? In return, Jedediah would offer the Ute people many fine gifts. The trappers would offer more gifts, finer ones, every time a hunting party came to Ute country. This treaty was to last forever.

Manuel now unwrapped some blankets and laid out the gifts—three yards of red ribbon, ten awls, a razor, two knives, forty lead balls, some arrow points, and a half pound of tobacco. Jedediah would have liked to offer more, but he couldn't afford it.

At great length, after discussing it with his Big Bellies, men of experience, Conmarrowap agreed. The burn in Sam's throat eased a little. He breathed deep, in and out. The next subject was touchy. Would the Utes make peace with the Shoshones?

Conmarrowap frowned, and some of the Big Bellies grumbled. Young Utes had earned their war honors fighting the Shoshones since before the memories of the oldest men. The Utes had enjoyed stealing Shoshone women and Shoshone horses for just as long. Sam knew another truth: In some ways the Utes defined themselves as those who always fought Shoshones.

Jedediah told Sam to sign these words. "The Big Bellies of the Shoshones have promised to stop the fighting if you will also stop."

The Ute leaders still weren't sure.

"Stop just for a time," Jedediah said. "Soon I will return and meet with both peoples and help make peace between you."

Conmarrowap hesitated, pursed his mouth, and made the sign for yes.

Now Sam's throat ached again. This next item terrified him.

The captain said, "We want to buy the two Shoshone women who were recently brought into your village."

Slave women. For now they were forced to sleep with their captors and act as servants. Soon, probably, they would be tortured and killed.

Jedediah wanted to save their lives, and was willing to spend good money to do it.

Conmarrowap's face was unreadable. Sam looked around at the red faces, without appearing to look. "We need women," he signed. He felt inept, like he was stammering. The Ute faces were stony. Sam's legs were ready to jump and run.

Manuel pitched in, speaking and signing at once. "They will do the camp work, the skinning . . ."

"You want them for your blankets," said a Big Belly across the fire in English.

Hell, the bastards have understood everything we've said to each other.

Sam's gullet spasmed now, and he tasted hot bile.

"Shoshone women are not so good in the blankets, but . . ." This was the Big Belly on Manuel's left.

All the Big Bellies chuckled.

Conmarrowap said, "We know why men want women." In the corner of his eye, Sam saw the chief was grinning.

He took a deep breath in and out. "We will pay you well for them."

Some of the Ute leaders traded smiles.

Sam made an offer. The first counteroffer was accepted. As it turned out, this was the easy part of the deal.

Sam's gullet relaxed.

Then came the last part.

"What do you know of the country to the south and southwest?"

The Utes looked at Jedediah like he was loony.

"South and southwest? No one goes there."

"Are there beaver in that direction?"

"There's nothing at all."

"What about rivers that way?"

"No rivers. No nothing."

Now the English-speaking Big Belly spoke up. The words sounded like he was talking to children. "To the north and east is good country. Lots of water, lots of deer and elk. Sometimes even buffalo." The man smiled big.

"I hear," said Jedediah, "that there is a great river leading to the south and west." Sam signed the words.

Several of the Utes shrugged or gave disgusted looks.

One said, "That way you will have to eat the soles of your moccasins."

Another said, "You'll travel many days without water."

Another said, "To the south and west ten or fifteen sleeps maybe you come to the end of the world."

Jedediah opened his mouth to speak again, but Sam said quietly to him, "They're about to lose respect for us."

Jedediah nodded. He knew that was dangerous. Sam could almost feel Manuel panicking.

So Jedediah spoke words of thanks and said he would set out many, many items on his blankets to trade to the people tomorrow. If all this worked as Jedediah planned, the Utes would talk for years about when they made the treaty with the Americans.

Outside, Sam tapped his leg and Coy came. Then Sam, Diah, and Manuel walked quickly toward their own camp, Coy perking along. Finally Manuel couldn't hold it in any longer. "Which direction we goin'?"

Sam already knew.

Jedediah smiled dryly. "South and west."

And maybe eat our moccasin soles on the way.

Three

A Trackless Desert

THE BRIGADE OF trappers had started from the rendezvous above the Salt Lake in the middle of August. The new fur company of Smith, Jackson & Sublette divided its forces for the fall hunt, and Captain Jedediah Smith was assigned the southwest. The fur men had a lot of good country to trap, but the British were pressing in from the northwest, the Blackfeet blocked the way to the north, and the Spaniards were coming up from the south. New beaver to the southwest, that sounded good.

"My ass," said a lot of the men. They knew Captain Smith. Maybe he liked to trap a beaver and make a dollar as well as the next man, but he loved one thing even more—seeing new landscape. During four years in the mountains he'd led men in every imaginable direction, a migratory bird covering miles, but without the ease. Searching for beaver, he always said. But the men watched the way his face looked when he topped a divide and gazed into a landscape no white man had seen before, and they saw rapture. Some called it obsession.

They also watched the way he spent his evenings. He didn't trade stories with the men around the fire, nor tipple with them, nor court Indian women. Always he sat off by himself, sometimes reading his Bible but most often making careful drawings of whatever hills and rivers he'd seen that day. It seemed like he cared for a book or a map more than his fellow human beings. And they concluded that this strange man fancied the color of a new lake and the shape of a new hill the same as they fancied the curve of a woman's thigh.

Yet they would follow him. He was the man, new to the mountains, who traveled alone three hundred miles past hostile Missouri River Indians to take a message to General Ashley. He was the man who got his head caught in a griz's mouth, came away a mass of blood, and coolly gave instructions for sewing his own ear back on. Most of all, he was the man who, late every afternoon, when the day's travel was done and the men felt beat to a pulp, rode or walked several more miles, to the top of the nearest big hill, to take a look at the country ahead. He was the toughest, most capable man any of them knew.

The trappers didn't know where Jedediah was heading. But they put adventure ahead of trapping and signed on.

Which got them into this pickle.

It was a mongrel brigade, and polyglot. As the couple of dozen traipsed along the desert far below the Great Salt Lake on a typical September day, they were strung out, plodding along on their mounts. Captain Smith rode in front with a distinctive expression, still as a waiting raptor.

This was a ragtag string of rough-looking men dressed in hides, and three women. The men led packhorses, and the women led a horse or mule with a pony drag behind. The packhorses bore the belongings of the fur company, items to give or trade to Indians, pay for passage through the country, or information, or guide services, or horses, or whatever else the outfit might need. It wasn't much. A better-outfitted brigade would have carried English blankets instead of American, kettles, wool cloth, cotton cloth, and all sorts of foofaraw for the squaws, from bells to vermilion. But this was a new company, and prosperity only a hope.

Trappers packed, Indians dragged. The drags, two poles with hide strung between, carried the possessions of the squaw—a buffalo-hide tipi, covers for sleeping, gear for cooking and sewing, and so on. These were her belongings, and if you lost the woman, you lost your house, your blankets, and your cooking and eating utensils.

Three of the men had wives, and slept in luxury in tipis.

Aside from Diah there were the other white-man hunters, including a Virginian who could read and so was the clerk; Americans from Pennsylvania, Kentucky, Indiana, Missouri, Ohio, and even New York; two Scots, a Frenchman, a German, and an Irishman; two French-Canadians, meaning men of mixed blood, red and white; a Mexican; three Indian men, a Crow, a Nipisang, and an Umpqua who was a slave; and a black slave named John. Around the fires at night, if you were sharp-eared, you could hear a new language being born. Trapper talk was backwoods English spiced with French, Spanish, and the words of several tribes. It was natural to them, a jumble and a tickle to outsiders.

None of these trappers thought much about the mixture of colors, languages, and nationalities. It was the way they did things.

To Salt Lake and on to Utah Lake the going was easy, well-known country with plenty of water and plenty of game, even if it was elk and deer instead of buffalo. They dried seven hundred weight of buffalo meat to bring along, and didn't touch it that first week.

And then the Utes told them they were headed into disaster.

The men talked about it that night around the cook fires. What was the captain's plan? Some guessed he'd hunt out the Siskadee, a river they knew well, and follow it south and west. Some guessed he'd stick to mountain country, where beaver peltries could be taken, what the men called "plews."

At their own fire in front of their tipi, where Flat Dog and Gideon Poorboy shared supper, Sam murmured, "It's a starving country ahead." He mentioned those moccasin soles. Then he threw some flesh to Coy, wondering how long they'd be able to spare meat for his coyote.

Two days later, after crossing a big divide, Jedediah turned the outfit southwest into as desolate a territory as any man of them had seen, dry, dust-colored country dotted by hills and mesas, the kind of land that makes you nod off in the noonday sun, and the horses hang their heads low.

They plodded and plodded and crossed another divide into a kind of world they'd never seen. Here was red rock in every direction, a gigantic, all-encompassing circle of pink-orange-red sandstone, with patches of dust and cactus and sprigs of grass running like streams between the immense stone monuments. But water? No sign of it. They rode along the dirt trails through the red rock, past weird shapes arising like hoodoos, alongside the sandstone that, strangely, had whorls in it, as though it was once butter but now hardened into eerie forms that hinted of . . . They dared not think. They rode, and camped dry several nights. Soon they were leading their mounts, knowing that little grass and little water meant dying horses. Sam was very protective of his saddle mount, Paladin.

On they walked. Only Gideon rode. He had one wooden leg from the knee down and couldn't peg well enough to keep up.

Conversation passed the time. "Armies march on full bellies," said John. "What we marching on?"

"Faith," said Robert Evans, a wisp of an Irishman.

Coy yipped, as though making a comment.

White teeth made a show in John's dark face. "What's faith?"

Evans looked sideways at John. The Irishman bore a face that told a tale, a love of a drink, a laugh, and a jaunty tune. Sam supposed that, despite his size, his nose had gotten crooked in barroom brawls.

"I leave faith to the priests," Evans said, "and certain American captains."

John laughed, and Gideon joined him heartily.

"Mystic prophets all," said Gideon.

Sam looked at Coy, thinking the captain often did come back from his scouting trips looking like he carried a secret, something hidden from ordinary men.

"Way I heard it," said John, "them prophets went out in the desert and thirsted and not all of them come back."

John turned to Sam. "Do you have faith?" Though he worked as willingly as any man, John talked a lot of sass.

"I do," said Sam.

"You one of them as admires the cap'n so much you'd follow him into hell on a one-way trip?"

"I guess I am."

"This beaver is the same," said Gideon.

"I like a bit of madness myself," said Evans.

Coy yodeled out a long call, or plaint. Sam loved his companion's eloquent howls, but their meaning was a mystery.

He stopped and poured a little water into his beaver hat for his pet.

THAT NIGHT THINGS changed. The brigade had been eating the flesh of horses and mules as they happened to give out. Now Diah gave the order to kill a horse, the weakest-looking one, for its flesh.

"That one wasn't gonna make it anyway," said Sam.

Coy whimpered at him, and Sam heard the forlornness in his own voice.

The rest of the men were too tired to talk. They caught the horse's blood in their hats and drank it.

Only John the slave seemed to have energy for conversation. He sat with Sam, Meadowlark, Flat Dog, and Gideon, who gathered together every night, right in front of the tipi Meadowlark put up for herself and her husband.

"What kind of name is Gideon?" asked John.

"Biblical," said Gideon. "Israelite. Means 'mighty warrior.'" Gideon looked at his peg leg, and Sam knew what he was thinking. He took off the peg and started carving it. He was making an intricate pattern of leaves and tendrils, and showing a real talent for it.

"I don't like my name," said the black man. "John. Every half ass be named John."

"Any man can earn a name," said Flat Dog. "So it is among Crow people."

Sam thought, *Or maybe a name chooses you.* That's the way he felt about his Crow name, Joins with Buffalo.

"I wish I had yours," John said. "Sam is a good-sounding name."

"We don't need two Sams in camp," put in Meadowlark.

"We could call you Black Sam," said Flat Dog.

"I'm not black," said John. "I'm purple."

Everyone looked at his face more closely. He was the color of an eggplant.

"The name I'd choose would be the one my grandpa had," said John. "Sumner. I like that one. Don't know what it means, but . . ."

"Captain," Sam called to Jedediah over at the next campfire. "The name Sumner—you know what it means?"

"'One who summons,'" said Jedediah.

John got a merry look. "Does that mean like a butler," asked John, "or like the angel who calls the roll at the Last Judgment?"

"Whatever you want," said Flat Dog.

"I'm the angel," said John, grinning.

"All right, Sumner," said Sam, "that's you."

"Listen here," said Gideon. "We're your friends, and we expect you to get us through zem pearly gates."

THINGS SPARKED UP. The outfit came to a handsome river, chest deep and sixty or seventy yards wide. It even had beaver sign. Diah called it Ashley's River, in honor of his former business partner, the man who had boosted the mountain fur trade into something important.

As they moved up the river, trapping on the way, they were struck by how shy the Indians were. Each family, when the strangers approached, lit a brush fire as a signal to neighbors, packed their belongings into baskets worn on their backs with a line around the forehead, and fled. Though Jedediah wanted to give them presents, he was unable to get close.

They also found that game was very scarce. They saw nothing but a lot of black-tailed hares and a very few distant antelope. The last straw was that the beaver seemed fewer than the sign. They left the river in favor of a creek heading up in the west. One look from the divide above the creek told the story: a bigger, emptier, drier country.

More dry camps. More horses killed or dying. The men had started with twenty-eight company animals, now were down to twenty. The free trappers, not bound to the company, had lost two of their eight. Now everyone missed the red-rock country. This piece of land was bland, the flats the color of a window unwashed for too long, the hills the color of cedars that rolled away endlessly, or of ocher outcroppings. Both dust-colored flats and cedar-green hills stretched away to infinity.

Sam watched Paladin carefully. He checked her hoofs at the end of each day's march and staked her on the thickest grass they could find. Some evenings, to keep her in training, he put her through her special maneuvers. Sam had taught her with the help of his Delaware friend Hannibal; he had once worked liberty horses in a circus. Liberty horses performed without riders, responding to hand and voice signals. Sam thought a demonstration like that would do a lot to impress Indians, and maybe save his life in a pinch.

This evening Paladin obeyed Sam's hand signals, prancing to the left or right, circling, curveting, or rearing. She came to his whistle. And Coy rode her. Sam was working on getting the pup to do somersaults on her back.

Now came the part that always drew an audience. He himself stood on Paladin's back, and the mare walked slowly in a circle. Sam was mastering keeping his balance for the walk.

His friends gathered around and had some fun.

"Get!" Gideon shouted.

Paladin ignored him. Sam thought it was good training for her, making sure she responded only to his voice.

"Run, you bugger," Evans shouted.

When Paladin passed close, Sumner gave the cluck that made most horses go to a faster gait.

At first some of these tricks had worked, but now Paladin ignored them all.

Flat Dog and Meadowlark watched in silence and admiration. Crows were great horsemen, but they had never seen any man, except Sam's friend Hannibal, ride a horse standing up.

AFTER DAYS OF worry and suffering the brigade came on another river, this one headed south through a canyon. Either Jedediah was seeing something with that glass of his when he walked up every night to scout, or he was witching their way along. This stream they called Lost River, because it kept disappearing in its own sandy bed, and then seeping up farther down the canyon. It didn't inspire faith, the Lost River, so they abandoned it for some rocky hills and then another valley running south, a parched valley.

Now the whole country was red again, and it seemed to Sam they were descending into a netherworld, dangerous but lovely to the eye, a world of rocks in purple and yellow and a bouquet of reds variable, rich, and delightful. None of this, however, hinted of water. For the first time Sam could remember Coy lost his bounce, and poked along head down, discouraged.

The question on everyone's mind was whether they would starve to death or thirst to death.

They were too exhausted to speak, except, occasionally, of beaver.

"We'll find beaver," said Sam.

"Don't think so," growled Gobel. The blacksmith stretched his enormous arms. He was the size of man you wanted on your side in a fight.

They looked at each other around the fire, the young Sam, his Crow bride, her brother and his best friend, the slave, the blacksmith. The fears and the dreads in every pair of eyes were different. But none flickered with hope.

A tune jinked up. Sam turned in delight and surprise.

Gideon played a slow, dreamy ballad, "Scarborough Fair," one that caressed every man's melancholy.

Then he gave Sam a look and jumped into another song. Cued, Sam sang the words:

The water is wide, I cannot cross over
And neither have I wings to fly
Build me a boat that can carry two
And both shall row my true love and I.

Everyone laughed at the water joke. Now the men from the other two fires gathered around, and even the Indian women and the children.

Meadowlark joined Sam in the part she liked.

O waly waly up the bank
And waly waly down the braes
And waly waly by yon burn side
Where me and my love were wont to gae.

Now Evans got out his Irish tin whistle and was ready to go. Gideon grinned broad and slipped into what he knew everyone wanted, a tune to dance to. It was a hop jig. Sam didn't remember the name of this one, but it was a three-beat jig instead of a two-beat, danced with a stiff upper body and feet very nimble and twice as quick. He and Meadowlark had learned it thoroughly back at rendezvous, and they led the way now. Others danced and fell all over themselves and had a grand time.

Evans was as deft with the tune as Gideon, and led the way to a second time through at an even quicker pace. The high, spiky pipings inspired everyone's feet. Evans had a way with the instrument, ornamenting here, bending a note there, to set the blood afire.

Sam noticed that one of the Shoshone women, Spark, was dancing in front of Gideon, directly to Gideon, as if they were a couple. Gideon's peg leg was bouncing up and down as fast as his bow, and his eyes locked with hers.

A new "marriage" is coming into camp, thought Sam, happy for his friend. After the amputation, Gideon had drowned himself in grief. Though Gobel had smithed a socket onto Gideon's stirrup, a place for the peg to fit, Gideon had trouble riding fast. "Injuns get on us," he said, "I'm a gone beaver." Only his music seemed to perk him up. Sometimes, in good spirits, he would carve on his peg.

The tune ended. Gideon drew his bow for one more song, but at that moment Jedediah materialized out of the darkness and stood among them half real. He'd been up the nearest hill again, looking ahead with his spyglass.

"Greetings, Cap'n," said Gideon.

"Greetings, dreamer," someone said at the other fire. The name was mostly a joke.

"I think I see a river," he said. "Maybe twenty miles."

Eyes regarded him, but tongues were silent.

Quickly, Gideon and Evans launched into a rousing version of "What Shall We Do with a Drunken Sailor," an old stamp-and-go sea chanty that set the feet to moving.

Then Evans made a proposition. "I have a new song I've been doodling on, a storytelling song about you, Captain Smith. Would you care to hear a bit of it?"

"Damn right!" and "Aye" rang out around the fire. Evans said, " 'Tis called 'The Never-Ending Tale of Jedediah Smith.' "

We set out from Salt Lake, not knowing the track
Whites, Spanyards and Injuns, and even a black
Our captain was Diah, a man of great vision
Our dream Californy, and beaver our mission.

"Now comes the chorus," cried Evans.

Captain Smith was a wayfarin' man
A wanderin' man was he
He led us 'cross the desert sands
And on to the sweet blue sea.

All the men chuckled at this, including Jedediah. Though he wouldn't say openly they were headed for California, all believed it.

We rode through the deserts, our throats were so dry
If we didn't find water, we surely would die
The captain saw a river, our hearts came down thud
The river was dry, and we got to drink mud.

The men liked that.

Now Evans played a bouncing version of the chorus on his pipe, with lots of florid ornamentation.

"The way the song goes," he explained, "you have a verse, a chorus, then another verse, and the pattern starts again—verse, chorus, verse, with an instrumental solo here and there. But this is as far as I've got."

"It shines!" called several men in the circle.

"So here is my idea." He looked merrily about. "Let's all do it together. Come up with the next verse, I mean, and then later on another and another."

"Every verse more suffering than the last?" said someone.

"Is this a tragedy?" queried another.

Still, they all pitched in, and that very evening they came up with one more verse.

We rode through a salt plain, not a creature could live
The captain saw a village, said the Injuns might give
Our stomachs were aching—we smiled and said "Please"
Our tongues were surprised when they fed us on fleas.

This wasn't quite accurate. Those Indians, Paiutes, had offered the trappers bugs, but not specifically fleas. Nevertheless, the verse got a big laugh—everyone loved it. Evans said "fleas" was poetic license.

LATE THAT NIGHT came a scratch on the door flap of Sam and Meadowlark's tipi. It was Jedediah. He didn't want to come in, just wanted to give Sam the news. Robeseau and the Nipisang were leaving the outfit. They wanted to go east, seeking better beaver prospects. Being free trappers, not hired company men, they had the right. Their wives, children, and horses would go with them, and the brigade would be that much weaker.

When Diah left, Sam looked at Meadowlark in the soft glow of the coals. "He doesn't get discouraged," he said, and sat back down next to her.

She gave her husband a lopsided smile and said, "Sometimes I wish he did." She snuggled her face into his neck, so he couldn't see her eyes. He held her tight. His wife was plucky, plenty damn plucky. Not many Crow women would leave their families for any man, especially not a white man. Fewer yet would want to set out across unknown deserts to get a look at the ocean-everywhere.

"You said you have dreams about the ocean," said Sam. "Tell me about them."

"Better not to talk about it," she answered. He could feel her stiffen up.

He thought about what she'd said before. In her dreams she went into the water and descended deep, she'd said. There were strange and wondrous creatures down there.

But she didn't want to talk now. She'd been moody lately. Touchy and moody.

The next morning matters were worse. The men woke up to find that Manuel Eustevan had run off. He took with him a good deal of company property—one Shoshone slave woman, the Umpqua slave, a horse, a rifle, and some ammunition. Manuel was claiming the slave woman for his own blankets.

Sam wondered whether Manuel took some of the brigade's confidence with him. Half the men talked about whether Manuel would survive, and all thought on whether they would.

Sometimes, in the evenings of days like this, Evans and Gideon would play tunes, or the brigade would work together on another verse of "The Never-Ending Tale of Jedediah Smith." Tonight they were moping.

Sam, Gideon, and Flat Dog were at the seep getting what water they could. The water didn't flow. You pressed your horn or kettle against the grass and mud, and water oozed into it. Mud too.

Gideon raised his head and looked at the captain legging his way up the nearest hill. "Dreaming," he said.

"What?" asked Sam, though he'd heard clearly.

"He's dreaming, I think." Gideon said it comfortably; not much upset him.

"The Buenaventura," said Flat Dog, drawing the word out slow, like a tease.

"Or is it Californy?" The French-Canadian had his own way of talking. "It" came out "eet," "this" came out "zis," and so on.

They all looked at Jedediah. He'd get to the top before sundown, but he'd have to find his way down in the dark. Coy yipped lightly, as though calling the captain back, or urging him on. Sam scratched the little coyote's belly, and Coy rolled onto his back for more.

Sam stood up and looked at Diah's back again. He shook his head, then his shoulders. No sense to anything these days, but Diah was Diah, and Sam wouldn't criticize him.

When they had enough liquid, they walked downhill to their horses and watered them.

Sam rubbed Paladin down with water too. He admired her looks again, white body with a black cap around the ears, a black blaze on the chest, and black mane and tail. The Crows called this kind of pony a medicine hat. She was getting gaunt from this desert travel, and Sam was worried.

When the horses finished the water, the men walked back to camp. Sam could hardly watch Gideon peg along. Just three months ago Sam had taken his friend's leg off, with a knife.

The brigade spread itself along a dusty, cactus-spiked flat in three campfires set a little apart. Its men were grousing, no need to ask about what.

"Diah don't make sense," said Gobel. The blacksmith laid down words like rings of a hammer, solid and sure. He was a practical, earthy man, not one to let himself become entranced by figments of imagination. "This ain't no beaver country, and there ain't no prospect on south."

He looked Sam, Gideon, and Flat Dog in the eye, including them in his challenge.

They sat down with blank faces. Coy growled. He didn't take to Gobel.

"California," said Robert Evans with the music of his Irish ac-

cent. Evans and Gobel, the smallest and largest, liked to brawl—
they saw it as sport.

"The Buenaventura," said Sumner with a sly smile, making the
word slide like a note on a fiddle.

These two words had become a muse, a siren, a force.

Oh, the Buenaventura. They knew one big fact: In the middle of California was a huge harbor where a big river flowed in.
That knowledge gave rise to mists of speculation. The river was
the connection between the west side of the Rocky Mountains
and California. It would provide a basic route from the United
States to the decks of ships that would trade in India, China,
London, and Boston. It was what President Thomas Jefferson
had dreamed of, but Captains Lewis and Clark had failed to
find.

The beaver men of the Rocky Mountains damn well thought
they would find it. Any hand of them knew the Rockies far better
than all the Lewis and Clark men put together. And they had
marched every which direction looking for it. They had been clear
to Flathead country in the north, Taos in the south, and the plains
of the Snake River, where some had been reduced to eating
grasshoppers, in the west. Now they were trekking to the southwest, thinking they might find the Siskadee, or Green River, and
that might take them to California.

If some of them were thinking the Buenaventura was a mirage,
like the water they sometimes imagined in this miserable desert,
they didn't say so.

California was also a mirage, a dream. Just as the Buenaventura
was Jedediah's big dream, California was the heart's desire of his
men. The sailors who had visited the ports of Alta California said
the climate was spring and summer all year round, and a farmer
might make two or three crops a season. They said the breezes
were balmy, the snows never fell, the women were willing, the life
easy, lazy, and good.

But now that name was also a joke among the brigade's men.

California meant the country you walk toward forever and never find, a never-never land you sometimes glimpse shimmering in the desert, tantalizing, always just beyond reach.

As one they looked toward the captain on the hill. He stood on the top, one dark vertical line tinged with the blue of twilight. *Solitary, the way he likes to be,* thought Sam. They could not see the single black horizontal line that would be his looking glass, which might also be called his instrument of dream-seeing. He would glass until he saw a couple of trees, some bushes, or a bit of grass that spoke of a chance of water.

"He don't look for water," said Gobel. "He prays for it."

"Maybe," said John with a smile, "he need one somep'n-somep'n stronger than God to pray to."

No one laughed. They didn't live in some far past, or in the future either. Last night they'd camped dry. Tonight they had a little water, tomorrow they might not. It was that kind of country. It was where their captain had led them, maybe following his dreams. Their life was the captain's dreams.

Four

To the River

IN THE END it was the Siskadee that saved them. Or was it Jedediah's dream?

They knew the Siskadee from where it came out of the mountains far to the north, almost to Jackson's Hole, all the way down to Flaming Gorge, where Ashley had boated it and got into trouble. The Colorado, Ashley called it, but the ordinary mountain man still called it the Siskadee, the Crow word for "sage hen."

First off, that hint Jedediah saw in his spyglass had in fact turned out to be a river—the Adams, he named it, in honor of the current president of the United States, John Quincy Adams. It was a dubious find, though. The men had exhausted their supply of dried buffalo, saw no game, and had nothing at all to eat the first night. Toward the end of the second day, though, came a hope—Indians peeking at the camp.

Jedediah went out alone with iron arrowheads as gifts. Diah knew these Indians probably had never before seen white men, or even horses. After much coaxing, one brave fellow came forward, visibly quaking with fright. The Indian gave Jedediah a rabbit. Diah patted the man and spoke soothingly. Soon another ten or twelve came close, bearing ears of corn as gifts. Corn! When Diah gave them the metal arrowheads, they were so delighted they ran off to get more corn, and even some pumpkins.

Farmers! In the red-rock desert! The trappers could hardly believe their luck. That night Jedediah wrote in his journal:

> Indifferent as this may seem to him who never made his pillow of the sand of the plain, or him who would consider it a hardship to go without his dinner, yet to us weary and hungry in the solitary desert, it was a feast, a treat that made my party in their sudden hilarity and glee present a lively contrast to the moody desponding silence of the night before.

Three days of rest, the captain said—Sam could hardly believe it. He felt like a gopher trampled by a herd of horses, breaded with dust, and fried by the sun.

Now, in the evenings, when dark protected them, he and Meadowlark played in the river together. This was a custom Sam taught Meadowlark, for Crow men and women didn't bathe together, not even couples. Mostly these two sat in the water up to their chins and talked, or just looked at each other. They wiggled their toes against each other's toes in the muddy bottom, and sometimes joined in love in the warm river. Sam taught her to splash water in each other's faces, dunk each other, and clown around. She loved it.

Each morning they woke to the light of dawn glowing through the hides of the tipi and made love. They took their time, touched each other in many ways, and afterward warmed up last night's vegetable stew and ate it and talked for a long time.

After breakfast each day Sam jumped in the river by himself, soaking up the water through every pore. Then he got Paladin and led her withers deep. He thought, dry as she'd been, even soaking the liquid through the skin would be good for her.

Coy stood on the bank while the man and horse bathed. Wary of the water, unable to understand why his master played in it, Coy yipped and howled the whole time, raising a coyote complaint.

Maybe it was Coy who called Sumner down to the river. "Why you do this every morning?" the black man asked.

"I'm a Crow," said Sam uneasily.

"And I'm an Irishman." Sumner laughed, slipped off his clothes, splashed into the water, and asked, "You serious about being a Crow?"

"Yes." Sam explained that Crow men bathed in the river every day, even in the mountain winter.

"That don't make you a Crow."

"I carry the sacred pipe." Sumner would know more or less what that meant. "I gave a sun dance." This was touchy but important. "I got a vision. I have a Crow name."

"Big doin's, huh?"

Sam nodded.

"Ain't for me." Sumner snorted. "Guess if I was a Crow, I'd still be a slave."

"No man oughta be a slave."

Sumner shrugged. "With Cap'n Smith it ain't bad." Sam eyed Sumner sideways and guessed he was just saying what he thought he was supposed to say. True, his only duties were around camp, but that made it seem he was a boy instead of a man.

"What do you want to be?" asked Sam, looking at him quizzically.

"A thief."

"What?!"

"Every tribe we meet, I filch something. It's a little dangerous, but that's the fun. For sure I put something in my pocket. What you think I trade to the women to get fun in the willows?" Sumner gave Sam a look. "Cap'n Smith don't supply me nothing to get poontang. I get it with stuff I done stole."

Sam couldn't help laughing.

"White man looks at me, he sees an ignorant Nigger and a slave." Sumner cocked his head saucily. "I ain't gon' say much, but don't you think you know me. I reads and writes pretty good, and one day I will do it real good. I'm a damned sneak." He gave Sam a shrewd look. "You read and write?"

Sam shook his head no. That was a sore spot with Sam.

For the first time Sumner gave Sam a wide-open smile. "Maybe you best turn into a sneak."

On the way back to the tipi, Sam thought about what he'd said to Sumner—"I am a Crow." He knew that his wife thought so. To her Sam was a man whose proper name was Joins with Buffalo, a name given him properly by a medicine man. Always, when they were alone, they spoke the Crow language and she called him Joins with Buffalo. He hadn't smoked his pipe in too long, though. The pipe was power. The way things were going, he and the brigade could use some power.

This morning Flat Dog was sitting with Meadowlark and talking about this and that, as he did most mornings. Sometimes Sam worried about how much they expected. Flat Dog saw Sam Morgan as a Crow warrior, with a full list of duties attached. They had fought the enemy Sioux together. They had danced the sun dance together. They had suffered together. They belonged to the same warrior society, Kit Foxes.

Yes, the three were on a great adventure—they all wanted to see the ocean to the far west, especially Meadowlark. Ultimately, though, being a Crow meant responsibilities to the village, to the people. They all knew where they belonged, in the end. Only Sam had to remind himself.

He reminded himself every morning, I am a Crow. It was confusing. A white-skinned, towheaded Crow. A Welsh Crow. Confusing.

"What are you thinking about this time?"

Meadowlark liked to tease him that he spent too much time cogitating, instead of just being and doing.

"Confused about what I am."

"I know that one. Let's see, you're a mountain man, have all those hunting and traveling skills."

"Yes."

"You're a Crow. You have medicine."

"Yes."

"These are true, you know. You really are both. You're something special." She rubbed against him to hint at a woman's response to his being special.

"You also waste time thinking." She smiled up at him and stroked his face. The breakfast fire was out, and today they didn't have to travel. "Tell you what, I'll teach you who you are. You want to know? Come inside with me."

And for the next hour he was in the right place on Mother Earth.

Later, Meadowlark built another fire to reheat their vegetable stew. Sam watched her fondly. Strange—though they were almost never out of each other's sight, he didn't feel like they got enough time together. She said she didn't either. Finding water, getting a few mouthfuls to eat, plodding across the desert in the parching sun, taking care of their animals, putting the tipi up and taking it down—these daily tasks were exhausting. When they lay down at night, they barely had the energy for love, and usually their coupling was silent and brief. Their words of affection were few, their cup of feeling no longer brimful, as in the first weeks, but just barely enough to slake thirst.

Oh, those first six weeks, all of July, half of August. As they tramped slowly and painfully across the desert now, Sam put his mind back in those times at the rendezvous in Cache Valley and their honeymoon.

There he woke up amazed every morning, amazed that she was next to him. He had stolen her away back in the spring, and they had several dazzling days together, a magical time there in Ruby Hawk Valley. They made love triumphantly, tenderly, playfully. He repented of his one terrible sin in front of her, getting her brother killed, Blue Medicine Horse, who was also Sam's best friend. For this transgression, there in Ruby Hawk Valley, she forgave him. She even used his own Bible words—"I give unto you beauty for ashes, the oil of joy for your mourning, the garment of praise for your spirit of heaviness."

Those short days felt like a time lived in the way people in stories lived, the Bible stories, or the King Arthur stories his father used to tell from the old country. To Sam this kind of life was why he left Pennsylvania, why he merely paused in St. Louis, why he came as a new man to the Rocky Mountains. In that act, that adventuring forth, he felt himself an Adam, abandoning the old world and searching a new, undiscovered world for a home. He wanted to live every day of his life like that, living what he felt inside himself.

Then her relatives came with rifle, spear, and arrow and sundered him from Meadowlark by force.

This brutal fact was as real as his dream, more real. They brought him back as a prisoner to a hostile camp. He was forbidden to speak to her, even to make eye contact with her. At last, at her urging, he left the camp to rejoin his brigade—he acted like a white man again.

Then, like a miracle, she came to him. She ran away, abandoning all for the towheaded Welsh Crow.

After their wedding ceremony, those six weeks at rendezvous . . .

Now Sam had two new human beings in the galaxy of his life.

Meadowlark was his love mate, housemate, playmate, partner in every way. He'd never realized, back at home, how much his mother and sister left his life incomplete. And Flat Dog was his brother. Plus Coy and Paladin. That summed it up.

At first Sam was surprised. Now he couldn't believe how much Flat Dog felt like a real brother. For instance, they could talk about anything.

"I don't get it," Sam said as they rode along, dust spitting toward their faces with every plop of hoof. Coy trudged beside Sam, each step looking wearier than the last. He looked at his wife, two or three horse lengths ahead of them, leading her pony.

"She was shy, demure, soft-spoken, a perfect lady. Now she's . . ."

Flat Dog's face rearranged itself into a lopsided grin. It was a face that could only be described as skewed, put together crooked. The effect made everybody smile.

Sam waited.

"Because she turns out to be stubborn?"

Flat Dog looked like he wanted to hoot. "Because she's not shy anymore?"

Well, hell, the way she joked with the other women, it was, it was even ribald.

"She's not demure?"

She treated the other men like brothers, laughing and cutting up.

"Soft-spoken?"

Sam's wife was plenty loud enough to be heard and to make her wishes known. In her realm, domestic matters, her wishes were not reeds but the trunks of cottonwoods.

Her manner even changed toward Sam. All of a sudden she was full of hoots and hollers, and even outrageous pranks.

"Fact is, she ain't changed a bit," said Flat Dog. Sam tried to teach him proper English, which Sam had copied from his mother, but Flat Dog picked up everyone's speech. "She's just like when she was a kid."

Sam raised an eyebrow at him.

"When she was maybe eight, ten, twelve, she was the family clown. She even liked fart jokes."

"But she was ladylike with me. Red Roan too." Red Roan had been her other principal suitor, the chief's son.

"Teenage girls, they have to be careful. There are rules, especially in front of young men."

"Now I don't know what to expect."

"Expect our mother," said Flat Dog.

Needle. There was certainly nothing held back about Needle, or hesitant, or circumspect. In fact, Meadowlark's mother's tongue could probably light a fire.

Sam nodded.

"Well?"

"Well, I have a beautiful, sexy, high-spirited, outrageous, outspoken, and terrific wife."

Flat Dog gave him a big grin. "Demanding too."

AGAIN, A FEW days farther down this river, they came on more Indian farmers. This time the brigade was able to trade not only for corn and pumpkins but squash and watermelons. They also got big news. One day's journey downstream a big river flowed in from the northeast. Jedediah said coolly and confidently that it could only be the Siskadee. And the Indians reported beaver only a few more days downstream. Jedediah observed something that struck him as even more important:

> I saw on these Indians some blue yarn and a small piece or two of iron, from which I judged they had some intercourse with the Spanish provinces.

California!

No one knew where the Siskadee went. Lots of American and British seamen, though, had sailed the coast of the southern part of California, and no big river came to the Pacific there. So maybe the Siskadee turned south into Mexico. But California was close, the men could see that. They were missing the fall hunt, essentially, and had almost no prospect of beaver, but . . .

The captain wrote in his journal, justifying himself,

> I might as well go on as undertake to return. Some of my horses had given out and were left, and others were so poor as not to be able to carry a load. The prospect ahead was . . . that I might in this moderate climate trap all winter and also purchase some horses. These considerations induced me to abandon the idea of returning to the mountains until I should have gone somewhat further in exploring the secrets of this thus far unpromising country.

The next day, when they came on the Siskadee, every man in the brigade was sure they would winter in California.

Five

Native Hospitality

NOW THE MEN were grumbling in their two-month beards. They grumbled even while they rested by the stream for a couple of days where there was a little grass. They felt as gaunt as the horses looked.

As they walked on, though, the going improved. The river valley was wide flats or low, gravelly hills, easy to follow. Indians lived on small farms dotted here and there.

The men kept a wary eye. These Amuchabas, as they called themselves, appeared to be farmers, and seemed to eat vegetables far more often than meat. (Some of them spoke a little Spanish, and Abraham Laplant had some Spanish.) They professed to be friendly, and said their main settlements nestled along the river some thirty or forty miles ahead. But Indians you didn't know were still Indians you didn't know.

Diah moved the outfit downstream slowly, gently, saving the horses. And when he got to the first large settlement, the brigade was treated, he said in his journal, "with great kindness. Melons and roasted pumpkins were presented in great abundance."

The men relaxed, but they kept their weapons handy.

Here, finally, they got their first real rest since leaving rendezvous back in mid August, nearly two months ago. Gideon gave the Amuchaba village an English name—Camp of a Much a Music and Romance.

THAT EVENING THEY made a real camp, one to spend a couple of weeks in. In the early darkness they ate roasted squash, not any mountain man's favorite food, but still a treat for tongues half starved. Gideon got out his fiddle and struck up a tune. "Who feels like dancing?"

Some of the men were hoping to have some fun in the willows later with Amuchaba women, but everyone was exhausted. Dancing with another man didn't sound like fun.

So Evans proposed some more song-writing. Everyone entered into the spirit of the thing.

"I wish we was drunk," said Gobel.

"Then let's just decide to be drunk," cried Evans. "Every man, just make your mind a drunken sailor." With that he sallied forth, slurring his words. He began:

We set out from Salt Lake, not knowing the track
Whites, Spanyards and Injuns, and even a black

and went rollicking through the first verse and chorus, ending with the dream of all of them,

And on to the sweet blue sea.

"Our male chorus is not together," said Evans, "because we have forgot most of the words." He rehearsed the next verse with them, teaching them to use the rhymes "mud" and "thud" as aids to memory.

The captain saw a river, our hearts came down thud
The river was dry, and we got to drink mud.

As they went on, Sam heard Sumner tossing out some words he knew were wrong, just for fun, and because the captain was close enough to hear. "Captain Smith was a lecherous man, a philandering man was he."

Jedediah was having too much fun to frown at Sumner, though Sam knew he heard.

We rode through a salt plain, not a creature could live
The captain saw a village, said the Injuns might give
Our stomachs were aching—we smiled and said "Please"
Our tongues were surprised when they fed us on fleas.

Sumner was still proud of his rhyme "fleas."
When they came to the chorus—

Captain Smith was a wayfarin' man
A wanderin' man was he
He led us 'cross the desert sands
And on to the sweet blue sea.

—Sumner sang his own version again, but Sam couldn't get it all. He heard some rhymes, something like "Captain he all goosey 'cause he never get no pussy."

But now they were to the hard place. New lines were called for. Where would they go? Who was a poet?

"Something about the Good Book," Sumner cried out.

"That's a dandy idea," said Evans, and began tossing out rhymes for "book."

"Get 'no water' in there," said Sam.

"Nor beaver," said Gideon.

"Get 'skirt' in there," declared Sumner. "No skirt."

Everyone started calling out words and phrases, Evans madly combining them into lines. What they came up with was—

We was lost in that desert, no beaver, no creeks
Don't worry, says the captain, we'll find water next week
He climbed up a hilltop to get a good look
And studied his Bible—was there a map in the book?

Here Evans piped a solo.

We parleyed with Injuns, we traded tobacco
We took gals to the willows, and made canyons echo
And only the captain, with morals full girt
Missed out on the fun—never lifted a skirt.

The men loved it, and Jedediah laughed as loud as any.

MEADOWLARK JUST BLURTED it out one morning, in the dawn light, in the tipi. She seemed to have been waiting for Sam to wake up. When he opened his eyes and saw her looking at him, he started to kiss her.

She put a hand over his mouth and said in English, "We will have a baby."

Sam hooted. "Hot damn." He considered a moment and half hollered, "Glory be." These were favorite expressions of his father's.

She clapped her hand back over his mouth and held it there.

They giggled. She tickled him under the arms. In a few minutes they started trying to make another baby.

"LET'S MAKE AN impression on these Indians," said Jedediah.

Sam raised an eyebrow.

"Let's show off you and Paladin."

It was a good idea. No trapper was all-the-way comfortable about camping with these Amuchabas, and a little awe would help.

Jedediah, Sam, and Flat Dog built the ring from willow branches. "Fourteen strides across, forty-two feet," said Sam.

"Why?" asked Jedediah.

Sam shrugged. "All I know is, that's the way circus people run their horses."

Before the evening meal, while the light of the late autumn day still lasted, they got the trappers and the Amuchabas assembled.

Sam was confident. Paladin knew what it meant when he led her into the ring and stood in the center, facing her. Laplant explained in Spanish that Sam was going to give commands to the mare by hand, and she would obey.

At a lift of one hand Paladin trotted around the ring counterclockwise. Another gesture and she shifted to a canter. Then, at a signal, down to a walk.

In response to voice calls she did all three gaits in the opposite direction. By now the Amuchabas were getting involved, and they oohed and aahed.

Suddenly Sam flung his right hand straight up. Paladin stopped, and reared, and pawed at an imaginary attacker. The hand came down to his side, and Paladin walked to Sam and stood, head down. At a flick of the wrist she walked across the ring and stood facing him, head down.

Next Sam got the mare to repeat all these same exercises in response to whistles.

By now the Amuchabas were agog. Jedediah said softly to Sam, "They think it's magic."

Now Sam crossed the ring and mounted Paladin bareback. With his knees alone he guided her through figure eights in the ring. Then he took to the edge of the ring, put her to a full gallop, slid far to her side, and waved at the audience underneath the horse.

The mountain men roared with laughter. The Amuchabas fell silent in amazement.

As a crowning trick, he stood up on Paladin's back and rode her around the ring at a walk.

Sam spoke to Paladin, and she cantered around the ring. He maintained balance perfectly, rising and falling with her rump.

At a word she stopped. Sam swept his hat off and bowed to his audience. The trappers whistled and clapped. The Amuchabas looked on gape-mouthed.

Later Jedediah said, chuckling, "I think it worked."

THE BIG ROMANCE at this camp was Gideon's. He and the Shoshone slave woman, Spark, had taken to disappearing into the willows together. Now Spark made the arrangement formal, in her way. She built a hut in the manner of the Amuchabas, of limbs thatched with grass. She traded for enough squash and pumpkins to feast the whole brigade and prepared them in the style of the Amuchabas—she cut a plug in each one, pulled the seeds out, buried the whole fruits under coals, and baked them. She also put Gideon's blankets and possibles into her hut. No matter how briefly they used their first home, in public view, this was now a marriage.

As she worked, the big French-Canadian perched himself on a waist-high rock nearby and accompanied her with boisterous fiddling. His peg leg rapped out the beat on the rock.

"What an odd name, 'Spark.'" Sam sat down next to Gideon.

"In Shoshone it no mean spark like the fire," Gideon said. He wiggled an eyebrow. "But she is."

Sam hoped the woman could make a bonfire in Gideon's heart and loins. Sam had felt uneasy around Gideon for months now. He remembered every detail of his friend's knee, every vessel and ligament and piece of cartilage, things no human being should ever see. Sometimes he imagined his hands still felt sticky with the blood. His ears still echoed with Gideon's screams. Oddest of all, he could still feel the dead weight of his friend's lower leg when he, a pretend surgeon, separated it from the body. Discarding that leg was the most bizarre thing Sam had ever done.

Worse, he remembered Gideon's anger about losing his leg. After the surgery, the French-Canadian changed his mind again. Beforehand he'd said loudly, for a week or so, that he'd rather die of gangrene than be a cripple. Then, one evening, he bellowed for them to cut the cursed thing off. So with the help of their compadre James Clyman, Sam reluctantly, carefully, did exactly that. The next few weeks Gideon reverted to complaining that he'd rather be dead.

This bear man had been the most virile human being Sam had ever known. One of the most interesting too—son of a Cree mother and Jewish father, born near Lake Winnipeg, raised partly in Montreal; master of woodcraft, plains craft, and mountain craft; speaker of Cree, French, English, and Sioux (but not Spark's Shoshone). Gideon was so electric you couldn't even imagine him dead.

Seeing the big man withdraw into himself, sink into black depression, had been painful. Diah's permission to come on this trip, if he could sit a saddle, had not been an act of hiring a good hand but kindness to a one-legged man. Gideon was still suffering.

Sam sat beside Gideon on the rock and soaked up the gaiety of the music. *He seems happy only when he's fiddling or carving. And maybe when he makes love to Spark.*

Gideon had finished carving his peg and had taken to carving stray pieces of cottonwood he found on the bank of the river. Now he was cutting a piece into a big sunflower on a long, slender stem, a beautiful piece of work.

The rest of the camp-wide romance enveloped every man but Sam and Jedediah. The Amuchaba women wore very little and took advantage to the fullest, both with their own tribesmen and fur men. If they had husbands, these men must have been busy having their own fun. Some of the women showed a preference for the men of the lightest skin, but they basically welcomed all the newcomers lustily.

ALL OF THIS made Sam nervous. Part of it was that the Amuchaba women flaunted their interest in the fair, white-haired Sam. The rest of it was that the men cast their eyes on Meadowlark.

Right now everything worried him. He fretted about his wife. The baby was due in April, the way they figured it. They'd worked out how his white-man months turned into her Crow moons.

What marched right into his mind and took a seat was, *This half starving and going without water, it's bad for a woman with child.* He said that or a near equivalent a half-dozen times. The thought of the way they lived on the way down here, the camps without water, the days without food—none of that could be good for Meadowlark or the child growing inside her. Being always on the move, that was bad too. He expressed this bothersome thought to Meadowlark almost every day.

She always said, "Crow women have been having healthy babies in hungry times and on the road since before the memories of the grandmothers of the oldest women."

That didn't do Sam much good.

Flat Dog told him the same.

"She's moody," said Sam.

"Big surprise," said Flat Dog, grinning.

"Sometimes she's grumpy."

"Welcome to married life," said Flat Dog. His English had gotten too damn good.

To hell with it, Sam said to himself. Here they were on the banks of the Siskadee. Back the way they came was five or six weeks of hard travel. In front of them, across that bad-looking desert to the west, was more hard traveling to some mountains, he didn't know how many days, and then more traveling to the Spanish settlements. Or so the Indians said. He thought, *We're between the devil and the deep blue sea.*

"Crazy me," he said to her. "I wanted to go everywhere and see everything. I wanted to stand next to the ocean. You just wanted to be with me. Maybe I've got us into trouble."

"You forget, my love. The one who wanted to stand by the ocean was me. And wade in. And swim down."

HE WAS STEWING again one morning, and Meadowlark was next to him sleeping, when a scratch came at the door flap.

Sam put on his breechcloth before he pulled the flap aside. Jedediah. The captain waited wordlessly outside while Meadowlark got into her deer-hide dress. Then they sat by the fire and accepted the tea she brewed for them—an Amuchaba woman had shown her how to make it from local herbs.

Then to business: "I want to teach you to lead a brigade."

Something in Sam's heart quickened. Meadowlark's smile told Sam she was happy about it too.

"I don't read nor write."

Customarily, the second in command was the clerk, who kept the records for the brigade. He noted the name of each man who bought powder and lead, and how much; who took tobacco for trading or ribbon as a gift for a woman; who brought in how many beaver plews, and the like. In due time many *segundos* became leaders.

"Doesn't matter," said Jedediah. "We can find a man to keep

records for you. Why don't you walk around with me today and learn some things?"

"Yes." Sam looked Diah long in the eye. "Good. Fine."

As the day went on, it wasn't just ambition that kept Sam with Jedediah Smith. He discovered something curious—his heart was opening to Diah. Though they'd known each other three and a half years, and had been through hardship after hardship together, they'd never been close, not really.

In just four years Jedediah had gone from green hand to top man. He'd set himself apart from the others. Never a comrade, never really one of the fellows, he was a distant figure, a man to be respected, not befriended. Now Sam, he was something like a . . . father.

They spent the day gathering intelligence about the country. The Amuchabas seemed to have no chiefs, really, but a lot of men knew some of the surrounding territory, and several knew a lot. Some Indians from near the Spanish mission to the west had crossed the desert to become Amuchabas, as of course any sensible person would want to.

Sam and Diah poked through the settlement for these men. While they poked, Jedediah talked about responsibility. A brigade leader, he said, takes responsibility for the well-being of every man. He chooses the route. Going into new country, he never sky-lines the party, seldom blocks its vision, stays aware of where cover is, keeps a sharp eye against trouble that might await, watches for water and grass. The leader can never just relax and have a good time. Alertness—wariness—those are his stances, always.

He must work harder than any of his men. Late each afternoon, when everyone else is worn out, he must ride or walk up a nearby hill to scout the terrain for tomorrow. If any man gives out, the leader must go back for him. When there is danger, the leader must go out first to meet it. If Indians approach, for instance, it is the leader who must walk out to them with the offer of friendship. The leader must even, said Jedediah, set an example for the men in his moral character.

Sam started to smile at Diah's idea of moral character . . .

But the look on Diah's face stopped him cold. Sam didn't smile or take exception, even gently—he valued their bond. Then came a remark that stuck with Sam, not only the words but the faraway look in Jedediah's eyes when he said it. "A leader is like a father," he said, "even a little like Our Father. He cares for his sheep, and tends to them."

They walked on a few more steps. "A distant father, though. Have you heard of Mount Olympus?"

Sam shook his head no.

"In the Greek idea of the gods—a pagan idea—the chief god, Zeus, ruled from a great distance, from the summit of Mount Olympus. He meted out justice. When a human being sinned, Zeus hurled down a thunderbolt. From afar, you see.

"That's the model for a leader—just, but still willing to discipline, kind but distant."

Something from another time or place, unreadable, swam in Jedediah's eyes. Sam had no idea what it was. He held his tongue.

By the end of the day's work they'd confirmed that the Siskadee did not run from these villages in the direction of the Spanish settlements—it went south to an ocean. The settlements were to the west. Yes, that desert could be crossed, but it was dry, very dry, and you had to find certain springs or you would perish. There was one spring a day's travel to the west, easy to find, but the others . . .

Sam didn't tell Diah about Meadowlark's pregnancy. He couldn't.

Several informants said some tribal members who used to live near the mountains beyond the desert would know the way. And two young men from the Spanish mission could say exactly. They were down there by the river, or on the other side of that hill, or . . .

"We must talk to these Indians," said Jedediah. But they found none that day.

*   *   *

"I'm taking Paladin down to the river," Sam said.

Meadowlark nodded.

He led the mare through the willows to the muddy stream, much more muscular than it looked. When he and Meadowlark played in the river each evening, they carefully picked an eddy. Now Paladin stepped into some shallows to drink. Coy curled up and went to sleep. Sam sat on the bank and watched the brown current beyond as it curled, swirled, and powered downstream.

His mind was somewhere else, everywhere else. Meadowlark. Diah. His father. The child on the way. Meadowlark. The hardships ahead, and behind. The child . . .

Before he knew it, his memory, or maybe his spirit, had traveled back to his time with Lewis Morgan, his father, especially the last day they were together.

His dad was Sam's first teacher. Not teacher of the mill business. In the world's eyes Lew Morgan was a miller, and the founder of a village, Morgantown. To Sam his father was the bearer of an older knowledge, now imperiled, the legacy of Lew's own youth, an understanding of the woods, of the four-leggeds and the flying creatures and the crawlers and the rooted—how all came together to make Earth work.

Father and son had a place in the forest where they went, their own place, it felt like. They called it Eden, and pretended they were the first people into this garden. When Sam was a kid, his father let him give all the creatures names, even the trees and bushes and grasses. Later, bit by bit, in morning after morning stolen from milling, Sam learned the right names, what made each bush or tree what it was, how it reproduced its own kind, and how it gave something to the other creatures, like the deer that browsed on the leaves, the birds that fed on the seeds and berries. Day by day, this world became a home to Sam.

His father also taught him skills, how to build a fire with flint and steel, how to feed on those same berries and leaves, plus roots and stems, how to find animals that offered meat, and how to take one of those animals to nourish your own flesh. It felt to

Sam like the one kind of knowledge that truly mattered to a human being, and he could hardly believe that others seemed bored by it.

He mastered woodcraft, and he mastered the long rifle. Even now he carried the rifle he'd inherited from his father. He'd had a gunsmith add a brass plate to it, bearing his father's nickname, Ⴀhe Celt.

Lew Morgan died on Christmas Eve, on Sam's sixteenth birthday. They were together in their place, Eden. And his father . . .

Coy's head came up, and he growled a little.

Paladin munched on grasses a few feet away. The riverbank offered good grasses.

As Sam was getting to his feet, a body blasted into him. Off the bank he sailed. He landed on his back in the shallow water with an Indian on top of him.

A stout teenager with a shell necklace choked him. A skinny fellow had hold of Paladin's lead rope and was pulling her into the river. Sam's head went under.

Coy barked and bit Sam's attacker in the thigh.

The choking grip loosened. Sam rolled hard. The Indian went underneath him, water roiling against his body. Sam elbowed him in the face and jerked away.

Paladin was fighting her captor. *Good girl.*

Sam had a quick thought of the pistol in his belt. Instead he grabbed for his knife.

Coy ran at the stout Amuchaba, but the Indian kicked him half a dozen feet.

Now Stout was holding his own knife low, advancing. Sam thought of a nice little trick. With his free left hand he slipped the hair ornament from his head.

Coy was whining and nuzzling his own ribs.

Paladin jerked away from Skinny and bolted into the river. Skinny splashed after her.

Sam made a thrust that wasn't his quickest. Stout blocked it hard, and Sam let his knife spin out into the river.

He backed off fast. Stout charged, but the foot-deep water slowed him down. Sam spun to one side and flicked his hand at the wrist that held Stout's blade.

A lovely line of red welled up, and blood weaved its way around the wrist.

Stout looked stupefied.

With a malicious grin, Sam held the small blade so the Indian could see it.

Stout was furious. He charged again, wildly.

Sam hacked a stiff hand at the knife arm. The weakened hand dropped the knife into the river.

Both men stood amazed for an instant.

Coy recovered and ran hard at Stout.

The Indian ran like hell toward the current. When he got there, he swam after Skinny and Paladin.

The mare was being swept downstream by the current. She whinnied in panic.

It's not me they want, it's her.

He bounded onto the bank and grabbed The Celt. As he leveled the rifle, he realized, *I got dunked, and both my powder horns went under. Wet powder.*

He couldn't abandon Paladin. He couldn't swim off and leave The Celt.

He got an idea.

He started running downstream on the bank, hollering like hell. "Help! Help! Help!" Coy followed, barking.

The current was taking Paladin away fast. That was one powerful river.

"Help! Help!"

Paladin was swimming toward the other bank.

He felt a spasm of fear. *Am I going to lose Paladin?*

He got downstream of the mare and the swimming Indians.

"What's the matter? What's the matter?"

It was the giant Gobel, with Sumner on his heels.

"They're stealing Paladin! Keep this!" He thrust The Celt at Sumner and set his pistol down.

Here the riverbank was high. Sam looked at the water and hoped it was deep. "Grab Coy and don't let him come." Then Sam made a clean dive into the water. Gobel cannonballed after him.

Wild, the current was wild. It slapped, it sucked, it bounced you, it tumbled you. Sam couldn't see over the waves. He was still downstream of the swimming mare and Indians, but he had a lot of current to cross to catch them.

And, *oh, goddamnit,* there was . . .

The current divided down below, on both sides of a cottonwood washed onto a shallow place.

Sam swam like hell for it. Either he'd get washed onto the tree, or sucked down and held against its branches, or the water would be shallow and he could stand up.

Gobel powered ahead of him. What was he doing?

Sam angled higher against the current, to give himself a better chance to get onto the tree. If he could get that far. *This damn current is killing my arms . . .*

Ten more strokes. Seven more strokes. His arms were failing. Five more strokes.

Big hands seized him, and Gobel stood him up.

Sam stumbled toward the dead tree trunk and heaved himself on top of it.

Paladin was maybe fifty yards above the tree, on the far side. At least she wasn't going to wash into it. Skinny was hanging on to her tail.

Sam whistled.

Paladin kept swimming toward the far bank.

Sam gave an earsplitting whistle.

The mare looked around.

Sam jumped up and down and waved.

She hesitated.

He whistled a third time.

She threw her head up and looked around crazily. Then she turned and swam hard toward the tree, towing Skinny.

Stout crashed into the upstream end of the tree, where the roots were, and disappeared below the surface.

Gobel ran forward, clambered along the roots, and groped downward. He saw a hand flailing above the water a couple of feet over. He flopped to the side and grabbed the bloody wrist. The other hand popped out and gripped Gobel's wrist. With a loud groan, and with agonizing slowness, Gobel heaved Stout half clear of the water.

Sam helped Gobel haul Stout all the way onto the roots.

Then he saw that Paladin was wading instead of swimming. He ran along the log and splashed out to her.

Skinny dropped Paladin's tail, stood up in the water, and hung his head.

Shots sounded from the east bank. Two bursts of black smoke spewed into the sky. Half the brigade waved at Sam and Gobel. Sam thought he could hear them cheering.

Scores of Amuchabas stood on the bank, silent.

THE TWO TEENAGE boys were properly hangdog about what they had done. Though Sam couldn't understand the words, their parents upbraided them loudly about it. His guess, though, was that their fathers would have slapped them on the back if they'd succeeded.

After the tongue-lashing, the boys disappeared into the desert.

That night the boys' families gave a big feast for the brigade. They made Sam and Gobel gifts of obsidian knives with beautifully carved bone handles. Sam was pleased. No blade was as sharp as obsidian.

As they walked back toward the trapper camp, Jedediah said, "I'd still keep an eye on that horse."

"Damn straight," said Sam.

They never saw Stout or Skinny again.

*   *   *

"ONE SPRING FOR every camp, people say." Sam was having a last drink of river water before bed. "It will be a tough trip. I'd bet one spring will be dry." Sam swigged deep from the horn. "They say ten camps, but a lot can go wrong." His face modeled worry.

"Oh, you men," Meadowlark said. She was sewing new moccasins.

He slipped into their robes. She set down her work and followed him.

The next morning, while the men gorged themselves on leftovers from the feast and started scouting for available women, Sam and Jedediah worked. Despite not being chiefs, some Amuchabas were more important than others, and they had more horses and more women. Curiously, they were uninterested in trading their horses for all the plunder in Jedediah's packs—blankets, tobacco, knives, even the odd musket didn't interest them, not compared to their horses. So the day's work came to this: Jedediah traded three of his poorer mounts for two that were in good shape.

On another day they traded for lots of the squash, pumpkins, melons, corn, and some of the bread the Indians ground and baked from the oversized beans of the honey locust. They found two of the Indians from the other side of the desert, and one from the mission, and got good directions to the first spring to the west. Ten or twelve sleeps to the mountains, these men agreed, and only one sleep beyond the mountains to a mission of the Spanish friars, with lots of horses and cattle and every kind of food imaginable— the Spaniards had abundance upon abundance, the Indians said.

But the Indians didn't want to go near the mission. Sumner had an opinion about that. "Probably them friars treats 'em like niggers," he said.

On other days Sam and Diah just talked in front of Sam's lodge. As Meadowlark came and went, busy sewing or making food, Sam tried to find out Jedediah's long-term plans. The captain said he intended to cross the desert ahead to get into a better country. Beyond that, he didn't know. Probably he would find mountains that would support hunters, and go north until they found beaver.

"I don't know where that might be."

So Sam forced it out. "Meadowlark's carrying a baby."

She made a stern face at him.

"How long?"

"Due in April," said Sam.

"Don't talk about me like I am not here," she told her husband. Diah waited.

"This whole thing scares me," Sam admitted.

Meadowlark made a wry face at the captain.

"Maybe she and I could stay here," Sam said, "with the Amuchabas."

"You know better than that," Diah said.

"Listen, both of you." Though she said "both of you," she was glaring right into her husband's face. "I want to see the ocean. I told you to start with, I came on this trip because I want to see the ocean. It's right over there"—she pointed west across the bleakest country Sam had ever seen—"and we're going."

AFTER TWO WEEKS with the Amuchabas the brigade made a raft, ferried men, animals, and equipment across the river in two trips, and started for California.

The first day was bad. The soil was sand. The vegetation, only a single kind of bush with oily leaves, sparsely placed. The mountains, absolutely barren, mere piles of rock, sometimes rust-colored, sometimes black. They looked to Sam like burnt meat.

They found the first spring without trouble, but everyone was uneasy.

Paladin had gained some weight with the Amuchabas, but was still a little gaunt. She needed sharp watching.

Diah squatted down by the fire with Sam, Gideon, Flat Dog,

and Sumner. Meadowlark and Spark came and went like ghosts. "What do you think?" asked the captain.

"Ze horses, they be not strong enough for this," said Gideon. "Not yet."

Diah looked at Flat Dog, but the Crow only shrugged.

Sumner pitched in, "Only white people crazy enough to do this with gaunt horseflesh."

Diah only nodded and looked at Sam.

Sam said, "Looks bad. I don't like it. Fact is, we don't know where we're going."

They waited. Sam knew the captain had decided before he sat with them.

"In the morning we head back," Diah said, and rose. "Recruit the horses more and get some guides."

They returned, and while the men rested in the village, Sam found potential guides, teenagers who grew up near the Spanish settlements, and brought them to Diah. They talked a long time. The men were helpful with information, but didn't want to go.

"They're afraid," Sam told Diah. Meaning, *We ought to be afraid*.

"It isn't the desert that worries them," said Jedediah. "It's the Spaniards."

Sam had to admit this seemed true.

Jedediah reminded the teenagers that they would see their families. He offered to pay them handsomely.

After another quarter moon and a few days more, the brigade set out on the raft again, this time with guides.

Sam said to Meadowlark, "That desert looks nasty."

She answered with a grin, "We're going to see the ocean."

Six

Across the Desert

IT WAS NOVEMBER 10 in this epic year of 1826, Jedediah and his
clerk Rogers calculated, that the outfit launched across the burning sands.

Man and beast plodded, head down. The day was warm. Sam
wondered what it would have been like in the summer. Blistering,
damn sure. No place for anyone to be riding or walking. He forced
a smile in Meadowlark's direction. She kept things simple, which
was good. Their job was to walk across a stretch of desert to a

spring, and to lead a pony dragging poles. Meadowlark's mind didn't wander. It didn't fetch up goblins or run wild with pictures of crawling across these sands, throat drier than a corn husk. It stayed with what was real.

Flat Dog's eyes glazed over from time to time, but he made no complaints, not even the joking cracks of the other men. His only comment, ever, was, "Where we live, in Crow country, we got lots of beaver and plenty of water."

Sam patted Coy. He guessed that the coyote had long since decided his people were crazy. This country was almost too arid for mice to catch. But Coy licked his sore ribs and stuck with his partner Sam.

Paladin walked along smoothly. She had an easy, effortless walk. Maybe she was the strongest of them, but Sam never forgot that she couldn't speak if she started hurting.

Late that afternoon, Sam was walking alongside Diah in front and thinking that the first spring would be in sight soon. From behind, Gideon bellowed, "Where's Spark?"

Sam looked up and down the line and didn't see Gideon's new mate.

Jedediah stopped everyone. Sam, Flat Dog, and Gideon walked the length of the brigade. All but Gideon were afoot to save the animals. They stood in the full sun, heads down, minds on nothing but water and shade. No sign of Spark. With air-dried voices they called to the knolls and bushes in the near distance. No answer.

"Where was she?" asked Diah.

"Walking with Meadowlark," said Gideon. Since these two were the brigade's last women, they usually stayed together.

"She went out of sight to pee," Meadowlark told Diah.

"When?"

"In the last dry wash."

Jedediah's mouth twisted. "Almost an hour," he said.

Gideon roared madly, "Has anyone seen Spark?"

Sam remembered how James Clyman used to tell stories by Shakespeare in the winter lodge, and one was about old King Lear lost on the heath (whatever a heath was), yelling thunderously at God. Gideon was booming thunder now.

"I seen her," said Sumner. After a pause, the black man added, "Yesterday."

Gideon humphed.

"Going into the willows with Red Shirt."

Red Shirt was probably the richest man of the Amuchaba settlement, named for the wealth that enabled him to possess a garment made of cloth.

"The willows?" said Gideon pathetically.

"Red Shirt, he got a big itch," said Sumner. The slave kept his head down, but Sam saw he was working to keep twitches of smile off his face.

Gideon turned both of his horses around, the one he rode and the one he led. Without a word he started on the back trail.

The brigade waited. They'd walked all day, and the spring beckoned. Gideon would never reach the river by dark. Coy ducked into the shade of a horse and whined. Everyone but him knew where Spark was headed.

Flat Dog said, "Gideon knows what answer he's going to get."

"If Red Shirt even lets him talk to her," said Sumner.

"If he can even cross the river," said Sam. A tired horse would have a hard time in that current.

"If some Amuchaba doesn't decide a lone white man is a tempting target," said Diah.

Sam, Flat Dog, and Sumner looked at each other. It was a small joke among them how Diah and most of the others called the brigade "the white men," when half of them were people of color.

When Gideon was a couple of hundred yards out, Diah mounted and rode after him. The two of them talked for maybe ten minutes out there, as the sun slanted toward the horizon. Coy fidgeted and looked an appeal at Sam.

Eventually Gideon came back with Jedediah. Diah's face was set, stiff and grim. Gideon was reciting words, unfamiliar words, foreign words. He made them into an incantation, a prayer, and they were mournful, words freighted with tears.

After a few moments Sam recognized the prayer. Gideon called it the Kaddish. He had said the same Hebrew words when the Shoshones killed their friend Third Wing. Sam and Gideon put Third Wing in a tree, where his body might go undisturbed, except for the sun, wind, and rain, and Gideon recited the Kaddish.

"He's doing the prayer for the dead again," Sam said.

"I remember," Flat Dog answered, shaking his head. "For a woman of a few weeks."

"No," said Sam, "for his leg."

Diah said, "For his life."

THE SECOND DAY every head in the brigade was down, Coy's and Paladin's included. The only sounds as they marched were the plopping of hooves and the cries of Gideon. These were a mystery. Sometimes they sounded like songs, sometimes like chants, sometimes like prayers, sometimes like ravings. Sam couldn't tell if the language was his mother's Cree, his father's Hebrew, or the French both parents spoke. Not English, for sure. Sam did know the meaning—grief.

Maybe Coy understood the meaning better than Sam, for Gideon's cries seemed more animal than human.

The outfit edged around the southern rim of a big valley, a route marked here and there by the passage of other travelers, Indians who also crossed this wretched piece of land, for reasons Sam couldn't imagine. Before evening the guides brought them to a small spring with a little grass. Sam took Paladin to the water for only a few minutes at a time, but often.

Flat Dog got out his pipe, took it to Gideon, and offered the ceremony of smoking. Gideon knew the power of the pipe—he himself carried one. But now he waved his friend away. Flat Dog walked into the evening to smoke alone.

Sam thought, *Long time since I smoked my pipe.*

At dark Sam, Meadowlark, and everyone wrapped themselves in their blankets without word or expression. *If the route gives no more grass than this, Paladin will die,* he thought.

And Meadowlark? The baby? He told himself that people were tougher.

The third day was worse. For November, the weather was hot. They tramped west and a little north, keeping barren mountains on their left, to an even smaller spring, which in fact turned out to be more of a hole. After taking water to drink and cook with, Diah let Coy at it, and then the horses, and they drank the hole dry. There was no grass.

Gideon had lapsed from moaning eloquence into morose silence.

Sam lay awake worrying about Meadowlark and their child. Their child. It felt like a big idea to get his mind around, their child.

He stroked Coy's head idly. If all the men died, the coyote would survive. And would Paladin? Would her nose take her to some small spring or seep the guides didn't know about?

In the wee hours Meadowlark wore him out with love, and he finally slept.

The captain roused the outfit early the next morning so they could travel in the cool morning air. At midday they reached another small spring and a little grass. The spring ran so little water that the animals lapped it dry several times, but the liquid kept seeping in and at last they had their fill. Sam made sure Paladin got all she could drink, a little at a time.

When the men had drunk, Coy eyed the spring, panting, circled around it, put a paw in it, rolled in it, got a coat of mud, and ran off acting afraid of being caught. Everyone smiled, but they didn't have the energy to laugh. Sam was envious of the cooling mud.

The men spent the afternoon squeezed into spots of shade, separated from each other. Talk would have been good. Music would have been good. A communal pot would have felt nice. Instead the men were isolated in ones and twos, napping or staring out at the desert.

On the fourth day they started early again, paused briefly at some holes of brackish water, set off across a lake bed of pure white alkali. It looked like the perverse opposite of a lake. The water had evaporated into the air or sunk into the sands, leaving only the powder.

To everyone's surprise, under the rough alkaline grain on the surface, barely farther down than the press of a horse's hoof, was a layer of pure salt, fine and white enough for any table.

They crossed the dry lake, which was shaped like a fat thumb. "Maybe fifteen miles the long way," said Jedediah. Sam looked north, the long way, but the white, flat lake bed melted mysteriously into the gray mountains—he couldn't have said five miles or twenty-five. He reminded himself to pay more attention, look at Jedediah's maps, and gain this skill. But in the evenings, in fact, he was too tired to do anything but pant.

That night, on the far side of the dry lake, they found holes with salt water. When they dug other holes, the water was better. The men boiled their corn and beans, and animals nibbled at a few strands of green. Coy prowled, hunting for small rodents that looked like pack rats.

Sam looked around the country in irritable amazement. The dry lake was perfectly flat and perfectly innocent of vegetation. Around its edges, mountains cut jagged lines along the horizons, or plains angled into infinity. The mountains, alone of all Sam had seen, were jumbles of rock, ashen or cinnamon-colored. Nothing at all grew on them.

Sam remembered Tom Fitzpatrick telling how a scientist had shown him a spoonful of river water in a microscope once, which was like a telescope. Thousands upon thousands of small creatures, much too small for an unaided human eye to make out, lived in the water.

On the dry lake and in the mountains nothing lived, exactly nothing. The broken flats were too barren even for cactus. There was no point in looking for game. No creature could survive without water.

Sam thought that the red-rock desert they came through, the

country north of the Siskadee, with its whorled red stone and the hoodoo shapes, was some of the most beautiful country a man could see, even if it was hard traveling. This country was hard, double hard, and triple ugly.

He stretched out next to Meadowlark that night without a word, and Coy curled up near his feet. They lay under the open sky. Putting up the tipi, or doing any other work, seemed too much effort. Like everyone else, Sam and Meadowlark didn't speak, because they thought that either the brigade wouldn't find water, or the food they'd brought would give out, or the horses would die and the men wouldn't be able to carry the food. Then the entire brigade would evaporate, or sink into the sands.

Sam supposed Coy alone would survive.

Tonight the only human sounds were Gideon's groans. Sam thought the bear man was only a step ahead of everyone else in his misery, and men's faces said they thought the same.

They had one wisp of hope. The guides said this lake was created by a river that sank into the sand. Couldn't be much of a river, they thought.

Tomorrow they would find the watercourse and start up it, however thin a trickle it was.

A thought jolted him. *My pipe*. Hannibal had said he should call it the sacred pipe, but those fancy words felt funny to Sam. *I should smoke my pipe and ask for wisdom.*

He didn't have a lot of words around his pipe. Living with the Crows, marrying into a Crow family, he'd become a pipe carrier. He'd given a sun dance. He'd seen something, and what he saw guided him well. That was enough.

He got the pipe out of his possible sack and carried it in its wrapper of deer hide out into the desert. He broke twigs off bushes, made a tipi of them, and with his flint and steel made a little fire. While it got started, he held the stem and bowl of the pipe up to Father Sky and joined the two. Then he filled the bowl with tobacco.

Waiting for coals, he fished his medicine bag out from under his shirt. He always wore this bag around his neck. It held a patch of buffalo fur, the thick fur from the skull, and a piece of paper with words handwritten on them. Now Sam unfolded the paper and looked at the words. Though he couldn't read them, he knew exactly what they said. At the rendezvous of 1825 he'd asked his friend Hannibal McKye to write them down. At a critical moment, they'd been very influential on Sam's life. Now he spoke them slowly, from memory:

"Everything worthwhile is crazy, and everyone on the planet who's not following his wild-hair, middle-of-the-night notions should lay down his burden, right now, in the middle of the row he's hoeing, and follow the direction his wild hair points."

This was the guidance that had brought him, ultimately, to this desert and these troubles. It had also brought him Meadowlark, the West, his life. "I still believe this," he said, putting the paper away.

He picked up an ember with two sticks and dropped it into the bowl. He drew deep. Ritually, he offered the smoke to each of the four directions, the earth, and the sky. Then he asked for help. He asked for a clear mind. He asked for wisdom. He asked to know what to do to protect his family.

Once all the tobacco was ashes, he tapped it onto the ground and went back to camp. Maybe he didn't have any bright ideas, yet, but he felt at peace.

Meadowlark was already asleep. At her feet, Coy whined through his slumber. Dreaming of water, Sam would bet, and crooning to it.

THE RIVER TURNED out to be a joke.

The teenage guides hadn't mentioned that, most of the time, the streambed was dry. Jedediah named it Inconstant River. But the standing water they came on now and then was a godsend. After everyone and every critter had drunk, Sam led Paladin into the water to stand. No way to get too much.

That night they ran nearly out of food.

The captain thought he'd brought enough food for ten or twelve days, easily enough to reach the mountains beyond the desert and the game that would be there. This was only their seventh camp. The lesson to be learned, Diah told Sam, was that men used to eating meat will gobble down a lot more vegetables than you think.

Sam told himself to remember, but he was too angry to care. Why should he try to train for a job when his wife and child were in danger? Why should he force himself to think when the whole brigade was about to evaporate into the parched air?

He gave a much bigger damn about Meadowlark. And the child in her belly, and Coy and Paladin.

The next day the guides disappeared on an errand. They returned to camp that evening with manna. Their people had cached some food nearby for an emergency just such as this. They bore several loaves the size of bread, but hard as rocks.

Sam chipped a little off with his knife. "Tastes like . . . candy!" He couldn't believe it.

The men broke up the loaves with an ax, and everyone set to. Candy for sure. Smiles everywhere.

Coy licked a little on the ground, sniffed at it, and turned his back, but Paladin ate it eagerly out of Sam's hand.

When the guides explained laboriously to Abraham Laplant in their limited Spanish, he told the captain that the crystalline loaves were made from cane grass. The Indians picked the canes, dried them, threshed the sugar off the leaves, and baked it.

Sumner said, "Wish they'd known about granulation."

Sam noted to himself, as he often had, that Sumner knew a lot of surprising words.

A couple of pounds of candy per man—a feast, and another feast tomorrow.

The next day they began to see sign of game, and Harrison Rogers, the clerk, killed an antelope. Coy lapped the blood that spilled onto the ground. Hell was easing into Purgatory.

That night one of the guides disappeared. His companions said he had expected to find his family here. Disappointed, he'd gone back to the Amuchaba villages. But the two remaining would stay with the outfit all the way to the mission, they promised.

Soon the brigade neared the foot of the mountain, and the guides led them to a small village of Indians, their own tribe. These Indians made the trappers welcome, fed them the first evening on acorn mush and pine nut bread, and then staged a big rabbit hunt to put on a feast the next day.

The brigade took that day to rest. This country was full of a kind of tree they'd never seen before, a big yucca with arms that twisted strangely toward the sky—like they were praying, some of the men said. Every man now was praying to get over the mountains and to California. Even Coy was perkier. It seemed like he knew that mountains meant better times.

On the third day beyond the small village, they came down from the mountains and into a fertile valley gleaming absurdly with small streams and, miracle of miracles, cattle. These bore a brand, which the guides identified as the mark of the mission.

The brigade was hungry again. When Jedediah in desperation decided to shoot a cow, he found that he had to hunt them like wild buffalo. But that night and the next the men gorged on beef, and there were plenty of scraps to throw to Coy.

Sam was relieved. Meadowlark looked fine. Meat, plenty of meat, was what her people ate.

Coy brought Sam a stick and pranced around until Sam threw it. They played fetch for a few minutes. Sam marveled at how Coy, however hard the times, perked up after one decent meal.

The men looked around. Yes, a mild climate, even in early winter. Plenty of grass. Maybe a man could grow crops year round, if he had a mind to. California looked good.

The thoughts Jedediah recorded in his journal, though, were less optimistic:

It would perhaps be supposed that, after numerous hardships endured in a savage and inhospitable desert, I should hail the herds that were passing before me in the valley as harbingers of better times. But they reminded me that I was approaching a country that was inhabited by Spaniards, a people whose distinguishing characteristic has ever been jealousy, a people of different religion than mine and possessing a full share of that bigotry and disregard of the rights of a Protestant that has at times stained the Catholic religion.

They might perhaps consider me a spy, imprison me, persecute me for the sake of religion, or detain me in prison to the ruin of my business.

As they got closer, the men passed a farm where Indians were working. Now Jedediah added another worry:

They gazed and gazed again, considering us no doubt as strange objects, in which they were not much in error. When it is considered that they were not accustomed to see white men walking with horses packed as mine were with furs, traps, saddlebags, guns, and blankets, and every thing so different from any thing they had ever seen, and add to this our ragged and miserable appearance, I should not have been surprised if they had run off at first sight, for I have often been treated in that manner by savages.

Arrived at the farmhouses, I was kindly received by an elderly man, an Indian, who spoke Spanish and immediately asked me if I would have a bullock killed. I answered that I would, and away rode two young Indians in a moment.

Part Two

CALIFORNY

Seven

The Mission

FATHER JOSE SANCHEZ, the head of San Gabriel Mission, was not what Jedediah expected. Elderly, rotund, and cheerful, he welcomed the captain genially. First he offered cigars to his visitor, and insisted the captain take the whole handful. Then, to Jedediah's distaste, the friar insisted on a toast with rum. Finally he treated Jedediah and Harrison Rogers to sumptuous meals, at which the friars got merry in their cups. Far from despising Captain Smith as a declared Protestant, Father Sanchez congratulated

Jedediah on having "escaped the gentiles," meaning the Indians, and reached a Christian country.

Meanwhile the men of the brigade located themselves in the quarters that were offered—rooms with actual beds, and candles to provide light. This was luxury. Meadowlark and Flat Dog took turns stretching out on the bed in Sam and Meadowlark's room— they'd never even seen a bed before. Coy looked at the beds like they were weird, sniffed elaborately, and hopped right up.

Then everyone inspected the mission, two thousand acres under cultivation with wheat, beans, peas, and corn; a vineyard, several orchards, a grove of about four hundred orange trees; two thousand horses and an amazing forty thousand cattle, plus mules, sheep, pigs, and goats. The mission compound itself featured not only buildings for worship and for living but storerooms, and shops for making blankets, soap, liquor, barrels, and other commodities.

"Incredible," said Sam.

"How many Indians you think they have?" asked Flat Dog.

"The corporal said twenty-five hundred," answered Sam.

"Treated as slaves," said Flat Dog.

"White men living good on the backs of other men," whispered Sumner. "That's what I see. Black slave, red slave, what's the difference?"

Sam noticed that Sumner loosed his tongue and spoke more freely when the captain wasn't around.

"We can speak as we want," Gideon said, half reading Sam's mind. "These Indians sure as hell got no English." Sam's friend rose out of his depression now and then, just enough to correct the behavior of others.

"You know what's strange," said Sam. "These people don't know who we are or what we do. They hardly know what beaver are, don't know why we trap them, don't know anything about life in the mountains."

"Don't know what way the stick floats," said Gideon. "Don't know what a possible sack is, don't know poor bull from fat cow."

"They must think we're madmen," said Sam.

"Maybe you are," said Flat Dog, laughing.

"Yeah," said Sumner, "maybe you are."

"Hell, even I don't know what we're doing," said Flat Dog. He shrugged and grinned.

Sam, Meadowlark, and Flat Dog went with Gideon to inspect the smithy. Gideon was interested in blacksmithing. The brigade had two blacksmiths who kept the horses shod. But this smith was doing far, far more. Right then he was hammering out intricate door latches with locks. On the benches behind him were door latches, an iron gate, candleholders (some to be fixed to walls, others to be carried), and one big chandelier. Gideon fingered them, and the smith proudly took the time to show Gideon his craft.

The smith was a man who appeared to be both black and Indian. He started explaining his work in what seemed to be excellent Spanish, but Gideon replied with the only Spanish he knew, "*No comprende.*" So the smith wordlessly pulled out hundreds of practical items he'd made, nails and screws, sickles, axes, hammers, wheel rims, and the like. Then he took time to show everyone how the finer work was done, not just the hammering on the anvil but the cutting, shaping, flattening, and welding.

Sam could see Gideon was fascinated, and he was glad for the bear man to be interested in anything, anything at all. Gideon kept looking into the fire, especially when the smith brought it up hot with the bellows, like fire was a magic crucible where transformations took place, rough shapes into useful objects.

The fire scared Coy, though—he kept jumping back away from the sparks and getting behind Sam's legs. Meadowlark and Flat Dog were getting itchy. "Gideon," said Sam, "suppertime."

"See you later," said Gideon, bending toward the anvil.

The entire brigade assembled, except for Gideon. The mission Indian women served up food, and plenty of it. Meat, vegetables, fruits—everything. The friars took care of guests right.

The women frowned at Coy, sitting on the floor next to Sam and looking up expectantly for food. "Coyote," they said with the

Spanish pronunciation. In the end they decided to let the Americans have their strange ways.

Sam thought he'd never get enough to eat. He'd probably lost twenty pounds on the journey from the Salt Lake.

Meadowlark, worse, looked like she hadn't gained a bit of weight in five months with child—she worried him. He'd say this for her. When food was in the pot, she ate. Or on the table. Seated at the first dining table she'd ever seen, on her first chair, with her first eating utensils, she was doing fine.

"Does look like the Indians do all the work," said Flat Dog.

"That's how the friars improve them," said Sumner.

"I saw a man whipped yesterday," said Sam. "Bad whipping."

"They whip them any excuse they find, I bet," said Sumner.

Meadowlark put in, "Those two boys who guided us, they threw them in jail. Said it was for running away from the mission."

"I'd run far, far away," said Sumner.

Sam wondered whether, now that they were in a foreign country, Sumner would run away from Jedediah. He looked about seventeen or eighteen. Sam had run away from home at eighteen.

THEY COULD ALREADY tell that the mission days would be dull. Nothing to do but wait. The captain was negotiating for permission to stay in the country, and the Mexican authorities didn't seem to be able to give him an answer. Jedediah said he might even have to go to San Diego, several days' ride south, to see the governor.

The next day, while Gideon went back to the smithy, Sam, Meadowlark, Flat Dog, Sumner, and Coy headed for the pueblo ten miles away. The mission, managed by men of God, was comfortable but boring. The pueblo, full of low types, might be a lot of fun.

The Pueblo of the Angels, as people called it in English, seemed to be fewer than a hundred houses, not counting the surrounding ranchos. The tale was that the original settlers, about fifty years ago, were blacks and Indians. Now a few rich Spaniards adjoined the pueblo on their grand ranchos, with fancy houses, beautiful saddle horses, and fine herds of livestock. The ordinary citizens irrigated their fields, grew a few crops, and fenced a few cows on sparse grass.

The streets were lined with hovels and cantinas that offered raw-tasting booze, whores, and gambling.

The first cantina swept the four of them out as soon as they sat down. "Coyote!" the woman cried, brandishing her broom.

"Coy probably got better manners than she do," said Sumner.

"I want to teach him more," said Sam.

"What?" asked Sumner, curious. "That's practically a trick dog now."

"I want to teach him to do flips."

"That be som'p'n to see."

They found a table in another tavern, exchanged coins for a little food and some brandy, and Sam pondered the impossible task of explaining to his wife and brother-in-law what was going on in this place.

First he had to tell them about money. The closest he could come was to compare it to beads.

"You know how you might give a trapper a buffalo hide for some beads?" They nodded. "Then, instead of using the beads yourself, you might trade them to another woman? Say, maybe for a tanned hide?"

They nodded.

"Then you're using the beads like money. Not something to use for yourself, just some, some . . . thing to trade for something else."

He didn't know how to interpret the looks he got back. Right now he hated the word "thing."

Flat Dog inspected the silver coins carefully.

"Reales, eight reales to a peso," said Sam. He added hopelessly, "A peso is the same as an American dollar."

Even Gideon had never seen an American silver dollar until Rogers, the clerk, had issued some to the men as back wages, everyone but Meadowlark and Sumner. "You'll need coins in town," he said. He added to Flat Dog, "Ask Morgan to help you with them, if you can trust him."

Flat Dog laughed.

This was the first money Sam had seen since he left St. Louis more than two years ago. Rogers said there weren't many coins in California anyway. Also no banks. For money people used receipts for cow hides. These hides, which the sailors called "California banknotes," were the fundamental commerce of the country, what the visiting British and American ship captains traded for. The province's paper currency was these receipts.

Sam decided, out of sheer stupefaction, to try another subject. "That woman at the bar," he said, "is a whore."

The Crows waited.

"Don't all women be whores?" teased Sumner.

Coy yipped, looking at Sumner and trembling with excitement.

Sam gave Sumner a dirty look and went on. "You give her a coin, probably a peso, and she takes you into the back room for fun in the blankets."

Meadowlark and Flat Dog looked blankly at Sam. What did coins have to do with this?

"I mean, she doesn't just do it because she wants to. She does it anytime with any man. For a peso. To her it's work, like blacksmithing."

Meadowlark made a face.

Flat Dog stood up. "Work?"

Sam nodded.

"Anytime?"

Sam nodded.

"Show me a peso." He held out his hand with coins.

Sam did. Meadowlark looked amused.

Flat Dog marched right up to the woman, who was dressed sexily but showed wear and tear. When he stuck out the peso, she took it without hesitation and led him to the back room.

"I got a peso for you," said Sumner, with a teasing eye on Meadowlark.

"I'll throw you over the moon," said Sam.

From behind came a voice. "Hello, my friend, would you permit a stranger to interest you in a small game?"

Sam recognized the speech, soft and silky, like a dove's coo. He whirled around.

"Grumble!" he shouted. Sam jumped out of his chair and clapped shoulders with a round, gray-haired man with a cherubic face. "Sam Morgan, Pilgrim," said Grumble, making it sound like a high title.

"Grumble, sit down and let us buy you a drink."

"I wish to make the acquaintance of the barkeep myself," said the cherub. He went to the bar, spent a minute or two chatting, and came back with the house brandy. Here you had a choice of homemade brandy, homemade brandy, and homemade brandy.

Sam introduced his wife Meadowlark proudly, then his friend Sumner, and reminded Grumble of Coy's name.

Coy wagged his tail eagerly, but Grumble gave him a jaundiced eye. The big cherub was not fond of animals.

"Grumble is the first person I met when I ran away from home four years ago," Sam told his wife and Sumner. "He got me out of trouble right off." Sam looked fondly at his friend. "And then got me into a lot of it."

"Not a bit of trouble," said Grumble. "Perhaps some adventure."

"You sound kind of like a friar," said Sumner.

"I was raised to be devout, and perhaps I am a sort of friar, a priest of low sacraments in vile places. Like cantinas and gambling houses."

Sam put in, "What are you doing in California?"

"Had to leave St. Louis," said Grumble. "In a hurry. Difficulties with the constabulary." He gave a conspiratorial smile.

"Stopped and did some business in New Orleans for a month or two, but I had the gold for passage and came around the Cape. I'd never been at sea, and I wanted to see California." Now the smile turned mischievous. "New opportunities. How did you get here?"

"Horseback across the country."

Grumble repeated it musically—"Horseback across the country?"

Sam nodded. "A lot of us mountaineers, we'd been up north toward the British territory, and down south to Taos. A little travel west said that was no way. There has to be a river going from the back side of the Rocky Mountains to the Pacific. So we tried southwest. My friends and I, twenty-four of us to start with, took off from the Salt Lake and came across the country."

"The St. Louis newspapers reported the discovery of the Great Salt Lake, and other new geographical features," Grumble said gently. He raised an eyebrow at Sam. He lifted his glass. "Here's to your splendid achievement."

They all drank.

"Was it an appalling trip?"

"The worst a man ever set out on." Sam launched into a description of the red-rock desert, then of the Amuchabas, and last of the white sand desert. Sumner poked in quite a few words, and even Meadowlark added some, all to the effect that it was one nasty, stinking journey. Coy whined right along with them.

Flat Dog walked back in, holding hands with the woman. Then he said something to her and walked to the table and sat. Introductions were made. Flat Dog bore a very self-satisfied look. Grumble looked at him and the woman, understanding.

"What will you do now?" Grumble asked Sam.

"We don't have any damned idea. What will you do?"

"Look for opportunities."

After some odd looks around the table, Sam said, "Tell my friends how you make your living."

"We who are quick of mind live by our wits."

"All right, Grumble, show them. Start with the boy with a hoop."

Grumble reached with a crimped-up hand into a leather pouch he carried on a thong.

"Flat Dog," said Sam, "you play. And tell us what you see."

Grumble drew out three playing cards.

Flat Dog eyed Grumble's hands and said, "His hands are . . ."

"Say it."

"They're . . . crippled." As a Crow he was embarrassed to mention such a thing publicly. "Also, they're small, delicate, and very clean. The nails are close-clipped and look polished."

The cherub with the monkish fringe of hair showed three cards, calling them out. "Gentleman, lady, and boy with a hoop. Now, Mr. Flat Dog, keep your eye on the boy with a hoop. If you can pick him out, you win. We'll pretend we've each put a coin in the middle of the table."

Flat Dog grinned. He loved to gamble, either the Crow hand game or trapper card games.

Grumble interleaved the three cards clumsily. Flat Dog had learned to shuffle a deck from trappers, using the waterfall method of shuffling, so it was weird to see a man have difficulty mixing up just three cards. Certainly it was no trouble to keep track of the target card.

Flat Dog gathered his curiosity and spoke as boldly as a white man. "Do you have arthritis?" That's what older white trappers called stiff joints.

Grumble gave a long-suffering smile and spread the cards on the tabletop facedown. "Pick out the boy with a hoop."

Flat Dog pointed to it immediately, the card on the right end.

"Turn it over—show us."

Flat Dog turned over the gentleman.

Meadowlark gasped.

Sumner snickered.

Merrily, Grumble turned over the boy with a hoop, which was

the card on the left end. "Mr. Flat Dog, you've got to keep an eye on that boy. Or would you care to try, Mrs. Morgan?"

Sam whispered to Meadowlark that Grumble meant her. "Oh, yes," she said.

Sam saw Flat Dog watching intensely this time. His expression said, *If my sister doesn't get it, I will.*

Somehow Meadowlark picked the lady, Flat Dog pointed to the gentleman again, and the boy with a hoop was the middle card.

Flat Dog looked completely perplexed.

Sumner tried twice, with determination, and got the same result.

"Maybe you would like Coy to take a try?" said Grumble with a big smile.

Then he fetched a full deck out of his leather pouch. He water-falled the cards. With fingers as nimble as any of them had ever seen, he turned up the ace of spades, buried it, cut the deck very rapidly a half-dozen times, and turned over the top card—the ace of spades, followed by the other three aces of the deck.

"Wow," said Sumner.

"And that's the least of what he can do," said Sam.

"The very least," agreed Grumble jovially.

Sumner asked carefully, "You can do about anything with a deck of cards, win near all the time?"

"And much, much more," said Grumble.

"I want to learn to be sly like that," the black man said.

"Sly?" Grumble drawled. Suddenly, interrupting himself, he rose to his feet, looking toward the door.

Sam turned and saw a female figure. In the dark cantina, with the figure against the bright light of the doorway, he needed a moment to realize who it was. Then Sam yelled, "Abby!"

He knocked over his chair jumping up, hugged her, and then the two of them did a little jig.

Meadowlark frowned.

Sam turned himself and Abby toward the group. In embarrassment he took a step away from her. "Meadowlark," he said, "this is the friend I told you about. Abby, this is my wife, Meadowlark."

Abby, in a lovely gown and carrying a parasol, made a small curtsy.

Meadowlark managed a smile.

Sam ordered a bottle of brandy for everyone.

MEADOWLARK WAS FASCINATED by the stories. Already she knew that Sam had come from a place called Pennsylvania down a great river on a boat for a long time, more than one moon, to a big village called St. Louis where they had buildings in the shape of boxes, like this village. She knew he'd had adventures on that journey, but had not imagined such an entrancing creature as Abby.

Abby was the most beautiful human being Meadowlark had ever seen. She wore a dress of pale, gleaming green, a silvery hat, and a handheld parasol of light blue. The parasol actually opened and closed—amazing! The dress had a very, very full skirt—you couldn't tell Abby had legs—and was form-fitted above the waist.

Sam said, and Meadowlark could tell from the stories they were telling, that Abby had no man or family. Instead she worked like white men did, what they called making a living. And the ways she made it were . . . Occasionally Abby had given men love for money, according to the conversation. Often she had other women as employees, as Jedediah employed Sam and the others for money, and rented them out to men for sex. Often she had gambled with cards as Grumble did. Mostly she had owned cantinas and sold men the mind-spinning whiskey.

In fact, that's what got her into trouble.

"Why did you leave St. Louis?" Sam asked. Apparently she owned the fanciest cantina in town.

"You remember Cadet Chouteau?"

Sam nodded.

"My protector found a new woman. Egged on by her, he turned into my persecutor."

So she had operated by running a drinking, gambling, and whoring house under the protection of a powerful man. And she looked innocent as a mountain flower. Well, until you looked very closely.

Now Abby, Grumble, and Sam took turns telling a story that gave Meadowlark's imagination a whirl:

When they were floating down the big river, Abby carried a lot of gold coins sewn into her dress, or into something called a corset, apparently worn under the dress. (Meadowlark didn't know why anyone would wear clothes under a dress, especially the sort of dress Abby wore, covering everything but face, hands, and shoes.) The boat crew saw her sewing the coins in and decided to steal them.

When Abby, Sam, and Grumble went out for an evening of drinking in cantinas, three crewmen caught them in a dark street. Two of the crewmen were huge brothers, Elijah and Micajah. Elijah, the leader, pointed a shotgun at the three friends. Since these friends were a woman, a teenager, and an old man, the thieves thought the conquest would be easy.

Coy woofed, as though it wouldn't have been easy if he'd been there.

But Abby had a trick. She lured Elijah into coming close enough to feel the gold coins and make sure they were in the corset. As instructed, she held her hands up on her head. Suddenly a tiny knife was in her hand, and Elijah's throat was cut. In the fight that followed, Abby shot one crewman with a "lady gun" and chased Micajah off by threatening him with the gun. Only Grumble was hurt.

"But not badly hurt," Abby said to him with a mean eye.

"Not badly," the cherub said with a smile.

Meadowlark sensed a story here and hoped she'd hear it later.

First she said, "Maybe you will show me this lady gun."

Abby fetched something out of the big cloth pouch that dangled from one of her wrists. It looked just like any pistol, except that it would fit in the palm of a hand. "Cute, isn't it?" said Abby.

Meadowlark started to pick it up, but Sam gave a small shake of his head.

"And the tiny knife?" Meadowlark asked.

Abby pursed her lips. "I don't want anyone to see where I keep it, but I'll show you something like it."

Sam gave Meadowlark a little nod and unconsciously touched the ornament he kept in his white hair.

Abby fished a finger-shaped object from her other wrist bag. It had very rough surfaces on both sides. Meadowlark turned it over and over, then held it up. "Your knife is such a size?" Abby nodded. "But what does it do, this thing, not the knife?"

"It's an emery board. You file your nails with it."

She demonstrated.

Meadowlark thought this was far more amazing than a gun or knife. She tried it herself, and it worked wonderfully.

"You may have it as a gift," Abby said.

Meadowlark made a little squeal of glee. She thought Abby was fascinating.

The six friends had supper, and more brandy, and floated on oceans of glee and laughter through the evening.

VOICES WOKE SAM, loud, harsh voices. They mixed with the other common sounds of the mission, men coming and going, horses clopping or whickering, but he thought he recognized them.

He slipped out of the bed with Meadowlark. He liked the idea of an afternoon nap for her. He was still fretting about her health, and the baby's. But he napped very lightly, or daydreamed, or worried.

He slipped out into the twilight, Coy at his heels. The sun set early on these short December days. He hated the short days near Christmas. He dreaded his own birthday, on Christmas Eve. Yes, the day he was born, but also the day his father died.

He walked past the kitchen where the Indian women were readying the food, always hot, always plenty. The friars were being very generous to their guests. He wound his way into an obscure, weeded area behind the smithy, where the voices led him.

Three figures—Jedediah, James Reed, and a mission soldier.

Coy barked and ran toward them yipping.

"Coy!" said Sam sharply.

The coyote waited for Sam to catch up.

Sam did not like the blacksmith Reed. Since the brigade got to the mission, the man had stayed drunk. In the months before he had alternated between boiling and cowering, depending on his mood.

But Sam also did not like the rest of what he saw. The soldier stood by with his sword out, and Jedediah raised a whip over Reed's bare back.

CRACK! Sam shuddered—what did such an awful sound mean about the man's flesh, his ribs?

"One!" said Jedediah.

Sam walked close. Coy growled. Sam quieted him with a hand.

CRACK!

"Two!"

Sam looked closely at Jedediah's face. It was fixed in neutrality.

"Three!"

The sound still made Sam jump. Coy was growling again.

"Four!"

Sam was horrified but transfixed. He couldn't walk away.

"Five!"

Jedediah noticed Sam now. He said, "You. Get gone. You don't need to see this."

Sam didn't move. He picked up Coy in both arms, to calm the coyote.

"Six!"

"All right, stay. Maybe"—he cocked the whip again—"you do need to."

"Seven!"

Sam turned away from the bloody mess that was Reed's back. He looked at Diah in fascination and revulsion.

"Eight!"

Perhaps the captain's eyes showed a hint more than neutrality.

"Nine!"

Maybe they were angry. Maybe they were . . . self-righteous.
"Ten!"

Jedediah handed the whip to the soldier, who walked away.

Reed didn't stir.

"Well?"

Sam had no idea what to say. Coy wiggled, and Sam put him down. Coy went close and sniffed at poor Reed's wounds.

Finally Sam emitted, "Why?"

"Reed, why did you get flogged?"

Reed rolled over onto one side. After a moment he opened his eyes and looked up at the captain, but he said nothing.

"Reed!" Now the voice was itself a lash. "Tell Morgan why you were flogged."

Reed squeezed out a word, but Sam couldn't make it out.

"Let us hear it!" said Jedediah. Sam was amazed at how the captain never raised his voice but still charged it with energy.

Reed lipped out the syllables one at a time. "Im-per-ti-nence."

"Exactly."

Jedediah walked away.

Sam bent over Reed, but the blacksmith swept him away with an arm. "I don't need the captain's pet."

Sam stood up, looked at Coy, and trotted off. He caught up with the captain. They walked along together for a bit.

Jedediah said, "You'd best watch that coyote. Don't forget he's a wild animal."

When they passed the kitchen, Sam finally spoke. "How did that feel?"

Jedediah's face snapped toward Sam. After a moment he smiled slightly and answered, "Firm. Distant. Olympian."

"JEDEDIAH WANTS US to go to San Diego with him," Sam told Meadowlark after supper. They'd been guests of the mission for nearly two weeks.

"Why?" said Meadowlark.

He smiled at the difficulty of explaining it to her. "We didn't ask the Mexicans permission to come into their country."

He saw in her face what Meadowlark thought: *What an idea.* No telling what "civilized" people make rules about.

His wife's thoughts and feelings, whatever they might be, were always ultra-vivid. He smiled at that too.

"Is the ocean at San Diego?"

"Yes." In fact, he'd heard it was a very fine harbor, well protected against the open sea.

Her eyes sparked.

"We can't go."

"I want to go."

"You need to rest. You've walked a thousand miles to get here, not eating or drinking half the time, and you're supposed to be eating and drinking enough for two."

She gave him that angle of head that meant he should straighten up and act right.

"We're not going."

She whirled away from him.

"We can go to the ocean down at San Pedro."

She turned to him with a look of immense disappointment, and he didn't know why.

"Hey, they say the port is poor, but it's ocean, and they'll have big sailing ships there."

"If you say so."

Sam said lamely, "I'm keen to see it too."

Her face softened.

"Abby and Grumble want to go with us."

Now she half smiled.

"There's something else mixed up in it too."

She looked at him questioningly.

"The governor, he sent for Jedediah. Wants to ask questions about why we came into California without permission. If Jedediah gets thrown in jail, or sent to face a higher authority in Mexico City, we don't want to go with him."

"That's for sure." She kissed him.

"And there's something else."

He told her about the flogging. He'd kept it inside for two days but could hold it no longer. For some reason, he didn't know why, it made him ashamed.

He gave most of the details. As he was skipping over just how really bloody it was, she said, "I saw Reed's back. I helped put a poultice on it."

Her eyes were sympathetic.

"It . . . It bothers me."

"Me too."

"Why?"

"Because your captain is like that."

That stung. Sam waited, but she didn't say anything more.

"I could hardly believe it."

She waited.

"I asked him how he felt after he did it."

"And he said?"

"Firm. Distant." Sam hesitated. "He said 'Olympian,' and he'd told me about that. It's a mountain where the boss god goes and looks down and throws thunderbolts at people who act bad."

Meadowlark couldn't help giggling.

"I guess Reed got thunderbolted."

Meadowlark said, "Men."

They held each other's eyes until Meadowlark smiled and kissed him lightly.

Sam said, "I'll tell him we're not going."

"We'll have fun instead."

Eight

The Pueblo of the Angels

GRUMBLE AND ABBY wondered if the Pueblo of the Angels was
their long-term place for sport and business. It did have some cantinas, and Abby could start another. "I want to start a fancy place,"
she said, "the sort of place they don't have here. Where rich people will come."

They were strolling through the town in leisurely fashion, Abby
and Grumble, Sam and Meadowlark, Flat Dog and Sumner. "The

people with money don't go to these cantinas," said Grumble, grumbling.

The friends saw plenty of the rich on their fine horses—and these Mexicans did have good-looking horse flesh. The dons galloped through town wearing huge Spanish hats over their dark faces, serapes over their shoulders, leather leggings, and boots with huge spurs. Flat Dog pointed out a handsome woman in a carriage, apparently with her husband, decked out in splendor. She wore a gown of scarlet silk, jewelry everywhere skin showed, and a high comb mounted in her hair, which was brown, not black. Her fair skin marked her lineage as Spanish, not Indian, surely a source of pride.

"You going to fall in with the style?" Sam asked Abby.

Meadowlark hung on the answer.

"My advantage is in being different," Abby replied.

"They say," said Grumble, "that the difference between these dons and ordinary folks is one drop of blood. If you can claim a single drop of Spanish blood, you belong among the gentry. Otherwise you're a peasant."

"Hell," said Sumner, "I'd claim that drop real quick."

Coy yipped, and everyone laughed.

"You and I must have a talk about what you may do," said Grumble to Sumner.

The streets were narrow, crooked, and dusty. Both sides were lined with hovels, but there were some proper houses built of sunbaked clay, which the local people called adobe. Probably half of the few businesses were cantinas.

"Plenty of vice here," said Abby.

"But you can't separate people from their money if they don't have any," said Grumble.

"What about the port town?" asked Sam.

"It looked like a hellhole," said Abby.

"Can we go to the ocean there?" asked Meadowlark.

Grumble saw the look in her eyes and understood. "Of course. Anything for a beautiful lady."

He turned to Sumner. "You want to start your apprenticeship now?"

Sumner smiled wryly and nodded.

"All right, the rest of you, go entertain yourselves. I must take Sumner to school."

"Your great advantage," Grumble said to Sumner as the others wandered on, "is that people will think you're dim-witted."

Sumner gave the white man the eye.

"If I thought that," Grumble said, "I wouldn't be teaching you. They'll assume, because of your color, that you think slowly. It is an enviable advantage.

"So here's a little game that makes 'stupidity' profitable."

In an hour Sumner had it down pat.

SAM CHOSE A cantina with three outside tables served by a Mexican woman whose black eyebrows bristled like daggers. Sam guessed that she woke up ready for something to be irked about.

He left Coy on a leash with Grumble and Meadowlark.

Sam more or less slid toward a table, appearing to balance carefully. He ordered a mescal, which definitely should have been one too many. Eyebrows went to get it, and when she came back, Sam clumsily hid, or actually failed to hide, a glittering object in one hand.

He tossed the mescal down before Eyebrows could take a step and ordered another to make the show good. Then he started admiring his bauble openly. It appeared to be a gold ring with a splendid ruby, probably a full carat in size, the sort of ring a man would give a very special woman. As Eyebrows approached this time, he slipped the ring clumsily into a velvet pouch.

Sumner sidled in, looking for a table. Sam gave him a foul look. Insolently, Sumner picked the table right next to Sam.

Sam tossed his second mescal down quickly and stood. With a nasty look at Sumner, he stalked out.

In the open on the table sat, temptingly, the velvet pouch.

In the corner of one eye Sumner saw Eyebrows step out the door. She looked after Sam, pivoted, and started to go back inside.

"Señorita!" Sumner cried. *Can't let her miss the little gift.*

Eyebrows came toward the black teenager.

"*Aguardiente,*" said Sumner firmly, meaning brandy.

But Eyebrows had spotted the velvet pouch. She eased slowly toward Sam's table.

Sumner was quicker. He leaned across and snatched the bag right out of Eyebrows's claws. He grinned big at her. Then he looked inside, drew out the bauble, and beamed with a delight possible only to the very innocent and dim-witted.

"Ain't it pretty?" said Sumner in the vile Spanish of peasants.

He tried to slide it onto one of his pinkies, and it fit like a dream. *Take the bait, idiot.*

"*No es tuyo,*" Eyebrows said. (It is not yours.)

"Oh, *que bonito.*" (Sure is pretty.)

"It is the gentleman's," said Eyebrows, continuing in Spanish. "He will be back for it." She held out a demanding hand.

Sumner shook his head slowly, teasingly. "Finder's keepers," he drawled.

Instantly, he realized his mistake—*I spoke English!*

He covered the error with anger. He balled a fist around the ring and rammed it behind his back. "You leave me alone," he said in Spanish.

"What are you going to do with the ring?" said Eyebrows. "Wear it? If one of the dons or friars sees it, you know what happens? They take it and give you ten lashes, *como un ladrón.*"

"A thief?" Sumner started to protest and then settled down. "They would," he said softly. "They would do that."

He turned the ring slowly in front of his eyes, seemingly mesmerized. "Finding this would be some luck, 'cept a black man, he don' get no luck."

"I'll buy it from you," said Eyebrows, shrugging lightly. "A peso."

Sumner was genuinely offended. This ring was authentic, probably worth a month of a working man's wages. "A peso? You think this Nigger is stupid? That's real gold there, that's a real ruby. This ring, it's worth twenty pesos, maybe more."

Eyebrows shrugged again. "You want to eat?"

Sumner ordered a big meal.

While Sumner waited for his dinner, Eyebrows found excuses to stay nearby, wiping tables, adjusting chairs. Finally, she couldn't stand it. "Let me see that ring," she demanded.

Sumner pulled the velvet bag out of the big, dirty pouch that hung inside his shirt. Gently, he opened the bag and held the ruby ring out to her. She touched the ruby, but Sumner held on to the ring.

"Give it to me," she said. "It belongs to the customer. He will come back for it."

Sumner gave a slow shake of his head.

She lashed him with a look. "Don't you need money? You want that flogging?"

"Black man always need money," said Sumner. He seemed to ponder. "I owes a man . . . I'd like to sell it, but I'm afraid to show it to anybody with enough money."

Eyebrows bristled off and came back with a big platter of beef and pork cooked in red chile sauce.

"Enjoy your dinner," said Eyebrows, "I'll be back."

In less than ten minutes Eyebrows and another Mexican appeared at Sumner's table. "Give him the ring," Eyebrows demanded.

"I won't steal from you," said the man gently. He was fair-haired, light-skinned, and so slender, his posture so slight, that at first Sumner took him for a woman. He held a magnifying glass in one hand.

What the hell?

Eyebrows said, "This man is an expert. Let him see it."

She thinks I don't know a magnifying glass when I see one.

Sumner drew out the ring and handed it to the stranger.

The man studied it. "This glass is ten power," he said, "very strong."

Finally, he handed Sumner the ring and said, "It is real, both ruby and gold."

With cries of "*Gracias*" from Eyebrows, the stranger was gone.

Where in heaven or earth did she find that fellow? wondered Sumner.

Sumner dropped the ring into the velvet bag and slid the bag back into his pouch.

"I give you five pesos for it," said Eyebrows. A week's wages.

Sumner shook his head. "I already said, worth twenty."

They debated. They bargained. Eyebrows asked to see the ring again.

Sumner pulled the velvet bag out again, except that now it wasn't the same bag. Grumble had said the timing was critical.

Eyebrows slid the ring onto her finger. She held it in several positions and admired it. In a few more exchanges they settled on ten pesos.

She put the ring on her finger and walked across the patio admiring her ruby, held high in the sunlight.

SUMNER RAN TOWARD his friends, he skipped, almost danced. When he got to their table, he held out the shiny silver coins. Coy gave a little yip, and Meadowlark quieted him.

Quickly Sumner gushed out the whole story, including the surprise appearance by the expert.

"Lucky break, that," said Grumble. "Actually, the trick works well done straight across the street from a jeweler's shop. The jeweler makes a good expert."

Sumner nodded his understanding.

"Altogether," said Grumble quietly, "well done." He didn't want to inspire any more exuberance. He divided the coins. "One for Sam the capper," he said, "four for Sumner the actor, five for me."

Sumner put an expression on his face, but Grumble cut him short with a word. "The teacher gets half. At least half."

Sumner smiled.

"The ring," said Grumble, palm out.

Sumner fished the bag out sheepishly and dropped it into Grumble's palm.

"Let me see," cried Meadowlark.

Grumble handed her the ring.

"Four pesos is enough to live on for a week," the cherub told her.

Sumner nodded, playing with his coins.

Good. Grumble wanted to keep Sumner dependent on himself. *He has talent.* A capper was valuable.

"This is the first money I ever earned in my life," said Sumner. "Thank you."

"Earned?" said Sam.

"The artist is worthy of his hire," said Grumble. "The beauty of this flimflam," he went on, "is that she'll probably never realize that we had a little fun with her, and will always be delighted with her bauble."

Coy whined.

Meadowlark tried the ring on several fingers until it fit the middle one of her right hand. She held it high and turned it in the afternoon sun. "So, so beautiful."

Grumble grinned at Sam. "You better quit beaver and join us flimflam artists."

The black youth held up his stack. "Freedom is coins in your pocket," he said.

Just then Flat Dog ambled up and claimed a seat. He'd been shopping, and they all took a moment to admire his purchase, a handsome red shirt with puffed sleeves, the first cloth garment he'd ever owned.

"By the way," Grumble told Sam, "our black friend speaks fluent Spanish."

Sam gave Sumner a look.

"I told you," said Sumner, "I am not what I seem."

Sam looked at him amazed. Those words had come out with the plummiest of British accents.

"This Nigger done talk low-life too."

That sentence was pure slave English.

"Maybe you should tell us all who you are," said Grumble. "Your teacher would like to know."

Sumner gave the broadest of smiles and spoke in plummy style. "I was born in Santa Domingo, on a big cane plantation. Since my mother worked in the big house, I grew up there, and played with the white kids. Our master was the second son of a viscount, or some such foolishness. I grew up speaking the king's English."

Now he shifted back to slave speech. "At night, though, down at our hut, we was with other Niggers, including my father and his brothers and their wives, and they all spoke Spanish, nothing but Spanish. So I grew up talking both tongues."

"Truly bilingual," said Grumble, no doubt thinking how to turn that to advantage.

"Trilingual," said Sumner. "In New Orleans I learned Nigger English. Safer that way."

Then he looked quick at Sam. "I'm doing the skip on Captain Smith. You're not going to tell him where I am, are you?"

Sam shook his head. "My Delaware friend Hannibal gave me the best advice I ever got. Hannibal, the man I told you about. He said every man should follow his wild hair. That sure as hell leaves out slavery."

Suddenly Sumner asked Grumble, "What's wrong with you?"

The lad was observant.

Grumble drawled, "We need to find that expert with the magnifying glass."

SAM AND MEADOWLARK knew the village, having rambled the streets. With an inquiry here and there the expert was easy enough to find—how many such men could there be in a small town? He was working in a small building adjoined to a smithy.

One look and Sam decided the jewel man was something odd, as much woman as man. He had a gentle voice and delicate hands.

Sumner made introductions—Grumble, Sam and Meadowlark, Flat Dog. Then he made Coy sit and shake hands.

Around the corner of the building came a surprise.

"Gideon!" Sam introduced his longtime partner to his old friend Grumble. Then he asked Gideon, "What are you doing here?"

The bear man looked like he wanted to give three or four answers at once. "I came to watch another smith, and I found Angel." He spread his arms theatrically and grinned. "Angel is an artist."

The shed was hung with examples of metalwork. Silver cups. Gold plates worked up fancy somehow. Copper plates . . .

"These are superb," said Grumble, and launched into teaching. "This is a simple copper plate"—he touched one with a finger—"gilded with gold in this intricate pattern you see, making something beautiful with the simplest of means."

He handed it to Meadowlark and took up another one.

"This one"—he held up a larger platter—"is silver embossed, or the more proper term is repoussé." He turned it upside down. "You see, the ornamentation is made by pushing out the reverse side." He showed them the front again. "Then it is chased, that is, punched with a hammer, for this effect . . ."

Gideon leapt in, holding up another plate. "On this one the chasing is in relief."

Grumble's face lit up with delight. "Here it's in intaglio."

Sam and Flat Dog rolled their eyes at each other, hoping Grumble wouldn't explain this too. Meadowlark was fingering the plate she held, almost with reverence. "Nothing for it," Sam whispered, "but to let them go crazy."

Coy slunk to a corner and lay down, bored.

"Ah!" Gideon grasped a jewel-encrusted crucifix and held it to his chest, modeling it for the others.

"Were you raised in the church?" asked Grumble.

"The priest who visits every two or three years, he baptize me," said the French-Canadian. "Our village, it was near Lake Winnipeg. I love his robe and his crucifix. *Le bon Dieu*, when I am at Montreal and am taught the words that go with the ceremonies, I am somet'ing less than charm-ed."

Grumble gave Gideon the look of a *compadre*.

Angel held a silver chalice and plate out to Grumble.

"The implements of communion," the cherub said, taking them and smiling hugely, "inlaid in niello." He held them out to Gideon. "Aren't they beautiful?"

On tables all around the room were many beautiful things made in silver—drinking bowls, spoons, frames for mirrors, picture frames, candlesticks, and plates, plus sacramental objects—chalices, censers, rosaries, crucifixes . . .

On the walls hung necklaces and earrings. Meadowlark modeled a gold necklace for Sam.

In halting Spanish Grumble asked Angel, "Where did you come by this skill?"

In halting English he replied, "I am apprentice to an artist in Seville and then I work in Mexico City."

"How on earth did you end up in California?"

"I don't end up in one place," said Angel, "but always journey forward. I wish to practice my craft. The bishop in Mexico City, he informs me that California has many missions, a great need for liturgical objects, and no artisans to produce them. So I come. I am travel—traveling?—from mission to mission."

"It really does look wonderful," Sam admitted to Gideon.

Tentatively, tenderly, Gideon murmured, "I would like to do this work myself."

Sam's heart pinged.

"I have promised to teach Gideon," Angel said. "I need an apprentice. It is my good luck," said Angel, "that so many enormous ranchos are very wealthy, and there are wealthy women who appreciate the beauty."

"Señor the goldsmith, let me treat you to a fine supper," said Grumble eagerly.

"I regret," said Angel, "but . . . Ah, here they are now."

A fine carriage pulled alongside Angel's shop. Two gorgeously dressed Spanish women alighted, one in her twenties and the other in her late teens, striking because of her tawny hair and gold skin. Angel made the introductions. The elder was Doña Reina Rubio y Obregon, the teenager Señorita Julia Rubio. They were sisters, and Doña Reina was married, Angel explained.

But no one noticed his explanation. Everyone saw that something extraordinary was happening. The looks between Julia and Flat Dog were bonfires. All stood stupefied for a moment. Sam noticed that Julia had remarkable green eyes.

It was Sam who broke the silence. At his instruction, Coy stepped forward, sat, and extended his paw to the ladies to be shaken. Charmed, Julia took it.

"Doña Reina," said Angel, "your necklace is finished." He fetched it from a drawer and handed it to the older sister. It was an emerald beautifully set in gold and suspended on a fine gold chain.

Julia and Flat Dog still could not take their eyes off each other.

Sam and Meadowlark hid their smiles.

Grumble leapt to the rescue.

"May I invite everyone to dine with me—you ladies, Angel, and my friends?"

Doña Reina seemed uncertain. "But where?"

"I don't know what in the village is suitable . . ."

"I believe nothing is quite suitable, really," she said. She spoke elegant, slightly overpronounced English.

Señorita Julia intruded. "Perhaps . . ."

Finally she took her gaze off Flat Dog. The sisters exchanged eye messages.

"Have you visited the Pacific Ocean?" asked the señora. "Near our Rancho Malibu it is very beautiful."

"We were going to see it at San Pedro," said Sam.

Meadowlark frowned at him.

"San Pedro is ugly," said the young girl.

"Perhaps you will visit us at our rancho," suggested Doña Reina. "All of you, Angel, Gideon, and you, our new friends. Our father, Don Cesar Bartolomeo Rubio, will be very glad to have you. You will be our guests for a night, and on the second day we will have a lovely trip to the ocean."

Julia and Flat Dog sparkled.

Nine

The Pacific Ocean

SAM AWOKE TO an amazing sound. Every few seconds a gentle roar, a kind of tender crash, drifted through his mind. Then a fizzy sound, or maybe silence, and another crash.

He knew what made the sound, for he had watched it carefully late yesterday afternoon, when he and Meadowlark arrived. Coy had chased the surf as it retreated, then fled from it as it crashed and then swished up the sand. Sam could hardly believe it would go on all night, a kind of chorus that rocked and pillowed his sleep at once, and go on all morning, all day, and forever.

He lay back and listened.

He and Meadowlark had stolen some time to be alone together.

Two days ago the whole party had arrived at the rancho. Julia's father was expansively courteous. "Call me Don Cesar," he told everyone. He showed them around his splendid home, which had more than a dozen rooms, most with fireplaces. Don Cesar particularly showed off his collection of weapons and items of soldiering—a conquistador sword and breastplate; a matchlock rifle; two fine dueling pistols; a cutlass from a pirate vessel; a jeweled dirk belonging to a Spanish grandee; several styles of whips and lashes, including a cat-o'-nine-tails and a knout. The cat, the don explained, was preferred by the British, the knout by the Russians. Since it had wire interwoven with the rawhide, it looked nasty. He tapped the handle into his hand with an air of satisfaction. His prize possessions were a garrote and beheading ax said to have been used during the Inquisition.

Sam looked at the breastplate and whispered to Flat Dog, "Wouldn't that thing bounce the arrows off?"

Then Don Cesar showed everyone to private bedrooms, and the party reassembled in the evening for a feast such as Sam had scarcely heard of.

After a sumptuous breakfast the next morning Julia asked to see Sam and Meadowlark's tipi, and Meadowlark quickly erected it for her.

Rubio was fascinated by Coy. "A coyote?" he repeated, giving the word the Spanish pronunciation. "Is he trained to attack?"

"I don't think he needs training for that," said Sam. "Not if I'm in danger."

Rubio pulled at his goatee and looked at Coy askance.

Sam called Don Cesar's attention to Paladin, and would have shown him some of the mare's tricks, but Rubio wasn't interested. "An Indian pony," he scoffed.

Julia told her father that Sam and Meadowlark wanted to camp on a beach somewhere.

"Splendid," he said. "You may make your camp in a fine place. One of my men will guide you. It is called Playa Topanga."

Sam was a little tickled at the dismissiveness of the term "camp." It was true that their tipi hardly compared to Rubio's fine house, surrounded by buildings for blacksmith, tanner, candle-maker, and so on. But camps were Sam's home, and Mead-owlark's, and the homes of the Crow people, one camp after another, endlessly. *One good place*, he consciously thought, *following upon another. Home.*

That afternoon the whole party rode down to this small beach suggested by Don Cesar. While everyone else returned to the lux-ury of the rancho, Sam and Meadowlark stayed at the beach, tak-ing a kind of honeymoon.

Now the gentle roar lulled Sam's mind again.

Coy scratched at the tipi flap, his way of asking to be let out.

Sam eased from under the blankets, careful not to disturb Meadowlark. He crawled to the flap, slipped the pegs out, and stepped into the chill morning, naked.

Before him spread the Pacific Ocean. Far to his left, the south-west, a point of land made a faint smudge on the horizon. Far to his right, the northwest, a similar smudge. Somewhere between them, straight out and across an unimaginable reach of blue water, lay the land the maps called China.

Here at Sam's feet churned the surf. He smiled at this strange doing, a soft whoosh of protest, perhaps, at water running up against land and being turned back. A protest made every few sec-onds through every day of every year through a past too long to picture, into a future he couldn't imagine.

Meadowlark stepped to his side, naked. They faced west. Sam's thought was, *The sailors say China is strange, a country beyond the mind's ability to grasp. I say, without knowing, that this sea is stranger yet.* He called to mind the kinds of creatures he'd heard of, inhabitants of the ocean depths. He was sure no shape he might dream up, no visage from his nightmares, was as weird, as alien, as the creatures who actually lived in the water before his feet.

He didn't say any of this to Meadowlark. He knew her thoughts, whatever they were in particular, played in the same fields as his.

Topanga Beach, the don had said. Topanga meaning what? he mused. He said aloud, "It should mean 'wonder.' "

Meadowlark smiled at him.

Coy struck a pose, nose pointed toward the far end of the beach. There a creek dingled into the ocean, and a figure walked, human, solitary.

The naked Sam and Meadowlark slipped back into the tipi.

He put his hands on Meadowlark's slender waist. She turned to face him. He brushed her nipples lightly with his fingertips and leaned forward to kiss her.

She feather-bussed his lips and said with a smile, "Later." She reached for a dress. Sam had spent his hard-earned brigade money for green cotton, and Meadowlark had sewn it into the pattern of the kind of hide dress she always wore. Therefore for this special day she flew an emerald flag against the light blue of the sky, the dark blue of the sea, and the lovely red-brown of her face.

Abby had promised to show her how to decorate the dress with some lace at the neck and the wrists, but Sam didn't think she could look more beautiful than she did now.

They set out to walk along the sand, Meadowlark barefoot and Sam wearing only a breechcloth. He stuck a butcher knife in his belt—no telling who that figure might be. Coy followed, chasing the waves in and out.

They walked away from the solitary figure and toward the point to the northwest. They zigzagged down toward the sea and up the sandy rise, more or less keeping their feet out of the water, and turning the zigzag into a dance. They also jumped over long litters of seaweed, at least Sam supposed that's what it must be. It was no longer rooted anywhere, and the waves must have flung the stuff up on the beach.

Small birds stilted along the sand and stuck long, curved beaks down among the grains. When Sam and Meadowlark got too close, these birds didn't fly away, but scooted off rapidly on long, sticklike legs.

White birds with dark wing tips drew curves across the crisp morning air.

They came to a rocky finger jutting into the water. "Look," Sam said, "the dunes behind show where the ocean sometimes rises."

"It's far out now," Meadowlark said happily. "We can see lots."

"This must be what they mean by a low tide." On the trip to Malibu the whole group had talked of nothing but the ocean, though only Abby and Grumble had ever seen it. Sam and Meadowlark were now full of unfamiliar words and wild surmises.

It was Meadowlark who noticed them first. In the tideland at their feet, half sea and half earth, were little pools, each separated from the others by rocks. What Sam was looking at in the dozens of pools, he soon realized, were individual worlds of life.

Meadowlark squatted, reached into the water, and picked up a star-shaped something.

Sam flinched. "That thing might bite, or sting, or . . ."

Meadowlark laughed out loud. The creature was the size of her hand, and it had five fingers, or arms, or spurs, or whatever they were. On top it was a hard, orange, spiky shell. On the underside it was as peculiar a creature as Sam had ever seen, fish-belly color, with long, open grooves running out the arms—these arms actually seemed to be hollow!

Meadowlark held it up and cried, "A fish star!"

"Starfish," said a male voice.

Sam whirled. He didn't know whether he was more startled by hearing any voice or by hearing English. He eased his hand to the wooden handle of his knife.

"Easy," said the stranger, grinning. "I'm a friend."

Sam looked for Coy. The little coyote was far down the beach, playing.

The stranger was an elderly man, gleaming white of beard and hair, very tan, and from his accent American. He carried a bucket and short-handled shovel. "Are you new to the ocean?"

"First time we've ever seen it."

"Sometimes it seems like I've seen nothing else," said the old fellow. He stuck out a hand. "Robert Cameron, able-bodied seaman, a hand of merchantmen my entire life, until I retired. Call me Robber."

Sam shook the hand.

"That starfish won't hurt you," Robber said. He reached out. Meadowlark hesitated and then gave it to him.

"Charmer, ain't she? I've seen these fellows small as a thumbnail and I've seen them two feet across. They're a wonder. Unlike you or me, they can break off an arm, or get it eaten off, and grow a new one. These tiny feet on the underside—see these?—they can cling to any rock, no matter how steep. That hole here, that's the mouth. Darned if I know how these creatures make babies." He looked at it lingeringly and set it back in the tide pool.

"Want me to show you what else is in here?"

MEADOWLARK THOUGHT EACH tide pool was a miracle, and this beach held many, many more miracles, more universes than she could ever explore.

Robber pointed out some blue-gray-green creatures called anemones, six of them.

"Very funny, very ugly," Meadowlark cried.

"They look like round globs of gray mud," said Sam.

Meadowlark touched one with a finger and cried out in alarm and laughed at herself. The thing was squishy.

"The round hole at the top," said Robber, "is its mouth. Since there's almost no water here, right now the mouth is closed. But that mouth has tentacles that . . ."

For Meadowlark he explained what a tentacle is, and said, "We've got to see one that's open."

He splashed out into thigh-deep water, bucket in one hand and shovel in the other. Meadowlark was quick behind him, emerald cloth dress or no, and Sam reluctantly behind her. Soon Robber found what he was looking for.

Meadowlark gasped. It looked like a huge flower in brilliant pink. Long, slender pink tendrils floated gently in the water.

"Like petals," she exclaimed.

"Beautiful, ain't it?" Then, with a change of mood, "It's the most beautiful things that hurt you."

Sam thought better of asking what he meant.

Robber went on, "if those slender tongues, if they catch something, they paralyze it. Then they put it in their mouth."

"Do they have bones?" asked Meadowlark.

"No bones. Squish all the way through."

"How do they make more anemones?"

"That's a mystery to me. Let's get back to the tide pools," said Robber.

They did.

"Are they rooted?"

Robber fingered another anemone gently. It closed its mouth. "No, they're not rooted—they're animals, not plants. They have a kind of disk at the bottom that holds fast to a rock, or something else hard. In fact, look here."

Robber fished around with his shovel and picked up a strange little object with the tip and dropped it into his bucket. It was a shelled creature with long, jointed legs, the front legs pincers. Meadowlark stuck a finger toward it and it jumped—sideways.

"Oooh," she cried out.

"A hermit crab," said Robber.

She stuck the finger back.

This time the crab pinched her.

"Ow!" She stuck her finger in her mouth, laughing.

"Look what's on his back," said Robber.

Meadowlark and Sam bumped heads slightly as they both bent to look, and smiled sideways at each other.

"See?"

"A tiny anemone!" said Sam.

"Exactly! Hermit crabs and anemones usually live together, and most crabs carry an anemone or two on their backs."

"A saddle horse for the ocean," said Sam. Then, "Look at that, eight legs."

"Speaking of ocean horse," said Robber, "let's look over here."

They splashed in shallow water or mucked in sand, boulder to boulder, tide pool to tide pool. Robber didn't say what he was looking for until . . .

"There!"

In a deep pool Meadowlark saw a purple-looking plant with a bunch of daggers sticking up, like an ocean cactus.

"Mildly poisonous," said Robber. "But don't look at the sea urchin, look at what's holding on to it."

Meadowlark gasped out loud. A small creature with a head like a horse's was clinging to the sea urchin with its . . . tail?

Robber laughed. "A sea horse."

"The head is like a horse," said Sam, "but the tail is like a monkey."

"Exactly. What a confused critter!"

Robber slipped on a glove and wiggled the spine of the sea urchin. The sea horse let go and . . .

"Is that the way it swims?" said Meadowlark. It inched its way forward upright and very slowly. There were whirring motions around its body.

"It has that armor, the ridges you see running around its body, and it has fins."

"Totally mixed up," said Sam, "horse and monkey, fins and armor."

They spent perhaps an hour playing in the tide pools, all three of them.

Suddenly Robber suggested, "Want to eat with me? I came down here to dig clams."

"Sure."

Sam whistled at Coy—the coyote was getting too far away.

It turned out that digging soft-shell clams when the tide was out was dead easy. Even Meadowlark took her turn at the shovel. While they worked, Sam and Meadowlark found out that Robber had abandoned ship here—"Where in the world will you find a climate so sweet as California?" he asked. He was unmarried—"I had a woman in every port in the world"—and had no family of any kind.

When the bucket was almost full of clams, Robber said, "One more thing. Nothing better with clams than a few abalone."

He led them out to the rocky point. At a low cliff edge, where the water was perhaps six feet deep, he dove in and started prying abalone off the rock with his butcher's knife. From the look of it, getting them off the rock was hard work. Robber would pop to the surface, get a breath, and go back to it. Eventually he would give one to Meadowlark and go back down. He took six.

Meadowlark made a face. To her they looked like giant half snails.

At last, Coy skittering alongside, they followed Robber up the small creek to a one-room cabin. In front of it Robber lit a fire, put a big pan of water on, and set to pounding the abalone like hell. He pounded and pounded.

Coy stayed well back. He seemed to have an aversion to both clams and abalones.

When Meadowlark asked for something to do, he pointed out some wild onions she could pick and wash in the creek.

"Doesn't Don Cesar object to you living here?" Sam asked.

"Not his land," said Robber. "The Mexican government is probably waiting for some other nabob they want to give this piece of God's good green earth to. It's one of the finest pieces on the planet."

While the water was coming to a boil, Robber told them about the creatures of the deeps of the ocean. According to him dolphins were the most lovable of animals, because they jumped free of the water and played around your boat and always seemed to be smiling.

"This is a seafood stew I'm making here," he declared, "clams, chopped abalone, and onions.

"The nasty critters are the sharks." Robber picked up a stick and drew one in the sand, so Meadowlark would know one if she ever saw that dorsal fin cutting through the waves. "I like to catch sand sharks and eat them. Getting even with shark-kind."

Sam laughed at that expression.

"Whales are the largest animals in the world, I'm pretty sure. In my whaling days, I saw things. . . .

"When you see a sperm whale pull a boat full of men through the water faster than a horse can run, and do that even with harpoons in his back—you know that's some hunk of animal."

Robber's favorite ocean-dwellers, though, were the octopus and the squid. He made a giant drawing of an octopus in front of the fire. "This one," he said, "can be as small as a joint of your finger. Or, believe it or not, as long as three horses hitched one behind the other." He gave them a look of amazement.

Now he did a drawing of an octopus as long as a man, most of it being eight tentacles dangling behind. "These tentacles have suckers on the bottom, and if the octopus catches anything, he never lets go."

Merriment played in his eyes. "He pulls you up into his mouth, which is at his bottom." Robber nodded in that direction. "That's where his tentacles join his head, and that's where he does"— Robber made a comical expression—"his eating.

"Now, here's the best part. When the octopus feels threatened, he squirts out a cloud of black ink, and while you're blind, he runs like hell."

The squid was similar, and just as small, but got even bigger.

"This sailor has seen some," Robber said, "that must have been fifty feet long. They have ten tentacles instead of eight.

"Know my favorite strange one of all? Jellyfish."

"Jellyfish," said Sam. Then he explained to Meadowlark what jelly is.

"Sure enough. They come in swarms, either thousands and thousands or none at all. Mostly they come at night, rise up from the deeps. They have lots of different shapes, but most of them look like the tops of mushrooms. On the sides they have these hangy-downs, things like strings that follow them. Actual, these are tentacles, and help catch food.

"Here's what I really like. Some of them, there in the dark, they glow."

Sam and Meadowlark stared at him.

"Glow, yes, they do. The ocean is dark," said Robber. "Think about it, farther down you go, the farther you get from sunlight. A hundred feet down looks like twilight. A thousand feet down, night. Ten thousand feet down, a darkness you nor I can't ever imagine.

"But up through the darkness come the jellyfish, glowing mushrooms trailing thin streams of light. The white ones look like half moons, glowing."

Meadowlark cut off an exclamation with a hand over her mouth.

"They swim through the incredible blackness, and they glow like lamps. Glow, I say . . ."

MEADOWLARK KNEW IT for a delicious dream:

She felt herself caressed by the gentle eddies of an ocean infinitely deep, as deep as her own mind and the mind of all consciousness. She undulated through the warm waters, slowly, her black hair waving behind her like the tendrils of an exotic undersea plant. Suspended in the depth, suspended in light, she nuanced her way forward.

Though she didn't feel that she moved, she swam through great columns of light, thick as trees. These trees were ethereal. She passed her hand through a column and looked in amazement at the glow of her skin.

In every direction, like downy thistles before a breeze, swam many-colored fish. Some were deep purple with yellow patches brighter than sunlight. Some were a rash of orange; some a scatter of green, others a luminous blue, or a hammered bronze. She turned in the water, and turned and turned, embracing them all with her eyes.

She swam a little toward the edge of this sunny area, swam toward where the columns of light faded in the darkness, and were almost lost. Here there stirred black shapes, shapes small and graceful, like flags blowing in a wind; shapes that darted like knife blades; shapes the size of sailing ships, cutting the water swiftly as any prow. The water out there, she felt sure, was cold.

She looked for the half-moons—she was sure half moons floated out there somewhere, glowing in the darkness. She turned her body in every direction, she shot her eyes this way and that, but she saw no half-moons.

Her heart ached a little.

Suddenly she was afraid. Then she thought, *How am I breathing underwater? What am I breathing underwater?*

Instantly the sea surged into her mouth, down her windpipe, into her lungs.

Meadowlark gagged. She stopped breathing. She gasped desperately for breath, and knew that she would find breath if she could find calm.

An idea seized her. She turned and swam back toward the brightest sunlight. In the light she relaxed. Then she told herself to breathe. *If you breathe, the water will be air. If you breathe, you will live.*

She sucked in—was it water, was it air? Either way, it filled her lungs with life. Ecstatic, she breathed deep again. Her body relaxed. The water again felt warm, friendly, balming.

She reached the brightest stretch in the sunny ocean that surrounded her, and bathed in its pleasures. She drifted into a school of lilac-and-red fish and was delighted at their sudden flight, this way and that, with sudden stops, then further rushes. They streaked the water with scarlet, then dotted it, then streaked it again.

She was happy. She lolled. She spun slowly in the water, her movements languid, her limbs sensuous, her heart soft and light.

HOOF CLOPS OUTSIDE the tipi.

Coy barked sharply.

Sam grabbed his pistol with one hand and his knife with the other.

The clops drummed up the memory of the last time he'd been surprised in his tipi. In Ruby Hawk Valley, where Sam and Meadowlark had spent their version of a honeymoon, Meadowlark's relatives and one of her suitors suddenly appeared with weapons pointed. They took Meadowlark back to her family, and marched Sam back to the village as a prisoner.

I damn near lost her forever.

Coy barked harder.

Maybe he remembers too.

So now he got the last peg out of the tipi flap fast and busted out naked and looked up beyond the horses' heads, each hand raised to fight.

Julia Rubio squealed with laughter.

Flat Dog gave his brother-in-law a severe look—*What in hell are you doing?*

Sam dived back into the tipi.

When Meadowlark opened the flap for her brother and the señorita, a small fire was started and coffee was brewing. Sam sat fully dressed in the position of host, behind the center fire.

"The others are gone back to the pueblo," said Flat Dog.

"I am come here with my man," said Julia. Then she added, "I knew of the instant, this is my man."

Flat Dog looked a little sheepish but said, "I feel the same way."

The two pairs of lovers gazed at each other across the low flames, dowsing themselves in the words and their meanings.

Sam and Meadowlark looked at each other. Considering what they'd done, they could hardly criticize anyone else. Sam did wonder why. *Flat Dog, you're kind of striking, tall and rangy like most Crow men, but that face of yours, it's more comic than handsome, and you don't have a dollar to your name.*

Flat Dog spoke to Meadowlark. "Will you let us use your tipi?"

Meadowlark nodded slowly. "Yes."

"We will give ourselves to each other and make the bond forever," said Julia.

I know how that feels.

"We'll go to the mission," Sam told Flat Dog. "Bring the tipi back when you're ready."

"Flat Dog will come when my father's men guess right and find me here," said Julia. "But we will never be finished, this man and I."

As they were packing up, Meadowlark said quietly to Sam, "The last two days, looks like they were something big."

Sam grinned. "She's a fire-breather, that one."

Ten

Banished

"THIS LITTLE GAME will show the advantage of race, subtle but decisive," said Grumble.

Sumner started to protest but thought better of it. He slipped into some dark shadows.

The others went into the cantina, Abby at a table by herself, Sam, Meadowlark, and Grumble at a table near enough to watch. Coy snuggled up to Sam's feet, being mannerly. This was the fanciest cantina in town, for the little game required a dupe with some pesos in his purse.

No sign of Flat Dog yet, and not a whisper from the Rubio family.

Abby was gorgeous. Today she wore a royal blue gown and a mint-colored hat, which set off her hennaed hair perfectly. If any observer questioned her wealth and breeding, doubt was banished by the fine brooch she wore, with a gold timepiece encircled by sparkling diamond chips.

Nearby the threesome ordered mescal and a big supper. They were playing the part of ruffians.

Abby's role was to sip at her brandy and wait, alone. Once in a while she checked her timepiece. When a man or two offered to buy her a drink, she dismissed them with withering glances.

In San Pedro Harbor were two British merchantmen, traders seeking to exchange their manufactured goods for hundreds of rawhide bags of tallow. The captains would do well. Sumner had reported that officers came into this cantina every evening to celebrate their good fortune.

At last a man strode in wearing the outfit of an officer of a merchant ship, plain blue frock coat with billed hat. Sam was tickled at the look Abby gave him. It was a come-hither so delicate, so subtle, that only its object would normally notice.

The officer walked smartly to Abby's table, bowed, and spoke, doubtless introducing himself.

Abby lit up, eyes dancing—her whole body bubbled a little. Sam looked at Meadowlark, who was smiling and shaking her head. "She's a wonder," Sam said softly.

The officer marched to the bar, bought a bottle of a special brandy kept for certain customers, and took it back to Abby's table. She poured for him generously, herself delicately.

They passed the time in animated talk, the language of the tongues meaningless, the language of the bodies sensual.

At last Sumner ambled in. He was turned out smartly. This was no slave certainly, but a free black and a man of means, even wearing a splendid ruby ring on one finger. He looked around the room, his eyes glowing with anticipation. They came to rest on Abby. He approached the table.

Sam couldn't hear the words. The officer at first stiffened at the black man's presence. Abby said something gaily—Sam caught the word "fun." The officer's back relented. Then Sumner stepped to the bar, and Abby leaned over to whisper in the officer's ear. Though Sam couldn't hear the words, he knew exactly what they were.

"Let's have some sport with him. We'll propose a game . . ."

SUMNER DIDN'T SEEM to notice that the man and woman never bet the same side of the coin. If Abby put her peso on the table heads up, the officer slapped his down with tails showing. Whooping it up, Sumner tossed his and let it turn heads or tails by chance.

The rule was that the odd man out won. So if Abby said heads, the officer said tails, or vice versa, and it didn't matter what Sumner said. Whichever one he matched, the other one swept the pot away.

A simple collusion. "No matter what the black man calls," she'd told the officer, "we win."

Sumner smiled at Abby too much, drank his brandy too fast, and generally had a very good time. He lost a peso on every flip, but he didn't seem to mind, and his leather pouch bulged with coins.

Abby encouraged Sumner's flirtation. She complimented him on the large ruby ring on his finger, and the gold ring in his ear. Sam heard her say, "Cedric"—that was the false name Sumner had chosen—"you are so . . ." So this and so that. Her eyes lingered on his muscular arms, and she held his glance a little too long. She laughed too loudly at his witticisms, whatever they were.

Occasionally she tossed a knowing smile at Officer.

Officer was trying not to gloat. Never had he been in on a simpler ruse, or a more effective one. Nothing more fun than encouraging a man to make a fool of himself and pay for the privilege.

Meadowlark whispered to Sam, "All because Sumner isn't white."

At last Abby protested. "Cedric," she said loudly, as though to a child, "you're having a terrible run of luck. Time to stop."

"Ah'm havin' fun," said Sumner. Whenever he played dumb or drunk, his English deteriorated.

She gave him an appraising glance, shrugged, and smiled merrily. "Well, a few more flips then, to see if your luck changes." She fished in the embroidered pouch that hung from her wrist and pulled out a silver coin dangling on a silver chain. She slipped it off and held it out. "Here, borrow this. My grandmother gave it to me for good luck. Use it to flip."

Cedric grinned and rubbed the coin. "Luck, you my gal. Luck, you my lover."

They each put a peso in the pot, then flipped, Cedric using the lucky coin.

Somehow he lost again. And again, and again, and again.

"That's really enough," said Abby. She looked at her timepiece, turned her face away from Sumner, and winked at Officer. "It's past time for me to go." She collected her lucky coin, spoke a few words of commiseration, and glided out.

Sticking to the plan, Officer stayed with Cedric. He did offer sympathy, unconvincingly. After one more drink, Officer excused himself and stepped into the night.

Abby was waiting, as promised, at a cantina around the corner. They laughed together and spoke gay words. Officer was getting confident of a kiss, and more. Carefully, they pooled their winnings and started counting the pesos out onto the table, one for the lady, one for the officer . . .

"What in hell!" came the booming voice.

Sumner stood over them. "Putting your heads together. You two done cheated me. You are flimflam artists."

Suddenly a lady gun was in his hand.

Abby gasped and put a hand to her mouth. Officer blanched.

"There's nothing crooked here," said Abby. "We were just . . . attracted to each other and decided to share a drink afterward."

"Exactly so," protested Officer.

"And split the take," said Sumner.

He pointed the barrel at the pile of pesos in the middle of the table. "Believe I'll just take that pile myself," growled Sumner.

"That would be robbery," said Officer quickly. "Armed robbery. The local officials will have you flogged."

Sumner hesitated. Then he nodded. "Black man don't like no law." He thought a little more. "Tell you what. You, missy, pick up that pile. We three will walk us back to the cantina."

"What . . . ?"

"Let's git," Sumner said sharply, the pistol pointed at Officer's chest.

They got.

SAM WAS HUGELY relieved to see them come in.

Sumner gave a huge, fake smile in the direction of their table. "Now look there. Them fellows, that Indian woman too, they saw us. We'll done ask them."

He put the pistol away, and Sam breathed easier. Meadowlark carefully kept her face straight.

Sumner told his story mostly to Grumble, ending with, "So what you think's going on here?"

"I know exactly," said Grumble. "It's one of the oldest ruses in the world." Then he explained to Sumner, a little slowly, just how it worked.

"I'll be damn," said the eggplant-colored man. "Whose idea was this?"

Abby said nothing.

"It was her idea," said Officer. "She did it. I never had such a thought in my life."

Sumner grinned at Abby. "That true, ma'am?" The "ma'am" rolled with fine irony.

"Certainly not. I know nothing of . . . chicanery."

"Which of 'em you think done it?" Sumner asked Grumble.

The cherub shrugged his shoulders. "Makes no difference. Report them both to the law."

"Surely that's unnecessary," said Officer.

"I can't believe you'd do that," said Abby.

It took a few minutes, but a deal was struck. In return for keeping all the money, Sumner would let them both go.

"That fair?" he asked Grumble.

The cherub nodded. "I think so."

Sumner scooped up the entire pile.

"If you'll excuse me then," said Officer. "Gentlemen. Madam."

The "madam" sounded edgy.

"I don't think he want your company no more," Sumner told Abby.

"Decidedly not," said Officer, and left.

Five minutes later Sumner came back. "He's in his lodgings," the black man said.

They all started hooting. Fists pounded the table.

The bartender looked at them like they were crazy.

Grumble started dividing the money.

FLAT DOG LIKED the roar of the waves. He got a kick out of how the water swooshed up the sand, paused to wet his bottom, and sucked back to the infinite sea.

Julia was stretched out next to him. He reached for her hand. She squeezed his but didn't open her eyes. She'd said she just wanted to enjoy the sun on her body.

The swoosh tickled his parts again. He thought about what this funny thing the ocean was. Water swirling up and back. Waves crashing down. Amazing what forever-and-ever noise the ocean made. It shut out the rest of the world and invited you to . . .

He looked again at the horizon. He liked the place where the dark blue sea smeared into the light blue sky. For a small distance you couldn't tell which was which. He knew people sailed out there—somehow they used the wind in their canvas sails and went wherever they wanted. They even sailed, according to Captain Smith, all the way to China, a place at least five thousand miles west. His home country was about one thousand miles northeast. The idea of sailing—traveling by wind!—five thousand miles! There you would find people with yellow faces. What a hoot.

Julia screamed.

Something whacked Flat Dog in the head.

He tried to spin and get to his feet. Groggily, he pitched to the sand.

A Californio stood over him, holding a pistol like a club.

Julia screamed and screamed.

Flat Dog got to his hands and knees and peered.

Men were dragging Julia across the sand. Her skirt rode up and exposed too much thigh.

They dropped her at her father's feet. He pulled her skirt down and said something abrupt in Spanish.

She barked loud words at him.

Flat Dog tried to get up.

A boot slammed him back down.

Rubio strode over to him, a whip in his hand. The Russian knout—Flat Dog saw the dried and hardened thongs of rawhide interwoven with wire. He remembered that the wire was sharpened so it would tear the flesh.

On hands and knees he charged Rubio.

Two men kicked him, and he felt ribs crack.

Julia was howling, but Rubio's men held her away.

In utter silence the don inspected his knout, and thumbed the wire tips. The savage gleam in his eyes and the contemptuous curl of his lips spoke for him.

Two men held Flat Dog, one gripping his calves, the other standing on his hands.

Rubio raised the knout high and spoke a single word. "Indio!" With that cry he lashed the whip down.

Agony beyond imagination.

"Indio!" yelled the don, and the knout struck again.

Flat Dog's mind sailed off somewhere, perhaps to China. Only his body was left to suffer.

Ten times the knout struck. Ten times the don shouted, "Indio!"

Much later, Flat Dog regained consciousness. The first thing he saw was that no one was with him on the beach except his horse. He didn't call out for Julia. He knew.

He wiggled. Then he didn't move again for a while. At great length and in great pain, he got to his hands and knees. He crawled and crawled until he came to the tipi flap. He struggled past it and collapsed. Tomorrow, or the next day, he would lie across his horse and ride toward the pueblo. Later, maybe, he would come back for the tipi.

JEDEDIAH'S TRIP TO San Diego confirmed his darkest prejudices about Mexicans. The governor was suspicious of him— "Why have you and your men invaded our country without passports?" Plainly, the governor suspected that these Americans were the vanguard of a host of Americans who would come and take this golden clime from the Mexicans. The Russians asserted their rights to some of it. The British coveted it. Surely the Americans, who shared the continent, would try to push their way in.

Jedediah explained patiently that he and his men were merely hunters. Finding themselves in a parched country, without enough food and water for the men, or water and grass for the horses, they were desperate. And their desperate solution was to cross what the Mexicans called the Mojave Desert to San Gabriel Mission, hoping to rest men and horses. There they hoped to trade for more horses, and be on their way again.

Several captains of American ships vouched for the truth of what Jedediah said.

The governor neither understood nor cared. Not knowing what "hunting beaver" could mean, he called them "fishermen." And he didn't want to take responsibility for dealing with interlopers. "You will have to go to Mexico City," he said. "There they will decide what to do with you."

Jedediah was perfectly aware that in San Diego he was half guest, half prisoner. But he refused to go to Mexico City. If he did, he might spend years in a Mexican jail. He confided to his journal that it was also an impertinence to demand that he make the journey at his own expense.

So the governor, always a politician, made a ruling. "You will have to wait until I send a letter to Mexico City and get an answer back."

Jedediah argued. "Don't you see, the delay will be ruinous. Think what I'll have to pay my men in wages while they do nothing. Think of my losses in beaver that doesn't get trapped."

Finally, influenced by those reputable ship captains, the governor granted Jedediah passports, on one strict condition—that he gather his men from San Gabriel and leave the country the way he came.

SAM WAS TALKING to Jedediah in the captain's room, which was a lot nicer than anyone else's room, when he heard a soft tap and a soft voice. "Sam."

He opened the door.

Meadowlark stood crying, head down, her shoulders shaking.

Sam held her.

Now she sobbed loudly, and her body quaked.

When she was ready, she led Sam and Jedediah to the room she and Sam shared. On their small bed the sheets were wild with blood. Then Sam saw that a head dented the pillow, and . . .

Meadowlark stopped them from pulling back the sheets hastily. Instead she peeled them off slowly. They were not stuck hard to the cloth shirt beneath. The first cloth shirt Flat Dog had ever owned was in tatters.

The back beneath it was a mass of red welts and deep slashes.

Sam looked at Jedediah, anger in his eyes, and said, "They flogged Flat Dog, the bastards."

Sam guessed who, and with what.

FATHER SANCHEZ CAME with a translator and a Mexican woman who had skill at healing, a *curandera*. She spent a long time cleaning Flat Dog's back and then gently rubbing salves onto the open wounds.

Flat Dog made no sound, no movement. Meadowlark held his hand and from time to time wept. Sam, Jedediah, Father Sanchez, and the translator watched gravely.

Sam told the captain the story, how Flat Dog and Julia Rubio were wildly attracted to each other, how Julia finagled an invitation to the rancho for all of them. How she and Flat Dog slipped away, came to Topanga Beach, and asked to use the tipi.

Jedediah gave Sam a stern look, though Father Sanchez did not.

"Looks like it was a bad idea," the captain told Sam.

"Rubio is a harsh man," the friar put in. "He has no respect for any authority but his own."

"He's also a bastard," growled Sam.

"I have seen this coming. His family rebels, especially this youngest girl. The harsher his rules, the more headstrong she gets."

"What makes me furious," said Sam, "is that Rubio thinks he's superior. He whipped Flat Dog like a slave, not a man."

Father Sanchez said softly, "I doubt that the don respects your American idea of equality."

The *curandera* gave Meadowlark what was left of the salve. She said some words, and the translator said, "Put this on his wounds again tomorrow morning. In a few days his back will be much better. I think a rib or two is broken. That will bother him longer."

Coy curled up beneath the bed and stayed until Flat Dog was on his feet again.

Sam and Meadowlark spent the days trying to get the story out of Flat Dog, but he wouldn't talk about it. They wondered what had happened to Julia, but at their questions Flat Dog just shook his head no.

On the fourth day he started moving decently and the spark in his eyes hinted at returning. Which was good, because tomorrow was the night of the celebration.

Eleven

Fandango

FANDANGO: THE MEXICANS turned the Pueblo of the Angels into a party. The beaver men didn't know what the occasion was and didn't care. Any excuse to dance, sing, holler, carouse, and romance the ladies was plenty good enough for them.

The beaver men called the affair a fandango. Sumner said *baile* would be a better word for it, but fandango sounded a bigger party to the trappers.

La música was at *la plaza*. Everybody came—Mexicans of the pueblo; dons of the ranchos and their ladies, plus their grown sons and daughters, the men who worked the ranchos; the many Mexicans who lived at the mission, and plenty of mission Indios. The plaza was throbbing with people decked in their *baile* best and in a festive mood.

Gideon said, "I will fiddle," and pegged toward the orchestra with his case.

"How you think the French-Canadian melodies mix with the Mexican?" Sumner asked Sam.

Sam smiled and shrugged. Tonight he was downhearted. Gideon had decided to stay at the pueblo as an apprentice to Angel and then travel with his new master from mission to mission, learning silversmithing and goldsmithing. The master was in his twenties and Spanish. The apprentice was in his thirties and French-Canadian. But all that mattered was the art.

Sam had to admit that making beautiful objects in gold and silver seemed good for the bear man. For a French-Canadian on one leg it was a definite step up from hunting beaver and fighting Indians. Still, in a few days Sam would lose his traveling companion of four years, four long years of every kind of adventure, times shining and sour, up to heaven and down to hell and up to heaven again.

Sam thought often of the terrible night when he cut Gideon's leg off at the knee. Sometimes he even dreamed about it. That night had changed Gideon's life forever. Sam's too. Now the man himself, his bright spirit, would be taken away.

Sam, Meadowlark, Flat Dog, Sumner, Grumble, Abby—as a group they made their way around the edge of the plaza, looking for a place to sit. But the cantinas were jam-packed, people raising their cups, crying out, waiters rushing here and there, all the hustle and bustle of a grand celebration.

Flat Dog was walking on tenterhooks, a man afraid that any step would bring pain. His back was a mass of scabs.

"I believe I will mingle with the crowd," said Sumner, starting to slip away.

"Come back," said Grumble. "You will not cut any purses. Tonight or any time."

"I'm good at it, I . . ."

"Sumner! Are you my apprentice? It's foolish to do things they flog you for, or put you in jail for."

"Take the jail, to hell with the flogging," said Flat Dog.

"The idea," Grumble said firmly, "is to create ruses and illusions, not commit crimes."

Sumner frowned and stayed with the group. He had declared himself free. Whenever Jedediah decided to leave, Sumner would make himself scarce and rendezvous later with Grumble and continue his education in the fine art of living by his wits.

Sam would help out. He would tell Jedediah that Sumner had stolen away, and no one knew where he was. If Jedediah insisted on going to the authorities, Grumble promised to buy Sumner from Jedediah.

"I don't care if it costs a hundred dollars," he told Sam confidentially.

Sam gave him the eye. A hundred dollars was half a year's wage for the average man.

"Or two hundred," Grumble insisted. "He will be worth it to me."

Sam smiled to himself. Grumble could not admit that sentiment played any role in his doings.

"Mr. Grumble," came the accented voice, "Miss Abby, will you and your friends join us?"

It was Don Francisco Avila, former *alcalde* of the pueblo and a friend of Father Sanchez whom they'd all met briefly. He rose courteously and opened his arms in welcome. His wife, Doña Emilia, and two granddaughters surrounded him.

The six joined the Mexicans. Room could always be made for the guests of the don of a great rancho, though the doña looked queasily at Coy.

"What great seats," Sam said. "Close to the orchestra." He tied Coy's leash to his chair leg.

Brandy, wine, and tequila flowed in the more expensive cantinas, mescal in the cheaper ones. Smiles flashed, songs were raised, and the plaza roared with color. Sam noticed that several wives and daughters of the big ranchos danced with their men. Sam had never seen women more in love with finery. Their gowns were silk, crepe, or calico, short in the sleeve and loose at the waist (Abby said something tart about the absence of corsets). They wore dainty shoes of satin or kid leather, mantillas, combs in their hair. Bright-colored sashes cinched their waists and extravaganzas of silver jewelry gleamed on their fingers, earlobes, and bosoms.

Suddenly Sam heard Gideon's fiddle play a solo introduction. The bear man was on his feet, swaying to his own magic. The orchestra was giving him a chance to show his stuff. A plaza full of dancers stood still, breath held.

Gideon launched into a vigorous jig. After a little hesitation, the orchestra pitched in with him, everyone catching the tune and harmonies. Before long the dancers bounced with the rhythm.

"A rhythm is a rhythm the world over," said Sam, feeling a tinge of envy.

Meadowlark held out her hand. "Let's dance." She and Sam knew this one.

They neat-footed niftily, smiling at each other. Sam had a fine time. For the thousandth time he thought, *How lucky I am to have such a woman.*

Then they heard the sound of another familiar instrument. Evans, the Irishman, had joined the jig with his whistle. He and Gideon faced each other like duelists. For a verse Evans drove the tune fiercely, adding ornamentation along the way. They rang out the chorus together. Then Gideon bowed the next verse, making it faster and at the same time more flirtatious, more fun. They roared through the chorus together, and Evans charged into another verse. The orchestra felt the fever and pitched in wildly.

Irish, French-Canadian, and Mexican all together. Sam danced exultantly.

When the jig ended, the dancers burst into applause. Men and women leaning against the plaza walls, or seated at cantinas, joined them. The two trappers took a deep bow.

Sam led Meadowlark back toward the table. He was breathless. "Over there," Meadowlark said, "I want to stand right next to the orchestra. To hear it better, the . . . whistling? Piping?"

They drew close to Evans, and when they did, Sam became entranced. It was like birdsong, the melody of this little instrument, high, pure tones with lots of turns and curls, a thrush's ornate, warbling style. He liked it.

"I love music," said Meadowlark.

He knew she meant not the music of her own people, but this kind of music, in her mind what white people played.

"Me too," he said. Sam had loved to sing as a boy. His father played the Welsh harp, and the whole family sang together each Sunday evening, their equivalent of going to Sunday worship, because Morgantown had no church.

The orchestra raised up another song, unfamiliar, entirely Spanish in spirit. Sam and Meadowlark rejoined their party.

As they did, a table and chairs were being brought onto the patio of the next cantina—room was being made for . . . Don Cesar Rubio and his family.

Rubio threw a contemptuous glance at Flat Dog, Sam, and Meadowlark. Sam nodded to him. Flat Dog pretended not to see him, but turned his chair so his back would face the don. The back sported a beautiful new calico shirt and showed no sign of injury.

A glance told Sam that the Avila family knew. Probably the whole town knew.

"Señorita Julia is not with her family tonight," said Avila. His eyes were on Flat Dog, his face compassionate.

"A toast!" cried Flat Dog. He jumped to his feet and raised his glass.

Everyone at the table raised their glasses.

"To love!" cried Flat Dog loudly.

Grins lit up the table. "To love!" they all responded.

Sam resisted turning his head to see Rubio's reaction.

Avila changed the subject deftly. "Do you know how to dance our fandango?" His English was precise, each syllable carefully enunciated.

None did.

"It is a dance of courtship, very . . . exuberant. No one knows its origin, perhaps Moorish, perhaps Gypsy. Watch carefully."

Couples faced each other. The music began slowly, its rhythm accented by castanets. Dancers clapped their hands, snapped their fingers, and stomped their feet. Gradually, now, the tempo picked up. Sam noticed that it was three-beat music, like a waltz, and it was getting fast.

Stop. A total pause in the music. Dancers froze wherever they were. Tension thrummed.

Music again! Animated by the notes, the dancers got wild. Passion surged through their poses. Arms and faces teased. Eyes, torsos, and hips challenged. Back and forth they soared, faster and faster, ever more passionate, ever more daring, and yet again faster.

When the orchestra stopped, silence clapped the ears. The dancers stopped—sexual electricity charged the air.

"When we open a cantina," Abby told Grumble, "we need musicians who play the fandango."

"Ah, romance," said Don Francisco, "it is the essence of this dance."

"Romance," said Abby, "I like to hear it called that."

They all chuckled with her.

Sam noticed that several couples, after the dance, joined arms and disappeared into nearby streets and alleys. He looked into Flat Dog's face. Normally, the Crow might have been heading down one of those alleys. Now he sat, apparently content. But Sam knew his friend. Flat Dog was on some kind of edge—he needed watching.

Sam looked at Meadowlark and saw that she was worried about Flat Dog too.

Yes, your back hurts, and your heart aches. What else?

Sam looked from Flat Dog to Rubio and back, so close together. He said softly to Meadowlark, "He's got to be boiling." Sam took a breath. "You think maybe he wants to get revenge?"

Meadowlark made a face Sam couldn't read.

"The only thing Flat Dog told me about it was, Rubio kept yelling out, 'Indio! Indio!'"

Meadowlark said softly, "I wonder if we will ever see Julia again."

The music lifted, round and round, forever bubbling.

Sam grasped Meadowlark's hand and led her out to dance.

She looked back at her brother. "It is a kind of madness, such love."

"He might do something that isn't smart."

"Let's dance."

When the song ended, she led him back to the table. Rubio sneered as they passed, and Meadowlark gave him her most dazzling smile.

Sam noticed that some couples came back into the plaza, separated, and danced feverishly with new partners. A shadowed corner, a useful serape, an act of love . . .

"Only the peasants behave like this," commented Doña Emilia to the whole company. Yet her eyes said she was tickled by the idea.

Sam saw the men of the brigade mixed through the cantinas and among the dancers.

Evans and the two blacksmiths, James Reed and Silas Gobel, were sharing a bottle. A couple of days ago Evans and Reed got into another donnybrook, a knock-down, drag-out affair, each man cursing the very breath of the other. They quit when each was too battered to go on, Reed angry and Evans cheerful. Tonight they were fandango *compañeros*.

Whiskey, thought Sam, *whether they're clapping each other's shoulders or busting each other's noses.*

He liked Gobel. The fellow had brutish strength, a face that blazed with brute passion, and a mind that was straightforward, if slow. He looked like a man born to bear arms, to protect women and children. If Sam had to leave Meadowlark in someone else's care, he would consider Silas.

Sam poured another brandy for Abby, Grumble, and himself. He looked into their eyes, first Grumble, then Abby, then back and forth. He raised a glass in silent salute, and they raised theirs. A few more days and he would be leaving these friends behind. He didn't know when he would see them again, if ever. They planned to take a ship to Monterey and see if that town suited their talents better than the Pueblo of the Angels.

Among scores of couples, Arthur Black, the odd Scot, was dancing alone. The blankness in his eyes probably kept him alone. He had a twisted smile on his face, as if he were watching angels fornicate and enjoying it hugely.

Another trapper, John Wilson, danced furiously with any available woman, and went to the alleys at least twice.

Peter Ranna, a French trapper, danced elegantly with a young woman and conversed politely between songs, as though he was courting her.

Suddenly Sam saw that Harrison Rogers, the clerk from Virginia, was leaning heavily against a nearby wall. Bottle in hand, he looked at the crowd, a sardonic expression on his face. Sam never knew what was on Rogers's mind. Rogers took a long pull on the bottle.

A young Indio woman approached him. All at Sam's table listened sharply, but no one could catch the words over the music.

Rogers glared at the woman and muttered something.

Her face changed like he'd slapped her. Fire flicked through her eyes. Then she laughed, shrugged eloquently, and walked off alone.

Sumner rose, went to Rogers's side, and in a moment came back.

"He said," said Sumner, imitating the clerk's Virginia mountain twang, "she asked him to make her a *blanca pickanina*. It would be an honor,' she told him."

Sumner stood there for a moment, grinning down at everyone.

"He told her," said Sumner, still dead-on with the accent, " 'As you are so forward, I have no propensity to tetch you.' "

Abby laughed the loudest.

"Madam," said Avila to Abby, "it appears that in this village it would be difficult to make a living as a madam."

They all laughed again.

Sam looked across at Rogers, scowling, and chuckled again.

Then he noticed Flat Dog was gone. The chair was removed, to make his absence inconspicuous.

Meadowlark suddenly clamped Sam's arm. She had just noticed too.

Sam whirled and glared at Rubio.

The don replied only with another sneer.

Twelve

A Ceremony

A RAP ON the door.

Sam rose blearily toward the surface of consciousness. He opened his eyes to a half-lit room, a candle still guttering. Meadowlark sat up and looked at him questioningly.

Two raps, softly.

Sam went to the door and spoke through the thick wood. "Who is it?"

"Jedediah."

Sam opened the door.

"Get dressed and come quickly. Father Sanchez's apartments."

"Something bad?"

Jedediah gave a dry smile. "I think you'll like it."

SAM AND MEADOWLARK took a couple of minutes, for they'd been sleeping deeply and happily. They'd left the fandango early, not long after midnight, for the lovely privacy of their bedroom, a luxury they wouldn't have much longer. There they loved each other to weariness. That was another luxury soon to be lost, Sam guessed, because Meadowlark was approaching her sixth month.

Father Sanchez's door was wide open. The good friar sat comfortably in a big stuffed chair. As Sam and Meadowlark stepped into the room, they saw the other visitors scattered on ladder-back chairs, Grumble, Abby, Flat Dog, Angel—Angel?—and Reina Obregon y Rubio—Doña Reina?

In the middle of this circle stood Flat Dog and Julia, holding hands. Julia wore a floor-length white dress, white gloves to her elbows, and a white hat. Within this frame her tawny hair and golden skin glowed. She looked like a translucent vase bearing the fiery liquids passion and beauty.

To Sam, Flat Dog looked so happy he couldn't see straight.

Sam and Meadowlark sat in the chairs left open for them. Coy slipped between the chair legs and peered out quizzically.

"Welcome," said Father Sanchez. The interpreter at his side rendered each language into the other for everyone. "Meadowlark, your brother has come with a request that deserves the most serious consideration."

"We want to be married," said Julia. Her strong voice vibrated with feeling.

Father Sanchez nodded at Reina. "And I support this marriage," she said. "It was I who helped Julia escape the hacienda tonight, and brought Flat Dog to her."

Sam smiled, thinking how that would rub Don Rubio exactly the wrong way.

"The Rubio family will support it, that is, my sisters. Father will not." Sam had met the four sisters of Julia and Reina. The mother had passed away. "We are tired, especially we sisters, of Father's tyranny. Julia, the youngest, will be the first of us to follow her heart."

"So we do not have the permission of the parents," said Father Sanchez. He raised an eyebrow. "You two are Flat Dog's only family in California. What do you say?"

Sam and Meadowlark spoke at the same time. "It's great."

They looked at each other in embarrassment. Sam added, "Whatever Flat Dog wants."

Father Sanchez nodded slowly, turned to Julia, and regarded her for a long moment. "Julia," he said gently, "I have known you for all of your seventeen years. I baptized you. I know you to be passionate. Look in your heart and tell me truly, beyond passion, beyond your excitement, do you find iron within yourself? Is there firmness of intention? Is there that which endures? My child, I tell you certainly, as a foundation for marriage, passion is not sturdy enough."

Julia didn't hesitate. "Father, I know my heart. This man is for me." She turned and looked into Flat Dog's eyes. "He and I will become one being, indissoluble, for all our lives long. I know that as I know the taste of my own breath in my throat."

Father Sanchez considered for a long moment. "And you, Flat Dog?"

"I knew nothing of love until Julia taught me. With her I am full of life. Without her I am as a dead man."

Father Sanchez pondered. "The rest of you, what do you say?"

Jedediah spoke immediately. "Will not Don Cesar send men after this couple, and take his daughter back by force?"

"If the mission decides to marry this pair, it has the ability to help them conceal themselves." Sam noticed that the friar stressed the "if."

Grumble spoke gently. "Father, I was raised most devoutly in the church. One of its teachings is that human passion is a reflection of divine love. I believe this passion to be so."

Abby said simply, "I support it." Sam thought he saw liquid in Abby's eyes.

Jedediah said, "I support it."

Sam wondered if Jedediah was taking pleasure in slapping the face of the Mexican establishment that had irked him.

Angel said, "I know Julia's heart, and believe this to be a good marriage. I have made a ring for the bride."

Julia glowed brighter.

"Let us talk of certain other obstacles to the union," said Father Sanchez. "You must become a Catholic," he told Flat Dog. "That means accepting instruction in the holy faith." The friar studied Flat Dog's face and probably saw puzzlement. "It means you will be expected to participate in the life of the church, its ceremonies, and its customs."

Flat Dog spoke with a surprisingly assertive voice. "I have seen my brother Sam join his wife's people, adopt our ways, and walk our sacred paths. I will do the same for Julia."

Sam was amazed and tickled, all at once.

Father Sanchez continued. "You must promise to raise the children of this union in the Catholic Church."

"I also wish that," said Julia.

"I promise," said Flat Dog.

Father Sanchez looked slowly around the room at all of them. "Give me a few minutes," he said, "to pray about this matter."

"Father," said Jedediah, "are there other questions we can answer? Fears we can allay?" He hesitated. "Are you afraid of offending Don Cesar?"

"That," said the friar, "is not a problem."

IN THE VAST church the cluster of people before the altar looked tiny. The dawn light coming through the windows lit up the priest's white and gold vestments brilliantly, so that everyone else seemed to be mere shadows.

The matrimonial couple knelt before the priest, each holding a candle.

A coyote crouched beneath the front pew.

First Father Sanchez exhorted the couple briefly. He urged them to realize that they would now be one person, joined through sanction of God the Father. He advised them to leave their families and make a new one, an entity with its own life, its own sanctity. He counseled them to learn from their differences in rearing and culture. "Such matters, instead of tearing at the fabric of union, can serve to strengthen it."

Then he asked, separately, for the consent of the bride and groom to proceed into this holy sacrament. Each agreed.

"*Ego conjungo vos in matrimonium,*" said Father Sanchez, "*in nomine Patris et Filii et Spiritus Sancti.*"

The translator said quietly, "I join you in matrimony in the name of the Father and the Son and the Holy Spirit."

Sam blew his breath out. He didn't realize he'd been holding it. Meadowlark squeezed his hand.

"The ring," said the friar.

Angel handed it to him. It was a simple circle of gold, needing no ornament.

Father Sanchez blessed the ring in Latin and handed it to Flat Dog. Coached step by step, Flat Dog put it on the thumb of Julia's left hand.

"*In nomine Patris,*" said the priest.

On her index finger. "*Et Filii.*"

On her middle finger. "*Et Spiritus Sancti.*"

And finally on her fourth finger.

Angel handed Flat Dog a platter covered with a beautifully embroidered cloth. On it gleamed two coins donated by Jedediah, one of gold and one of silver. After the translator, Flat Dog repeated these words: "With this ring I thee wed. This gold and silver I thee give, with my body I thee worship, and with all my worldly goods I thee endow."

Then Father Sanchez quoted a series of short verses from the Psalms. After each verse the Catholics, Julia, Angel, Grumble, and Abby, spoke the responses learned in childhood.

Father Sanchez announced that he would now proceed to the nuptial mass. During this ceremony he enunciated a number of collects, which were prayers of invocation, petition, and conclusion.

After the "Pater Noster" he spoke a solemn blessing on the new husband and wife, and gave another blessing before his benediction.

He then administered communion to the Catholics, who now included Flat Dog, and declared the ceremony complete.

Finally he stepped close and spoke a few fatherly words to the bride and groom.

Sam looked at Meadowlark. He was in awe. He looked, fully, at the commitment he had made to this woman. He grasped it with dimensions and textures new to him. And he loved all that he saw and felt. He took his wife into his arms, and felt the child of her belly nuzzled against him.

Flat Dog and Julia led the procession away from the altar.

Where are they going? thought Sam. His heart swelled. *To what happiness? To what tragedy? To what life?*

He touched the medicine pouch he wore around his neck, thought of the piece of paper inside, and the words on it: "Follow the direction your wild hair points."

Part Three

EXPLORING

Thirteen

California Mountains

JEDEDIAH TRADED HIS beaver hides for horses. The ranchos
had great horse herds roaming superb grasslands, herds so vast
most dons didn't know how many head they owned. Horses that
would have brought half a year's wages in the mountains sold for
a week's wages. Soon Jedediah had forty-eight new mounts, more
than two per man. He hoped he'd need the horses to carry all the
beaver they would trap.

"Do you know we're going to have another horse come spring?" he asked Sam.

"What do you mean?"

"That mare of yours is going to foal."

Sam felt a thrill. "You sure?" He knew some horsemen had an eye for it.

"I'm sure."

"When?"

"Spring."

Sam thought. Meadowlark was expecting the baby in what white folks called April. "A new human and a new horse about the same time."

"You're a progenitor," said Diah, and then explained what his big word meant.

Sam decided to pick out a gelding from the new company mounts. No need to ride Paladin near her time. In fact, he would get Coy to ride Paladin, so the pup would be the complete master of balancing on the horse. They were a striking pair, the coyote riding on the back of the white mare with the black markings.

A week after the captain's return from San Diego the brigade set out. The other men picked out saddle horses and hitched their possibles onto others.

Right off, the herd stampeded eight or ten miles before the men caught them. The ride was exhilarating, and the men made camp in high spirits.

That night Captain Smith and clerk Rogers rode back to San Gabriel Mission for a final dinner with Father Sanchez and the other friars. At this farewell the head of the mission offered them many gifts, and told them they were free to slaughter and dry all the beef they wanted for their return trip.

On the way back to camp Jedediah and Rogers talked it over and agreed that Father Jose Sanchez was one of the finest men they'd ever met, a true Christian gentleman.

And a devil of a contrast, thought Jedediah, *to the damn governor.*

*   *   *

THE NEXT EVENING Flat Dog and Julia quietly joined the brigade.

Rogers put on a sour face, but the other men welcomed the couple. "Ah," said Evans the Irishman, "a beautiful woman makes the world seem finer."

Meadowlark got out the tipi she had made for them from cow hides, and she and Julia put up the poles Sam had cut. "Damn poor ones they are," he apologized to Flat Dog, "when you compare them to lodgepole pine." Though California and the ocean were exciting, Flat Dog and Meadowlark missed the Yellowstone country, home of the Crow people.

Flat Dog grinned and the men relaxed, watching the women do the work. In good Crow fashion, Meadowlark wouldn't have tolerated male help for an instant. Julia, though, clearly would have embraced anyone's help, or encouragement. She was all elbows and knees. Sam wondered if she'd even made a bed before. *That's what you get, growing up rich.*

The next morning Jedediah looked at his outfit, the surrounding countryside, the world. He told himself he should be pleased. He'd brought his brigade safely across nearly a thousand miles of terrible desert. Though he'd earned almost nothing for the company of Smith, Jackson & Sublette so far, he'd found a route to a good country, one that now had prospects of proving profitable.

Several times, over cigars and brandy, Jedediah had asked Father Sanchez about the Rio Buenaventura.

"There is a great river perhaps a hundred miles to the north," said Father Sanchez through his translator. "It flows on to the north. On the east side of this river, a *grande sierra*, a range of mountains, running north and south. Or this is what the Indios say. The mountains, they have eternal snows on their summits."

Which would mean plenty of beaver.

Riding back to camp that night, Jedediah ran it over and over in his mind. This was his chance to turn the expedition from catastrophe to bonanza.

His passports said he had to go back the way he came.

He could fudge that. The governor and the whole Mexican government be damned.

Jedediah had told the governor he was hunting beaver. He hadn't mentioned the elusive Buenaventura. Now he was going after both.

BACK OVER THE mountains the way they came and onto the flank of the great desert that stretched to the Colorado River. Every man looked out across that desert and hated it. They remembered it less with their minds than their bodies. Dust in the teeth. Tongues turned to rawhide. Sand wherever your clothes fit tight. Skin parched. The taste of alkali in what little water you got. Eyeballs scoured and aching.

So every man, plus Meadowlark, the one woman who had crossed the Mojave with them, was happy about the captain's decision to travel north instead. He said they might find a river that way, and travel along it back to rendezvous. The plan was to trap the spring season in the mountains reported to rise ahead, and follow the Buenaventura back to rendezvous in midsummer.

A fine plan. California was a good country—the blacksmith Reed and the slave Sumner had slipped away from the brigade to stay there. Most of the men, though, favored mountain doings. Buffalo. Indians, their kind of Indians. Hunting and trapping. The Rocky Mountains.

Flat Dog liked roaming but was eager to be home again, and show his native country to Julia. Meadowlark was downright homesick. Now she had seen the big water everywhere to the west. She said to Sam, "I'm ready to be in my own village, with my mother, my father, my brothers and sister."

But there was no question of heading for home yet. Not and go back across the Mojave. Not traveling in a small party. They would go when Jedediah decided to go.

"We go to rendezvous after the baby is born," said Sam. If they found beaver, he knew, the captain would want to trap through April, at least.

Meadowlark made a face and turned away. Sam watched her walk around camp, bend over the cooking pot, stoop to pick up firewood. Her body was changing. Her breasts were fuller, her hips wider, her belly a little bulged. She was beautiful.

He thought, *In three more moons she will bear our child.* April. In Crow country that would be when the snow melts and the grass greens up, a time called *awasiia,* "earth is visible." Who knew what it would be called here in California, where grass stayed green all winter?

What would they call the child? In the Crow way of things, he would be known as Snub Nose, or some other silly and endearing child's name. (Sam wanted a son, though he hadn't told Meadowlark that.) Later the lad would be given a boy's name, not a child's name, and later yet, much later, a man's name, a name he would earn through a vision, or by a deed in war.

Sam thought about seeing all those changes, as the child went from toddler to boy to youth to man. Sam had to chuckle at himself, though. As he imagined his son growing up, his picture of himself, the father, stayed the same, a vigorous fellow in his twenties. It didn't add up.

Now in his imagination he watched Meadowlark put her child into her parents' arms, a gift. He watched that over and over.

Sometimes he wondered what kinds of changes were taking place in Paladin's body. He didn't know. When he'd seen mares foal in the past, he hadn't known a foal was coming until the tits waxed up, just a few days before she dropped. He'd be damn happy to have a colt.

Northward along the desert's edge the brigade rode, and then over a low range of mountains. Now they were back on the west side of the mountains, the well-watered side. Somewhere toward the setting sun, only a few days' ride, the Pacific Ocean heaved, the friars oversaw their missions, and the dons ran their horses and cattle.

Somewhere to the north, probably, flowed a great river and rose a great range of mountains. And there they would find beaver.

They set their faces north.

The two couples lived in a world of their own making. Flat Dog and Julia honeymooned. Sam and Meadowlark passed their days and nights in the romance of young married love and the anticipation of the child.

Every night Sam and Meadowlark sat and looked at each other. They lay beside each other, arms and legs entwined. They dived into anticipation that was deeper than thought. Each had memories of family, each had expectations about family, each had powerful wants stirred by the thought of family. Different in their hopes, similar in their hopes, they were drawn forward by the child, a powerful current, into the unknown. They held each other in the realm of the known and dreamed a kingdom of grace.

IN ABOUT THREE weeks the brigade saw their range to the northeast, and it was huge, full of snows that were eternal for sure. Soon they came on a big river that hurried out of the mountains and calmed as it turned north. Was this the Buenaventura?

Jedediah followed it doggedly. The river appeared to come out of the mountains on the east.

They got some information from local Indians. Yes, the Indians confirmed, the river had its sources in those mountains.

That meant it didn't drain the entire desert, all the way from the Salt Lake. It wasn't the Buenaventura. Jedediah rode off to the top of a hill alone and sat and thought things over for an evening. He admitted it to himself: The Buenaventura was a desert mirage. *It doesn't exist. I have chased that mythical river for more than two years. Now it is dust blowing in the air.* Disgusted, he named the new river the Peticutry.

Sam, Meadowlark, Flat Dog, and Julia were sorry about their captain's disappointment. But the geography of the heart seemed more important to them.

The other men of the outfit worried. If we don't find the Buenaventura, will we have to cross the Mojave Desert again?

Soon the trappers got back into the routine of a beaver outfit. Men rode up creeks and set traps, rode down creeks, pulled the drowned rodents out of the water, and skinned them. In camp Meadowlark, Julia, and others dried the hides and prepared them for transport. Trapping was hard work.

Julia surprised everyone by pitching in with a will. She took pride in working as hard as anyone—she fleshed hides with a scraper, stretched them on hoops made from supple limbs, bound them into packs that rode on the backs of the pack-horses.

During what Jedediah said was February, what he said was March, they trapped their way north through the foothills of the great mountain range. Mount Joseph, Jedediah named it, after the friar of San Gabriel Mission, a man they would remember forever for his generosity.

One by one, they passed the big rivers that came roaring west-ward out of the mountains, rampaging toward the Peticutry and then the sea. The Indians called those rivers Nototemnes, Tuolomne, Appelaminy, Mokelumne.

"Musical names," said Evans the musician. "Beautiful."

Jedediah gave them new names and fastidiously inked them onto the maps in his journal.

Sam chuckled to himself about this. *Like they weren't real until they had white-man names and were set down in some book.*

The Indians of the region were strange. They fed, apparently, on fish, roots, acorns, and grass seed. And they were skittish as any wild animals. "Might as well be blackbirds," Diah told Sam, "for all we can talk to them." When they saw Indians, Jedediah made signs he meant as friendly, walked out alone, and laid presents on the ground. The Indians ran away.

The captain was frustrated. He wanted to ask about a passage across these mountains.

"I'm thinking of a more northerly route across the deserts to the Salt Lake," he told Sam.

Jedediah was back to tutoring Sam as a captain in training. Sam told Meadowlark it made him uneasy.

"We need a way back that's not so hot or dry," she said.

Their eyes met, their minds full of the newborn they would be carrying across the desert.

THIS DAY'S INDIANS made Sam feel edgy.

They came near camp, and he staked Paladin even closer. The Indians appeared in ones and twos on ridgetops a couple of hundred yards away. There they stood and looked into the camp. Hannibal had told Sam about working for the circus, which showed wild animals in cages, animals no one had seen before, like Bengal tigers, or chimpanzees, or elephants. And people would come and stare at the animals, strange creatures from alien lands.

Not for the first time in California, Sam felt like one of those animals.

Jedediah watched the Indians to see how close their curiosity would bring them. Finally he took a blanket, some tobacco, and some beads, and rode in the direction of some he'd glimpsed. He picked a clear spot, in the open away from timber or brush or hills, where he could see anyone who approached. Then he laid out the blanket and put down the presents and sat down to wait. Though his pistol was in his belt, his rifle was back in camp.

Soon a skinny Indian stilted in from the captain's left. Sam watched the captain open his arms and gesture to the presents. The Indian watched for long moments and suddenly was gone.

The captain waited.

Two Indians, one short and fat, the other just plain small in every direction, walked toward Jedediah from straight on. Thirty or forty yards out, they squatted and looked. They called out in a language none of the trappers knew. They smiled big.

Jedediah opened his arms wide. He made the sign of friendship toward them, though the trappers suspected these California Indians didn't know the sign language of the plains and mountains. He waited.

They babbled, waved their arms, and ran off.

Flat Dog eased up beside Sam, holding both of their horses on leads. The two of them watched carefully, rifles in hand.

Jedediah sat and waited.

Sam thought for the hundredth time, *He has incredible courage.*

Time got boring. Jedediah stayed put. Everything stayed the same. Even the heavy air didn't stir. Birds didn't sing. Leaves didn't flutter. Seemed like the sun didn't make its arc.

Sam wondered how the captain felt, out there by himself.

SCREAMS! An incredible racket, a wild clamor.

Indians sprinting toward Jedediah, bristling with bow and arrows, spears and clubs.

In one motion the captain pulled the picket on his mount and vaulted into the saddle. He rode like hell.

Sam and Flat Dog rode like hell too. Without thinking, Sam fired over his mount's head. He wouldn't hit anything at this distance, but the boom and the whoosh of black smoke might scare them off.

He reloaded on the fly, pouring too much powder down the barrel and setting the ball by banging the Celt's butt plate on the saddle.

The captain came on pell-mell.

From behind Sam heard another shot, and the tatter-tat-tat of hooves. Other boys were riding.

Jedediah galloped up to them and wheeled his horse to a stop. He looked back at the blanket, and at the Indians poised halfway between their bush hiding places and the presents. "To the devil with it," said Diah, strong language for him, and rode on.

Sam didn't think to the devil with it. One look and he and Flat Dog agreed. They whipped their horses straight toward the blanket.

Other trappers caught them. Rifles roared, and a couple of Indians went down. The rest ran off.

Sam gathered up the blanket and gifts, rode back, and presented them to Jedediah.

"Good thinking," said the captain. "We give, but we don't let them steal."

Sam watered and rope-corralled the mount, haltered Paladin, and led her to water.

"Sam! Flat Dog!"

Julia's voice. Desperation in it. "Sam! Flat Dog!"

Sam jammed Paladin's stake into the ground and ran toward the two tipis. Meadowlark was curled in the dust, Julia bent over her.

Meadowlark had one hand tented over her eyes, the other clutched at her belly. She moaned.

Sam bent over her. "What's wrong? What's the matter?"

She answered in the Crow language, "I can't get my breath."

Quickly Sam lay next to her and circled her with his arms from behind. Her chest heaved and spasmed. He'd never felt so helpless. *What can I do?*

He felt her body soften. Two or three easy expansions of the rib cage came and went.

"I'm better now," she said weakly.

Sam just kept holding her.

As it turned out, Meadowlark had been hiding troubles. She had a blinding headache. Her stomach hurt, and had been hurting for days. Off and on for the last week, she'd had difficulty catching her breath. "Even just sitting still or laying down," she admitted. "Can't get my breath."

Now that she was calmed down, she spoke English again, but her voice was wan, her skin pale, her face glistening with sweat.

Julia checked her hands and ankles. For sure, they were swollen.

"We need to talk," Julia told Sam firmly.

He kissed the top of Meadowlark's head.

"Talk with me," she told them. She gave her husband an I-mean-it look. "Talk with me too. My body, my child. My life."

The talk was complicated. Julia wanted other minds to hear, so Jedediah and Evans also sat in. Julia's cousin had gotten sick like this, late in her pregnancy. The same symptoms, swelling of the face, hands, and ankles. Terrible headaches. Pain in the stomach. Shortness of breath.

"*Convulsiónes*," said Julia.

Jedediah, Evans, and the translator Laplant kicked it around; Jedediah came up with English words they knew and dreaded. "Puerperal convulsions."

"My cousin," said Julia, "she died of it. Her daughter they saved, but my cousin, she went into convulsions and died."

For Sam, that was enough.

Fourteen
Going for Help

THEY WERE ON some river called the Appelaminy in front of a
huge range of mountains. Where they were in relation to the
Spanish towns or the missions Sam had only a vague idea. Some
Indians here had talked about the missions, so . . . Somewhere to
the west was the ocean, somewhere west the towns and missions
that dotted the coast. Sam would damn well find them.

He told Meadowlark she wasn't allowed to lift a finger,
women's work or any other. He loaded up their belongings. The

missions and towns along the ocean would have women who understood being with child. Women who knew how to heal. He searched his mind for the word. *Curanderas*. Or midwives.

Abruptly he thought, *The Indians will have healers too. These Indians. Any Indians*. Then he rejected that. The Indians were unfriendly. He wanted a Spanish healer or midwife.

He made a litter for Meadowlark, a pony-drag behind her mount with blankets lashed across. Her pony would pull the drag, and Paladin would come unburdened, on a lead.

Not until he was nearly packed did Sam realize that Julia was packing up too, and Flat Dog was ready to go.

"Too dangerous to go alone," Flat Dog said.

"Meadowlark needs a woman," said Julia.

The captain helped Sam with the last knots. "Come back when you can," he said. "Meanwhile, here's your pay." Sam took the coins and swung into the saddle.

Jedediah gave another stack to Flat Dog and said to both of them, "I won't dock your wages while you're gone. Take whatever time you need."

Flat Dog looked at the coins and said, "This is a year's wages."

Jedediah nodded.

Flat Dog asked quietly, "When will you start across the mountains?"

"A month," said Jedediah. "When the moon comes back to half." He hesitated. "We must."

He stepped to Sam and reached a hand up. "Take care of her," he said.

Sam chucked at the horses.

THEY GOT THEIR first sight of the mission five days later.

Sam had alternately rushed and forced himself to slow down. They rode down their mountain river to the Peticutry, crossed the big river and the plains beyond, pushed up a low coastal range of mountains, and eased down their west side.

They found ranchos, and people told them that the mission at Monterey was run by a kind friar who would help.

From the top of the mountains they could see the big bay, a broad expanse of the Pacific calmed by the embrace of the land. Sam wondered whether what lay ahead would be like the peaceful Pacific or the stormy one. He tried constantly to calm the terror that chewed his mind.

Meadowlark sometimes insisted on riding, so she could see the beautiful waters ahead. Now her headaches were less frequent and her stomach pain less severe, but her face, hands, and ankles were still puffy. Sam watched her constantly.

The mission was imposing, and the four visitors were shown to bedrooms even before the friar arrived.

"Padre Enrique," he said by way of introduction.

Sam spat out their names and rushed to the point. "My wife needs help."

This friar had some English. "A woman has already been sent for, a *comadrona*, what you call a midwife."

Meadowlark was put on a bed, and Mexican women fussed over her.

Sam faced the friar, pursing his mouth. "We could have some trouble. We don't have passports. We're beaver hunters. Our outfit is in the mountains four days' ride to the east, not in California."

At least it was Jedediah's theory that Mount Joseph wasn't in California. Who knew how far to the east the province extended?

Sam looked his will at the friar. "We came here to get help for my wife. No other reason." He paused. "I would appreciate it if you kept it to yourself. The news that we're here."

The friar smiled gently. "Christian charity," he said, "takes precedence over the edicts of governments."

Sam sorted out the Spanish accent and the big words and smiled.

*   *   *

THE *COMADRONA* SLIPPED past Sam into the room where Meadowlark rested. Rosalita was a young woman of remarkable beauty, blue-black hair, dark skin, and a face delicately scribed.

Sam wanted to trust her but didn't know if he could. "Seems like she's too young to know anything," he told Flat Dog.

"Like you're too young to know about hunting beaver?" said his friend.

After a few minutes of examining Meadowlark, Rosalita called Sam, Julia, and Flat Dog in. "Meadowlark, she has the sickness that maybe leads to convulsions. You must take it very seriously." She was to stay in bed all the time, all the way until the baby came. "*Solo*," Rosalita added, with a glance at Sam. "Alone."

Flat Dog grinned at the word, but Sam didn't have any grins inside him.

Rosalita would come every day, early in the afternoon. Meanwhile, she gave them three pouches of herbs to help Meadowlark. "This is hyacinth. Put this bag around her neck and leave it there. This one is saffron. Put this bag around her waist and let it hang on her belly." She handed over a third bag. "This is raspberry. Make a tea from it two or three times a day and be sure she drinks it."

Rosalita started away and turned back. "And in return you will give me something for medicines and my work," she said directly.

Flat Dog handed her a coin or two. Sam left that up to him.

"In bed *all* the time," she repeated as she left. Her beautiful face looked grim. "Until the baby comes."

Meadowlark lay in a kind of sweet daze. Occasionally, she napped, but mostly she lay gently awake. Coy curled up around her feet and gave her a poignant look, seldom lowering his eyes. Sam sat on the edge of the bed and told her lots of stories, mostly about his father Lew and the days upon days his father spent with Sam in the woods, roaming. When Sam was small, he said, he and his father had a special glade in the forest they called Eden. He explained to her again what Eden was, how the first man and woman came from there, and how they were perfect while they were there, until Eve committed a sin and persuaded Adam to do the same.

Meadowlark stuck out her tongue, as she always did at that tale. "Stupid story," she said. Coy mewled.

Sam told her the one about the game he and his father had, naming all the plants and animals, like Sam was Adam. Then, when the boy had learned about each creature, Lew would tell him its real name.

Meadowlark had heard this story before, but she liked it, and it seemed to make her peaceful.

He told her as well about his younger brother Coy, the one that Coy the coyote was named after, the brother who died. Sam recalled their favorite ways of playing. One way was tumbling and the like. Coy loved to do somersaults, headstands, handstands, cartwheels, things like that. He even developed a sort of flip where he put Sam in a frog position, ran up full speed, planted both hands on Sam's back, and did a turn in the air, landing on his feet. Sam did all the same things, except for the turn. He was never as good at them as Coy.

Whenever they talked about the original Coy, the coyote on the end of the bed would thump his tail.

He told her again the story of the last time he saw his older brother, Owen, the one who was interested in the business and in the world of commerce, but completely uninterested in the woods and the way the real world works.

When Sam ran away from home, because Owen got the woman Sam wanted, he took the family boat. But, Sam always emphasized, he left everything else the family owned, the mill, the store, the house, the acreage. He abandoned it all to Owen, though by right half was his.

The next night, while Sam was exploring Pittsburgh, the constables tried to arrest him for stealing the boat, and stealing the Celt, the rifle his father had left him. Sam drew a word picture of Owen telling the sheriff these lies.

Meadowlark always smiled as the ending of this story came. Nearly two years later, back home for the first and last time, Sam paid his brother back with a big fist to the chin. He hit Owen so hard that the older brother toppled backward over the sofa and lay unconscious on the floor.

Meadowlark giggled at that.

Meadowlark wanted to tell stories too, the old stories of her own people. However, everyone insisted she keep as quiet as possible, so Flat Dog told several.

Among the Crows storytelling was regarded as a high skill. A good narrator filled his stories with verbal wit, puns, and tongue-twisters, phrases like "Peter Piper picked a peck of pickled peppers." Flat Dog was in high form. Though Sam's Crow was far from perfect, he caught onto the wit.

This tale was one of the many tales about Old Woman's Grandchild, a mythic hero of the tribe. Flat Dog made it long and extravagant and funny. Later Sam remembered it like this:

"Old Woman's Grandchild was going to his lodge, and he knew the snakes were waiting for him there. They would tell him stories, and if they could make him fall asleep, they would kill him. He would try to do the same to them.

"He was worried. On the way to the lodge he met Jackrabbit, and that gave him an idea. He traded eyes with Jackrabbit. That way, even if he fell asleep, the glassy stare of Jackrabbit's eyes would make him look awake, and the snakes would not kill him.

"In the lodge the snakes spoke first, in lulling phrases: 'In the spring when cherry and plum blossoms are in bloom, when we kill a deer, we cook it on the sunny side of a cherry tree thicket. In the spring when there is a little wind in the daytime, we sleep well.

" 'In the fall when it is cool, we are out a long time, and when we come back to our tipi and find it warm, we go to sleep right away.'

"These phrases, and others like it, the snakes recited.

"Old Woman's Grandchild was in fact fast asleep. But the jackrabbit eyes made the snakes think he was awake, and they dared not attack him.

"Before starting, Old Woman's Grandchild gave a special bidding to his four magic arrows. When the snakes thought they had failed to put him to sleep and it was his turn to charm them, one of the arrows was to fall on his face and wake him up.

"Now the arrow fell. Old Woman's Grandchild woke up and began to recite his own hypnotic words:

" 'In the summer, when the rain strikes the tipi and there is a rattling sound, we sleep well.

" 'In the fall, when it rains, we can hear the rain on the tipi, and we sleep well.

" 'In the fall when there is a little breeze and we lie in a shelter, hearing the dry weeds rubbing against one another, we generally get drowsy, don't we?'

"Now half his listeners were asleep.

" 'When out hunting in the mountains, when we have killed a buffalo or deer toward evening and built a fire and cook, while we are cooking, it grows dark. We are very tired. We take our cooked food and eat it. Rain comes, and when we lie down to sleep, we sleep right away.'

"Now most of the snakes were asleep, but not all.

" 'In the daytime, as the drizzle strikes the lodge, pattering, and we lie warming the soles of our feet, we fall asleep, don't we?'

"All of the snakes appeared to be asleep now, but the boy had to make sure. He spoke four more lulling phrases. They truly looked asleep.

" 'Attention!' cried Old Woman's Grandchild.

"No snakes stirred to his words.

"So he proceeded to cut all their heads off."

Meadowlark laughed and clapped her hands.

Julia didn't understand the Crow language. While her husband told stories, she brewed the raspberry tea for Meadowlark, or made trips to the kitchen to get the sick woman broth, with a little meat in it.

Sam was struck hard with this thought: *Julia is a good sister, a good wife, and a good human being.*

After a few days, though, Sam couldn't stay in the room all day. He was antsy. He was jumpy. As a matter of fact, he was angry. When he began to pace, Meadowlark, Flat Dog, and Julia threw him out.

He walked the streets of Monterey fiercely. It was a pretty town, facing the bay like an amphitheater. Sam found a cantina with a view of the ocean and sat for hours one afternoon, gazing at the water. He drank endlessly the strong café they brought him—he didn't want to be even slightly drunk.

He sat on the beach with Coy. He wondered what the little coyote thought, following Sam everywhere he went, now sitting by the waters where Coy could see no food for either of them. Maybe Coy didn't think. What a relief, not to think, or imagine, or dread the future . . .

Sam tried not to think. Instead he stared at the water and pictured the many creatures that Robber described within its depths. He discovered that the waters of the Pacific did something to soothe the waters of his spirit. The moment he and Coy walked back toward town, though, or toward the mission, Sam's spirit was riled. Sam Morgan was working himself up to be very angry. If anything happened to Meadowlark or their child. Angry at the world. Angry at God.

He decided to try to find Grumble, Abby, and Sumner.

A barkeep remembered them. A beautiful woman, he recalled, an older man, and a . . . He didn't say the word. "They were looking for a cantina to buy," he went on in hesitant, melodic English. "There were difficulties. An immigrant, he, she is maybe Catholic, or become Catholic. The black also. They must take a pledge of loyalty to Mexico, all three. And then"—the man gave a shrug—"I only am cantina. Me, I don't want to sell."

Sam put himself down at night on the floor next to Meadowlark's bed at the mission. He noticed that the earth's soil was not as hard as man's floor. He was a little envious of Coy, who got to sleep on the bed, next to Meadowlark's feet.

She seemed better. If she had ever been in serious danger, maybe she was moving beyond it. Sam sat every morning with her, and wandered during the afternoons. After lunch Julia and Flat Dog made him go for a walk. Their nice words meant, *Get out of here and stay gone for a while.*

Usually he checked Paladin first. One day he noticed she was waxing up—she would foal in a few days. He left jauntily on his walk, and near the buildings he got a terrific surprise—he recognized a voice.

He darted back around the corner of the building at a run. Sure enough—Gideon Poorboy. The bear man was bent over something he was working on, and cussing in French.

"You boys got any time for a trapper who doesn't want to buy a thing?"

Gideon looked wide-eyed at Sam, handed the platter to Angel, and ran to give Sam a bear hug. Even in that crush Sam thought, *He's sure moving better on that peg leg now.*

"*Mon ami.*" He held Sam at arm's length—Sam was a rag doll in the big man's hands—"*Amigo!*" Gideon exclaimed. They were getting into a regular stew of languages.

Angel gave Sam a warm handshake. "He must finish this embossing while everything is right," said Angel.

Gideon went back to it. Sam could see a geometric design had been drawn on the surface of the metal and outlined with a tracer. Gideon turned the platter over and put it facedown on an asphalt block. The outlinings were visible on the reverse side. These he then hammered delicately, so that those areas would be raised on the front side.

Angel watched carefully. "Good. Very good . . . Just so . . . A little less . . . Nicely done. *Nicely* done."

Now Gideon turned the platter over and put it back onto the yielding asphalt. This time he re-embedded the background of the design, so that only the crucial parts were raised. The process required an eye, a delicate touch, and artistry. Sam felt proud of his friend.

Gideon held the platter up and regarded his handiwork. His

eyes were busy, his smile broad. "*Le bon Dieu*," he said, "I do it."

"Bravo!" said Angel.

Sam asked to see more of Gideon's work.

Gideon showed him, murmuring, "These are only the efforts of a beginner, they . . ."

Sam could see, though, that the work was beautiful, done with a fine eye and deft fingers.

"I make something maybe special," said Gideon. He brought out a wood carving, a bear, Sam saw. The bear was reared up on its hind legs and roaring. It was very well done, with lots of detail and a sense of motion.

"He has a flair for this carving, your friend," said Angel.

"I'm glad," said Sam.

"He also has maybe a patron."

"The don, his rancho is near and he is rich, he say California is the land of many bears, and I am the bear man. So he ask me to carve bear for him—golden bear."

"Golden?"

"*Oui,* I gild it. Here, I show you."

Sam was tickled at his old friend's enthusiasm.

Gideon brought out a small book and showed the very thin sheets of gold interleaved in the book.

"These we beat by hand," said Angel, "very delicate."

"First I will prime the surface with a flat paint, then size it," said Gideon. "Then the part I am nervous about. These leaf of gold, they must be pick up with this pointed tool and this brush and place gently on bear."

"I help him with that part," said Angel.

"Bear country, bear man, golden bear," Gideon said happily.

"Bear man, you are some," said Sam. "Let's go to supper?"

It was a big event for Sam, an hour with his oldest friend from the mountains, a drink with men other than friars. He learned about Gideon's new vocation. "From trapping to the art, from the cold creek to the warm climate, from the hardship to the money,"

Gideon said with a big grin. "Not bad for a French man grizzly bear, no?"

Sam clapped him on the shoulder.

"We have business plenty for two," said Angel.

"This California, she is shining time," Gideon said, his florid face suddenly shifting into . . . Sam didn't know what.

"Me, I pour us all to drink," Gideon said. He filled their wine glasses.

Gideon proposed a toast. "This is thank you," he said. "This is thank you, Sam Morgan. You cut off my leg."

Awkward silence. Angel nodded and said softly, "He tell me all about it."

They drank.

"Another one," said Gideon firmly. He poured.

That terrible night by the Green River, the gangrene, the smells, the constant requests for sharp knives, the flesh, the blood, the tendons and ligaments, the blood, the cartilage, the blood . . . Sam could still feel, in his hands, the dead weight of his friend's leg, severed from the knee down, a piece of useless human being to be . . . What? What do you do with a friend's severed *leg?*

"Sam, I never yet say thank you. My heart, she was not good. Me, this child, I wanted to die. I make self miserable-miserable, all the way miserable."

Gideon lifted his glass high.

"Now I say, Sam Morgan, thank you. You save my life. You save my life. Thank you!"

They drank.

Sam felt damn good.

"So I make you gift." He looked proudly at Sam. "First I make one like practice for me. Now I make very, very good one for you." He fixed Angel with his eyes. "Let me show you."

Gideon reached for his belt buckle, tugged, and off came . . .

Out of the belt came a dagger, very sharp. The buckle was in Gideon's fist, acting as a handle. He handed it to Sam. The buckle was a silver rectangle with the silhouette of a bear scribed into it.

"Watch again." Gideon popped the dagger back into the end of the leather belt, which acted as a sheath. The little prong that kept the belt at a certain length (Sam didn't know what it was called) seemed to work in the normal way.

Now Gideon showed him how it worked. Clever. "It is Angel's invention," said Gideon.

"Many smiths have done it," said Angel.

"Is good. Now we measure." Gideon used a piece of twine and a knot. The big man didn't mark down inches because he didn't read and write. "Two days, you see, I have something special for you.

"You have knife in hair. Now you have dagger in belt. Maybe next time we give you very dangerous earring." They all laughed.

"I like that idea." Sam realized he was a little drunk. Normally, he didn't talk about his hair weapon, but . . . These were friends, and Angel admired things that were well crafted.

He reached to the back of his head. First off, every morning of his life, he tied his shoulder-length white hair back out of his way and fixed the tie with this deadly ornament.

He brought it out and handed it to Angel. The goldsmith admired the polished walnut, the four painted circles—"For the four directions," said Sam—the smoothness of the join, the sharpness of the blade. Angel handed it back.

"A friend gave it to me," said Sam.

"You should meet this Hannibal," said Gideon to Angel. "A most, most remarkable Indian." He turned to Sam. "This bear man will have your belt dagger for you . . . two . . . maybe three days."

Sam put his ornament back into his hair. He said his thanks several times, and meant them. His happiness for Gideon, his fun in being with his friend—these were big.

But he wanted to get back to Meadowlark.

Gideon and Angel promised to come to her room the next morning, to wish her well.

*   *   *

GASPING, GASPING.

Sam looked around in his dream—he knew it was a dream—but he couldn't see air anywhere. Air! Where was air? What color was air?—he couldn't remember.

Gasping, gasping.

He turned this way, turned that way, searching, desperate.

Realization—truth—crushed the dream.

He leapt to his feet, dizzied, bleary. He looked at Meadowlark in the gray light that leaked through the cased window above her bed.

She was laboring for breath—whooping, wheezing, whooping. Coy was licking her hand.

Sam grabbed her. "Meadowlark!"

She trembled. She shuddered. Then her whole body, lips to fingertips to toes, began to shake.

The shaking came in waves, larger and longer and larger and longer.

Madness.

Sam grabbed a boot and pounded on the wall that was in common with Flat Dog and Julia's bedroom.

He seized Meadowlark by the shoulders, and she quavered, all up and down the length of her body she quavered. Her entire body was like chattering teeth. Her hands went wild in the air. Her feet tatted out a bizarre rhythm on the bed.

Sam held her tighter. Futile, but he held her tighter.

Julia and Flat Dog rushed in.

"Convulsion!" Sam shouted.

Flat Dog grabbed Meadowlark's feet. One foot got away and kicked him in the chin. He grabbed them again.

Julia dipped a corner of her skirt in the water pitcher, knelt by Meadowlark, and held the cool cloth on Meadowlark's forehead.

Meadowlark trembled.

From time to time she earthquaked.

Her husband and brother held on, and she shook. And shook. And shook.

Sometimes she only trembled. Sometimes she gave way to long tremors that racked her entire body.

Sam had a wild fear that she was going to break in half from bottom to head, and the baby would spill out. "Meadowlark!" he cried over and over, urging her back.

But her mind was far away somewhere, stampeding.

AT DAWN THE *comadrona* came in. Meadowlark was sleeping fitfully.

While the midwife examined the patient, Sam fetched Julia.

"Rosalita," said Julia, "how did you know?"

The *comadrona* gave no answer. She was not due until after lunch.

Sam wanted to spit out something like, *Why didn't you come quicker?*

Rosalita knelt beside Meadowlark, felt of her cheeks, forehead, hands.

Meadowlark was asleep, maybe.

"*Convulsiónes?*" said Rosalita.

"*Convulsiónes,*" affirmed Julia.

Rosalita studied Meadowlark's face, started to peel back the sheet she lay under. "*Hombre, vayase aqui!*" she ordered.

"Out!" exclaimed Julia, brushing Sam away with her hands.

He was already on his way.

FLAT DOG WALKED up. "Paladin has a filly," he said.

Sam pushed his back harder against the closed door. "The women are attending to Meadowlark. I can't go now."

"Good-looking filly. Marked same as her mother."

Another medicine hat—Sam wanted to smile, but he couldn't. "I'm not going one step down the walkway, either direction."

Flat Dog went into the bedroom he shared with Julia. Just as Sam was feeling relieved to be left alone, Flat Dog came back.

"Let's smoke the pipe," he said. He had his pipe bag in his hands.

Sam gave him a wild look.

"That's what it's for, times like these. Ask for help."

Ask for help? Sounded crazy to Sam.

"The friars are praying their way, and we're going to pray ours," said Flat Dog. "Come on."

Flat Dog guided Sam, almost pulled him, to the fountain in the center of the courtyard. There they performed the ceremony— the offering of smoke to the directions, the earth, and the sky, the ritual handing of the pipe from smoker to smoker. Sam didn't know what Flat Dog's silent prayers were. He himself could scarcely calm his mind enough to form any words, any requests, any pleas.

When they were finished, he felt a little more calm. Within a couple of minutes his mind was rampaging with fear again.

This was the longest wait of his life. At first he threw himself up and down the walk in each direction, pounding on the mission walls with his fists. After a while he grabbed the door latch and held on as a drowning man holds to a timber. He refused to budge. Mad energies raged up and down his body.

Coy was inside with Meadowlark. Maybe he was a comfort to her.

Suddenly Gideon and Angel walked up. Sam wanted to clap his friend's shoulder, but he couldn't.

"The friar says this is a bad time," said Angel.

Sam nodded.

"Then we only leave you a gift and go."

He stuck out a belt to Sam. The buckle was a silver rectangle, and scribed into it was a buffalo. "For Joins with Buffalo," said Gideon.

The buffalo was gold.

"Not solid gold," said Gideon, "is gilded."

Sam looked up into his friend's eyes. For the first time that day his heart remembered warmth.

"Is t'ank you, big t'ank you," said Gideon. "You save my life. With courage you save my life."

Sam embraced him.

Julia opened the door.

Sam rushed in.

Meadowlark was sleeping. Or in a coma. Who knew?

Coy mewled. Over and over he mewled.

On her knees beside Meadowlark, Rosalita murmured something in Spanish.

"She says the baby must come today," said Julia. "Must. It comes or we get it."

"Get it?" Sam raged.

"Again the convulsions? Next time they probably kill her . . ."

Sam collapsed into the only chair. His feelings leapt from rooftop to rooftop, and made stomach-lurching drops into black holes between.

He waited. He wound his legs around each other, he wrapped his arms around his chest. He tossed like a speck of foam on seas of mad emotions, and he waited.

Twice more, each instance separated by a couple of hours, Rosalita made him leave the room.

When he came back the second time, Julia brushed past him and charged down the corridor. Flat Dog followed her.

Sam stared after them, then ran to Meadowlark. Still no change. He whirled on the *comadrona*.

"*Agua,*" said Rosalita, "*agua caliente.*"

"Hot water," said Sam. He'd heard those words plenty.

"*Trapos limpios!*"

"What?" snapped Sam.

"Clean cloths!" snapped Julia from the doorway.

"*Cuchillos afiladas!*"

"Damn it, woman, speak English."

Rosalita came to Sam with eyes wide and touched the handle of the butcher knife at his waist. "*Cuchillos afiladas!*"

"Get her some sharp knives," said Julia. "That's what she's saying. Sharpen several knives. She is going to cut the baby out."

SAM SAT NEXT to Flat Dog in the pleasant courtyard, Coy curled between them. Walkways lined the four sides, hedges kept the world out, and a fountain spouted serenely in the center. Its water soared into the air, captured faint afternoon sunlight, and dropped it back to the pool below.

For Sam nothing moved. The water was frozen as a mud puddle in winter. The air was fixed, stagnating, rotting. The sunlight didn't slide upward on the northern wall. The shadows in the courtyard were graves.

Time was held in a death grip, by his fierce command. Nothing happened. The world stopped, except for the motions of one woman, either a healer or a killer. One woman bent over the sleeping or dying figure of his wife, wielding a knife.

Sam's imagination tortured him. He had cut human flesh, and seen it part, seen it bleed. He knew the thousand little wellsprings of blood that were violated, each leaking Meadowlark herself onto the blade, onto the hands of the surgeon, and onto the dead boards of the floor. He knew too much, and too little.

Sometimes he tried to picture exactly what was happening. The tip of the knife slicing from the navel down. The thin line of blood. The second, firmer cut, through all the layers of skin to . . .

To what? His imagination swam in blood, blinded. Something within Meadowlark, some flesh that cradled a child, as every human child was held for a time, some . . .

Hands delving deep into Meadowlark's belly, into Sam's soul. Hands urgent and bloody that would hold up . . .

He could take no pleasure in the thought of the child. What he had desired for months now felt alien. What his heart longed for, his hands yearned to hold, his eye hoped to feast on, all was turned to . . . Blood. Black blood. Death.

He fixed his mind on those hands, rising scarlet from the darkness, and raising up life or death.

JULIA'S VOICE FLOATED from behind them. "You have a daughter."

Sam and Flat Dog jumped to their feet.

Sam's eyes searched Julia's face.

"Meadowlark is doing well," Julia told both of them.

Sam leaned against his friend, Meadowlark's brother. He had not known until now how good it was to have Flat Dog standing beside him.

"She's asleep. You may see her if you want. And your daughter."

Sam ran into the room and looked down on the two of them. His feelings stormed across his inner landscape, like stampeding buffalo. He looked on Meadowlark's face, serene now. He looked at her body under the sheet, relaxed. He looked at the naked infant sucking at Meadowlark's breast.

Rosalita picked up the infant and handed her to Sam.

A girl, yes, he confirmed. He held her against his chest. She felt good. Then, suddenly, holding her felt . . . wrong. He gave her to Flat Dog, who put her back at Meadowlark's breast. The child went back to sucking with a vigor that almost scared Sam.

He stood and watched for a while. The others brought chairs and sat and waited.

When Sam turned away, Rosalita spoke, and Julia translated. "The danger from the convulsions is past. We did what had to be done, and she has survived that. If she does not get a fever, she will be fine in a few days."

If she doesn't get a fever. Any woman might get childbed fever, Sam knew that, and any woman might succumb to it.

"With the surgery," asked Sam, "the risk of the fever is greater?"

"*Sí.*"

His mind spun like a wheel. *What are the chances? What are the odds, like the odds of making a lucky draw at cards?* Your hand cuts the deck of fate. A heart brings your wife back to you, a spade and she's dead. Such thoughts raced through the tumult of his mind. He despised himself for them.

When he turned to ask the *comadrona*, one look silenced him. He didn't want to make her more cross.

Rosalita left them a fresh poultice of herbs and mysterious other ingredients to treat the wound, and then said, "I want to see your new filly."

MARE AND FILLY were nursing in the corner of a mission corral. The filly spun away from her mother and pranced a few steps, as though showing off. She was a beauty.

Sam looked at Paladin with huge pride. A splendid young female sea-changed into a mother, both mother and daughter beautiful.

"She's going to be a graceful one," said Flat Dog.

"I have done much work," said Rosalita. "I want the filly."

Sam and Flat Dog looked at each other. After a moment Flat Dog said, "Leave this to me."

Sam nodded and walked away.

In five minutes Flat Dog found Sam sitting by Meadowlark's bed again.

"Tomorrow morning," Flat Dog said, "she'll come check on Meadowlark and take the filly." He waited. "Best deal you ever made," he said, "a filly for your daughter."

When Sam didn't say anything, Flat Dog went to the room he shared with Julia.

Sam sat down to wait. He made up his mind not to leave Meadowlark's side until she was out of danger, not for a minute.

Every couple of hours Julia slipped in with the baby and laid her at Meadowlark's breast.

Sam watched his daughter, greedy for milk, greedy for life. He watched his wife, exhausted, perhaps ill, perhaps balanced between . . . As he watched, he didn't know whether he was swamped with feelings or empty of all feeling.

Wait. Wait. Footsteps clomped through his mind, loud and unnerving. Life, said the first. Death, said the second. Life. Death. Life. Death.

They didn't get softer and they didn't go away.

He set his eyes on Meadowlark's face. He took her hand in both of his. He waited. And waited. And waited.

Fifteen

A Voyage

ON THE SECOND afternoon Meadowlark developed a fever. It didn't feel high, not to Sam's hand, but it was a fever.

They sent for the *comadrona*.

Rosalita said it was not a good sign, but her face said it was not unexpected. She went over the methods of keeping a fever down, cool, wet cloths on the head, if necessary cool, wet sheets around the entire body. "You never know about fevers," she said. "Usually they pass."

Flat Dog and Julia brought the cloths. Sam stayed next to Meadowlark and held her hand.

MEADOWLARK SWAM THROUGH great columns of light, thick as trees. She remembered these trees well, they were her old friends. As before, they were magical, they were ethereal—roots, trunks, and branches of pure light. Instead of amazement at the glow on her skin, she felt . . . The columns were hot, very hot. She snatched her arm out.

Then she realized. The water itself was warm, too warm. She swam to another column and touched it—hot, burning hot.

With a start she realized how hot she was. Awful. She writhed. She swam painfully among the columns of light, casting her eyes about. Somewhere it would be cooler, somewhere . . .

When she became aware again, she was far too hot. She looked for the dark areas, outside this region thrust through with swords of light—cool, shadowed regions for relief. But she saw none. On every side, as far as she could see, her seas roiled with light and heat. She tried to bring back the memory of the cool expanses of sea she swam in last time. She tried to cool herself by re-creating their memory, by picturing and feeling again the cool. *I want to glide into your wet coolness and hide.* But to no avail. Nothing helped. She floated through the hot water, miserable, panting . . .

When she was aware again, a hand held hers, yes, even so far down in the water here, a hand held hers. It was too warm, it raised her temperature. In an odd way she liked it, but it made her hotter still.

Now she remembered again what, in her half consciousness, her mind had been reaching for. Somewhere outside this bright area, the water was cool. She remembered that, yes, she could bring it back into her mind, yes. Somewhere out there the bright columns grew fewer and fewer, and the cool darkness would bring blessed relief.

She would find it. Yes, she would find it. Things would be better. She wouldn't be so hot, so intolerably hot.

She forced her body to swim. Somehow, even in the swimming, she felt the hand in hers. That was good, there was something good about the hand, she liked it, even if it was hot. Hot.

Swimming, though, swimming didn't seem to work. She swam harder. She thrashed. She struggled.

And as she swam harder, the great columns grew brighter and hotter.

She doubled her efforts. *Somehow, somewhere, if I can find the cool, dark waters . . .*

She came to consciousness again. She realized, *I am deeper, and the water is not so hot here. I am deeper. If I don't try, if I let go . . .*

She floated farther down. She lost consciousness. She drifted.

The next time her mind stirred faintly, she was aware of very little. The great columns of light and heat seemed well above her. She could see them, but they were remote, far away, too far to matter.

Now she was surrounded by a wonder. Half-moons floated in her seas, thousands of them, and they trailed light behind, like beautiful white hair. Her husband's hair, she remembered, was also white. These thousands of half-moons were a glory. She remembered someone had told her about them, told her that these glories illuminated the depths of the sea.

She was much deeper, she knew that. The depth was cool, the depth was relieving her body of the terrible heat, and she was getting comfortable. She relaxed and drifted farther down.

Now she felt a river take hold of her, a river within the ocean. This river was coldly delicious, like the drink of lemon, sugar, water, and creek ice the rich Mexicans drank. Oh, delicious. And it was taking her somewhere new, somewhere of perfect cool, perfect deliciousness. It was not dark—it was bright with the glow of the white half-moons, half-moons everywhere now, like bubbles on the surface of a tumbling creek, a world of bubble moons.

The river felt strong, and she welcomed its strength. *Oh, bear me along, you are cool, you are dark, you are good. Ride me to a new ocean, a good ocean, cool.*

She hesitated in the river. One small matter held her back. The hand. The river would take her beyond the reach of the hand, she knew that. The hand, it was nice, it was loving, but the river, the new ocean, and the wondrous half-moons . . . She wanted to surrender, to ride this delicious river, to swim forever among these beautiful, luminous moons.

She gave the hand a little squeeze. *Good-bye.* Then she let go and gave herself to the strong hands of the undersea river and the glorious light of the moons.

Part Four

JOURNEY INTO NIGHT

Sixteen

The Unimaginable

SAM FELT THE squeeze of the hand. He knew. He *knew*.

He lay down next to Meadowlark and folded her in his arms. Now in the wee hours of the morning no one else was here to see, no one to tell him no. And it didn't matter now.

He held her.

He held her, and slowly, he wept out all feeling, all feeling. With his tears flowed away all his love, all his life.

Not until the predawn light slipped into the room did he acknowledge that she was cold.

He lay still and held her.

Julia and Flat Dog came in. They said some things, did some things, he didn't know what. Soon Flat Dog started unwinding Sam's arms and legs, separating him from Meadowlark. He let it happen. He knew the world would never be the same again, but he let it happen.

He sat on a chair next to the bed, blind, deaf, and dumb. He sat there while the friar said his ritual words, whatever they were. He sat there while someone, strangers, took Meadowlark away.

Julia put his daughter in his arms.

A somnambulist in a nightmare, Sam handed her back to Julia.

He rose and walked as in profoundest sleep into the courtyard. There he sat on a bench. The fountain splashed. Birds twittered. The sun rose and made shadows. Coy lay beneath the bench and watched the world.

Sam knew none of it. Unendurable. Today, unendurable. Tomorrow, unimaginable.

He sat, stupefied. He stared into the day, blank.

Twice during that day he arose to go to the bathroom. For some reason he found these trips a humiliating experience, and shambled back to the courtyard as fast as a sleepwalker could.

At dark Flat Dog led him to the bedroom where Meadowlark had died. Sam refused to lie on the bed where she had been. He lay on the floor in a single blanket and bored his eyes into the darkness. For him it was the same as staring into the day.

ON THE SECOND or third day Sam stood by a hole in the ground and watched them lower a plain pine box into it. With Flat Dog, Julia, Gideon, Angel, and Father Enrique as witnesses, he saw priests put Meadowlark into the hole. It was obscene, what they did, but he said nothing. He cared about nothing.

He motioned all, please, to leave. Coy looked questioningly at

Sam, then padded to the edge of the hole and looked down. Sam stepped up beside him and looked down. Just looked, both of them. After a while Sam took the shovel left by the gravedigger and threw dirt on Meadowlark. Blade after blade, each one as full as he could get it, he dumped the dirt on her. He worked methodically, automatically, like a machine. When it was done, he hurled the spade, point first, into the mound of loose dirt and walked off.

As requested, he went to the room where the friars dined and sat with the group. He partook of food, indifferently. He watched his daughter nurse at the breast of an Indian woman, and he did not care. He walked back toward his room. He didn't notice his companions, Julia, Flat Dog, and Coy. He was an automaton.

On the outside walkway a man waited for them.

Without thought, Sam sized him up. Young, handsomely turned out, swelled with the arrogance that the Mexican dons flaunted so dashingly. Now came the first feeling Sam had since his wife died—anger.

"Señorita," said the man formally, addressing Julia.

"Señora," she answered.

"Señora . . ." He mouthed the word ironically. "Señora Flat Dog, I believe."

"Yes," she said in English.

"A gentleman wishes to speak with you." His eyes roamed over the trapper, the Indian, and the coyote. A hint of amusement touched his lips. He was speaking in Spanish now, and his voice changed, as though calling attention to the introduction of a higher language. Julia translated.

"And you are?" she asked.

"Agustin Montalban y Romero."

"Who wants to speak with me?" she said.

"Joaquin Montalban y Alvarado. My father."

"An old family friend," she told Sam and Flat Dog.

"A friend who offers help in a time of need," said Montalban.

"Where?"

"Outside." He nodded to the wall of the courtyard and its gate.

But what waited outside was an open carriage, three riders, and an elderly driver. Sam saw Julia stiffen. They all knew what the carriage was for.

"Thank Señor Joaquin Montalban for his kind concern, and tell him I will receive him this evening at the mission."

Montalban gave the three riders a look. They dismounted and flanked him. Sam suppressed a bitter smile. The gentleman was provided with ruffian bodyguards, just in case.

"You will come to him now," said Montalban. "Your friends are welcome. However, if they wish not to come, we will understand that their bereavement . . ."

"Tell your father," said Sam, "the lady *and her husband* await him here." He was amazed at the sound of his own voice, like boulders falling.

The gentleman inclined his head and said, "Not possible." He put his hand on the handle of the pistol in his belt. "You are unarmed. Señorita Julia will attend my father . . ."

Flat Dog and Sam looked at each other, understanding.

The pistol barrel rose.

The bodyguard on the gentleman's left reached out to take Julia by one shoulder.

"Coy," said Sam, "attack."

In one jump the coyote had the don's crotch in his teeth.

Flat Dog knocked the man flat, and the pistol flew.

Sam popped the buffalo belt dagger out. He was insane with rage.

A knife flashed from his left. Instantly he seized the wrist and pivoted behind. With the dagger he ripped the ruffian's throat from ear to ear. Blood sprayed like his rage.

Sam roared, "It is a good day to die!"

Flat Dog shouted, "It is a good day to die!"

As another bodyguard cocked his throwing hand, Coy leapt at him. The knife glanced off the throat-cut body and swished past Sam.

The dying legs in their spasms tangled with Sam's legs. Both bodies went down. As Sam untangled himself, a boot caught him right on the nose.

Blood gushed, and with it a feeling boiled out, pure and wild. Sam got his feet under him. He saw a living bodyguard recover his knife. Sam launched himself, riding the wild feeling like a stampede.

He knocked the knife aside with his left hand and butted the fellow with his head. The man splatted to the ground. Sam leapt on him, but the fellow rolled away and got to his feet.

Coy bit the man's knife hand. The ruffian bellowed and slung Coy away.

Sam slashed the man from shoulder to hip. Tunic and skin ripped. Sam bellowed, "Buffalo dagger!"

The ruffian looked gape-mouthed at his own blood, then at Sam.

Seeing the man still puzzled at a small belt buckle weapon, Sam laughed. It came out huge and crazy. Sam laughed wilder, thinking, *If I heard me laugh, I'd run like hell.*

He attacked. He used the buffalo dagger like a rapier. A cut straight across the forehead. A slash to the belly.

The ruffian's knife rose. Before it touched Sam's ribs, Sam's hand darted. The ruffian's wrist sprouted blood. The knife flew and rattled against the wall. The man stumbled after it.

As Sam turned to look at Flat Dog, a body from that direction knocked him over.

With a crazy glee he rolled and rolled. Getting his feet under him, he saw the crimson flood from his nose all over his body. He laughed. He yelled like a madman, "It is a good day to die!"

He dived to one side and kicked. This new bodyguard jumped on Sam's feet and trapped them.

Sam bent and stabbed straight into the man's throat. When Sam jerked the knife out, blood gushed.

Suddenly: wild stillness in the midst of melee.

Sam whipped the ornament out of his hair and flashed the blade out.

Montalban was hoisting Julia onto the carriage. Flat Dog grappled with him, and Coy bit his ass.

Sam got knocked down from behind. The ground whoofed the air out of him.

Reaching back, he sliced his attacker's side with the hair ornament. The man screamed and rolled away.

Sam attacked furiously with both blades, his hands whirling dervishes. He saw the look of astonishment on his foe's face and spewed laughter. Killed by a hair ornament and a belt buckle!

He kicked the man in the balls, pounced on him, and slit his belly until gut oozed out.

Springing to his feet, Sam dashed toward the carriage.

Montalban was trying to get his pistol pointed into Flat Dog's face.

Flat Dog was choking Montalban.

Julia was wrestling with Montalban's arm.

Coy was preventing the don from ever siring children.

Sam bellowed and crashed into the four of them.

The pistol exploded.

All four people rolled to the earth. No one was struggling any longer.

Rolling away, Sam saw.

Montalban's head was a mass of blood.

Flat Dog's was black with burnt powder, but he was laughing.

Julia was crying.

The elderly driver hopped down and ran.

Coy sat coolly and watched the driver flee.

Friars hurried out, their robes fluttering helplessly.

VERY QUICKLY, SOME things were sorted out.

Rosalita was sent for.

Father Enrique said last rites for Montalban, and offered the opinion, whether or not anyone cared, that the soul had not yet left the body.

To Sam's surprise the friar then said last rites for the other attackers.

"You killed all three of them," said Flat Dog.

Sam looked into the smoke-blackened face. He didn't know whether the words were said in blame, in awe, or what. He didn't give a damn.

Rosalita told the friar to stop saying words over the gut-slit attacker. "I'm sorry to say," she told them, "that this one survives. I will sew him up."

"I will have a man take him to the rancho in the carriage," said Father Enrique, "with the body of Montalban."

"Tell Don Joaquin," Julia told the wounded man sharply, "that I decline his most gracious invitation."

Sam and Flat Dog whooped.

Sam looked at his friend. They laughed louder, and Sam heard meanness in his own laugh. A thought whipped at him. *Maybe, now that she's gone, I will always be mean.*

Coy nuzzled Sam's leg. Rosalita inspected Sam's nose. "Broken," she said. "I must set it."

Julia took Sam's hand. "You killed two men for me. *Gracias.*"

Sam looked at her, rocked with strange feelings.

"Thank you," she repeated.

He nodded.

"There is very little time," the friar told Rosalita.

The *comadrona* tore pieces of cloth, rolled them, and forced them up Sam's nostrils.

He bellowed, laughing at himself. Coy whined.

"Leave these in place for a week," she instructed.

Sam started to protest.

"Breathe through your mouth! Leave the cloths!"

"I see what happened here," said Father Enrique. He surveyed the scene again with regretful eyes. "Yes, I understand it. Yes. What you did, it was necessary."

He looked from one to the other, Julia to Sam to Flat Dog.

"I must advise you to be gone quickly. Very, very quickly. Your horses are being brought."

Julia and Flat Dog got their few belongings. Sam brought Paladin and the other horses around.

"I'm sending a man with you," said Father Enrique. "He will show you where to stay tonight. Tomorrow I will send a wet nurse with your daughter."

Sam shook himself. *I damn near forgot about my own daughter.*

They swung into their saddles.

"You feeling all right?" said Flat Dog, looking at Sam sharply.

"I don't care about one damn thing," said Sam.

Seventeen

Lost in the Wilderness

THE RIDE BACK to the camp was emptiness.

First they hid in an outlying farmhouse. The wet nurse brought the baby. The farmer slaughtered a pig for a feast, and gave them the bladder as a substitute for a mother's breast.

Sam hated the sight of the cussed thing. But Julia learned quickly to use it, and was pleased with herself. The farmer gave them a goat that was fresh to provide milk, a gift from the mission, he said.

Sam asked Julia to give the girl a name.

Julia offered Esperanza. "My mother's name," said Julia. "It means hope."

"A good thing, hope," said Flat Dog, looking at Sam.

Sam shrugged his shoulders.

Coy rubbed himself against Sam's legs. The coyote stayed even closer to the man now.

After two days they set out. Sam's nose ached, and having his nostrils blocked was a nuisance, but he was indifferent to everything, even to being back on Paladin. He blocked her foal out of his mind.

"Don Montalban is looking for us," said Flat Dog.

Coy made friends with the goat, and it followed on a lead without trouble. Sam hated the goat. He half hoped Montalban's men would find them. He wanted a good fight, one more damn good fight, an apocalypse.

THE CAMP ON the Peticutry River where the Appelaminy flowed in was empty.

They found a stake, and signs of digging. They knew what it would be. Buried beside the stake was a letter wrapped in deer hide. Sam looked at the piece of folded paper. "I can't read," he said, and held it out to Julia.

"I don't read English," she said. "I learned to speak but not read."

All three started laughing. This was funny. The three of them were on the run together, a white man, an Indian man, a Mexican woman, and a mixed-blood child. Their companions had gone off, leaving a note to say where. And none of them could read the note.

Julia took the paper with her right hand. These days her left arm was occupied, constantly, by Esperanza. "It is written in English and Spanish," Julia said.

Laplant, the translator, had anticipated the problem.

"I have taken the brigade north in hopes of finding a route to cross the mountain. If we have good fortune, we must say farewell. If not, we will come back here. In the hole is a bonus for work well done."

It was signed, Jedediah Strong Smith.

Sam dug a little more and found gold pieces.

So they settled down to wait.

Julia spent her days on the baby. Flat Dog spent his wondering whether he would be stuck in California for years.

Sam spent his days on nothing. He stared a lot. Sometimes he looked at the mountains. They were full of spring snow, and most of these peaks would bear eternal snows. Didn't look to him like any horse party could cross those mountains, not now. But he didn't say that. He said nothing.

Coy stayed closer to Sam than he ever had, not even playing with Paladin or hunting small animals in the evenings.

Flat Dog and Julia tried to bring Sam back to the living, but they finally gave up.

On the sixth day the brigade rode into camp.

TIME HAD WORRIED the captain. When he left his partners at the rendezvous of 1826, he said he'd probably come back to Cache Valley for the winter, and certainly would return for the 1827 rendezvous. If he didn't appear, they were to assume he was dead, and all the men and equipment lost.

So getting to rendezvous was essential. His partners deserved to know how the trapping had gone, and they needed to ship his packs of beaver plews back to St. Louis to reduce the company's debt. All the trappers would be keen, and keener than keen, to know what the country southwest of the Salt Lake was like, and especially what California was like.

The month of May was at hand. Less than two months to get to rendezvous.

The captain looked at the snow-clogged mountains east of him. He didn't know how deep the snow was, or how compacted or loose it might be. Worse, he didn't know how wide Mount Joseph was—three days' ride? A week? A month? Thirty miles? A hundred? Two hundred?

He knew the dangers. He had led men across South Pass early in the season, the earth deep in snow, the winds full of flying flakes, and the clouds dark with portents of terrible storms. He gazed up at the mountains, high, cold, forbidding.

I shouldn't. I want to.

He took the brigade up the Appelaminy for a couple of days, then turned north in hope of seeing a clearer path across the mountains. After a few days, spying no better route, he headed east anyway.

The going was terrible. It was steep. The horses sank into the snow past their knees, even with the men on foot. Jedediah saw no sign of a pass. One horse died of exhaustion.

So Jedediah Smith did what he had often done. He climbed a high hill alone. There he could see better with his telescope, yes. He could also commune with himself, and with his God.

The summit view was nothing but discouragement.

Jedediah wrote in his journal:

Far as the eye could see on every side, high rugged peaks arose covered with eternal snow. Turning to the east, the frozen waste extending rough and desolate beyond the boundaries of vision warned me to return. Below the deep rocky ravines resounded with immense cascades and water-falls where the melting snow and ice was fast hastening to the fertile plain. The sight in its extended range embraced no living being, except it caught a transient glimpse of my little party awaiting my return in the snows below.

It was indeed a freezing desolation, and one which I thought should keep a man from wandering. I thought of home and all its neglected enjoyments, of the cheerful fireside of my father's house, of the plenteous harvest of my native land, and visions of flowing fields of green and widespread prairies of joyous bustle and of busy life thronged in my mind to make me feel more strongly the utter desolateness of my situation. And is it possible, I thought, that we are creatures of choice and that we follow fortune through such paths as these? Home with contented industry could give us all that is attainable, and fortune could do no more.

He tromped grudgingly down the hill and told the men they were turning back.

Robert Evans joked, "That means there's no ending for our song."

BACK IN THE camp at the junction of the Peticutry and Appelaminy, Sam supposed he was glad the brigade rode in. Didn't seem to matter much. Greetings were exchanged, shoulders slapped, smiles flashed like knives.

Sam saw Jedediah and Flat Dog put their heads together and knew they were trading news—the brigade had failed to get across the mountains, and in Monterey the unmentionable had happened. Sam stayed far enough away that he wouldn't have to hear the name of the one who once was his wife.

It was a hangdog afternoon in camp.

Robert Evans cheered the camp in the evening by getting everyone to pitch in on "The Never-Ending Tale of Jedediah Smith." They were still putting it together as Evans suggested. When the outfit was in the mood, he'd play all they'd composed up to that point, and the whole bunch would write a new verse together, based on what had happened since the last verse, however wonderful or miserable it was. Everyone would pitch in suggestions until, as Evans put it, "the rhymes do chime."

When they got the new verse written, they sang the song lustily and far out of tune, further out than sober men should be capable of. Sometimes Coy joined in, and they all laughed.

THE NEVER-ENDING TALE OF JEDEDIAH SMITH
We set out from Salt Lake, not knowing the track
Whites, Spanyards and Injuns, and even a black
Our captain was Diah, a man of great vision
Our dream Californy, and beaver our mission.

(chorus)
Captain Smith was a wayfarin' man . . .

They sang the verse about near dying of thirst and getting to drink mud, marched to the verse about getting to eat fleas, and rolled on to the chorus once more.

We was lost in that desert, no beaver, no creeks
Don't worry, says the captain, we'll find water next week.

They sang with enthusiasm the lines about Diah, with morals full girt, never lifting a skirt.

On through the jubilee held by the Mexicans they rambled, and it sure did sound fine now.

It was grand, Californy, a life of pure ease
It was warm all year round, with a sweet-scented breeze
There was plews in the creeks and mountains to roam
Only one problem—we couldn't get home.

"We can't finish it," said Evans. "Not yet."

They all looked, through the luminous May twilight, at the mountains that barred them from their home in the mountains, Cache Valley.

They wondered what the captain would do. He'd spoken of backup plans. From here they could travel north to Bodega Bay, where the Russians had a trading post, and get resupplied. They'd trade their pelts for everything they couldn't make themselves, all the goods General Ashley usually mule-packed to rendezvous— gunpowder, lead, gifts for the Indians they might meet, and those essentials of mountain life, coffee, sugar, tobacco, and whiskey. After that, with the snows mostly gone, they would start for the depot, as the captain called it, the cache in Cache Valley. Not a man of them wanted to cross that desert again, not at that time. It would be July and August.

They looked at Mount Joseph, choked with snow. They remembered the bitter conditions that turned them back. They wondered.

But they needed to get to the business of the evening—each group listening fully to the other's story.

Jedediah told of the failed attempt to cross the mountains, how the outfit mounted the west side of Mount Joseph higher and higher, until the horses floundered. At last the outfit turned back, leaving five horses and mules dead on the mountain.

Next, Jedediah and all the men listened with big hearts to Sam's tale. In fact, though it was his story, after a bumbling start Sam wouldn't tell it. Couldn't. Flat Dog and Julia had to do that. Sam could not imagine himself saying, *Meadowlark died.*

All through the telling Sam's friends watched him. Sam felt the eyes of Jedediah, of Evans the Irishman, Gobel the smith, Laplant, and of Rogers the clerk that Sam found cool and remote. It irked him to be pitied.

He thought how many men, and women, who started on this trip were gone. The three Spaniards and their wives and children who left voluntarily near the Hurricane cliffs. Manuel Eustevan and his Shoshone woman. Spark, lost to the Amuchabas. Wilson, discharged by Jedediah. Reed, who made himself disappear. Sumner the slave, who freed himself. Gideon, transformed from mountain man to Californio.

Meadowlark. Except that Sam didn't even think her name. He permitted nothing of her into his mind, not her name, not her face. All he ever did, when it came to Meadowlark, was sense the hole in his heart and sit next to it.

He didn't bother to wonder whether he would ever get back to Cache Valley, the Rocky Mountains, and the life of the beaver hunter. He didn't give a damn. He couldn't be bothered, these days, even to notice Coy and Paladin.

"WE HAVE TO move out," said Jedediah several times.

Sam never thought about that. He was sitting by a fire on a cool, misty evening, listening to the gurgle of the two rivers coming together and staring into his black coffee. Jedediah's voice made him jump.

"We're leaving for rendezvous tomorrow," he said, "me plus three men. We'll carry as much food as we can for the horses. Maybe a small party can get across the mountains."

The captain hesitated. "At any rate, we're going to try."

Flat Dog, Julia, and Irish Evans looked at the captain and waited for the punch line.

Jedediah tapped the heel of one boot against the toe of his other, which was his habit when he felt reluctant to say something. "I'm taking Silas Gobel." The blacksmith was at a nearby fire. "Also you, Evans. And you, Sam."

Sam spat hot coffee back into his cup. "I'm not going anywhere."

Sam looked into Julia's and Flat Dog's eyes and saw that they too were uncertain about him.

He got up, strode to some bushes, pulled the wrapped cloths out of his nostrils, and hurled them away. When he came back, he controlled his voice carefully. "I've got other things to do." *Like mope.* "I've got a daughter to take care of."

Julia spoke softly. "Esperanza is safe with us."

"That's right," said Flat Dog.

"She's *better* with us," Julia went on, "for now."

Sam glared at them. "You already talked this out with the captain."

"*Sí.*"

"The whole brigade will stay right here," said Jedediah. "This is the outfit's camp until we get back."

Sam thought Diah was speaking too lightly. To rendezvous and back would be several months.

"Caring for Esperanza will be our duty and our pleasure," said Julia.

"My duty too," said Sam irritably. But he didn't look at Diah when he said it.

"Sam," Flat Dog said, "you got to do something. *Do* something. Something hard. Get her off your mind. You can't sit around here for months and go crazy."

Sam whined to the captain, "Diah, I'm not ready."

"Sam, you're going."

Flat Dog added, "It will be good for you."

Coy squealed, but Sam couldn't tell whether he agreed with Flat Dog or not. Nor did Sam care.

LATER THAT EVENING Jedediah made commitments and left instructions with Harrison Rogers, the clerk. If the captain did not return by September 20, Rogers was to regard him as dead, lead the men to the Russian fort at Bodega Bay to get re-outfitted, and then ride to Cache Valley. If return by land was impossible, Rogers was to book passage for the men to the United States via the Sandwich Islands.

If Jedediah did return, he would be bringing more men, more horses, more everything. His tone implied, *And I'll damn well be here.*

Sam sat and quarreled with himself about tomorrow morning. He could quit his job. He could take Esperanza and . . . He could . . . *Go back into California, with Don Montalban and the Monterey constabulary looking for me? And the entire California government looking for all of us?*

He looked at Coy and thought about asking the pup. But he didn't feel playful enough for that.

All right, dammit, I'll go. Funny—Sam had to give a crooked smile. Crossing Mount Joseph in the spring snow, where you were liable to get frozen to death or starved to death or killed by an avalanche or God knows what else—that was less dangerous, maybe, than the settlements of California. *And for sure easier than sitting every day next to the big black hole in my heart.*

ON THE SECOND day the going got hard, the mountainsides steep and the way rugged.

On the third day they left the river canyon for higher ground. Sam rocked along on Paladin's back, uncaring.

On the fourth they camped on the divide between the Appelaminy and the south fork of the Mokelumne River.

The next day they waded into four feet of snow, though it was compacted enough to bear some weight. At this elevation, in this depth of snow, the likelihood of encountering Indians or game was next to zero. They walked the horses, to keep from jamming them into the snow up to their bellies.

Jedediah led the way in silence, and from long habit stayed unnecessarily alert, his eyes constantly on the move. Gobel, huge and silent, let volatile feelings animate his face. For some reason Sam felt that in any kind of emergency, Gobel would shed his blood protecting them all. Evans chattered like a morning bird, always chipper. Coy trotted along on top of the snow, the only member of the party not to sink, perky as ever.

The next afternoon the snow started falling. During the night the storm got violent, and the temperature plummeted.

Jedediah recorded the events of the next day, the seventh of their journey:

The storm still continued with unabated violence. I was obliged to remain in camp. It was one of the most disagreeable days I ever passed. We were uncertain how far the mountain extended to the east. The wind was continually changing and the snow drifting and flying in every direction. It was with great difficulty that we could get wood and we were but just able to keep our fire. Our poor animals felt a full share of the vengeance of the storm, and two horses and one mule froze to death before our eyes. Still the storm continued with unabated violence, and it required an utmost exertion to avoid the fate of the poor animals that lay near but almost covered with the drifting snow.

Night came and shut out the bleak desolation from our view, but it did not still the howling winds that yet bellowed through the mountains, bearing before them clouds of snow and beating against us cold and furious. It seemed that we were marked out for destruction and that the sun of another day might never rise to us.

Savaged by his inner storm, Sam barely felt the pain. He stirred himself only to feed Paladin and lead her in small circles to keep her blood circulating. He rubbed his broken nose, which ached in the cold. Later he curled up with Coy at his belly. The memory came strongly to him, how they lay like this the night they met each other, in the belly of the buffalo, and survived. Sam wanted Coy and Paladin to survive.

On the other hand, Evans kept his own spirits high. He played ditties on his tin whistle, his eyes smiling as he ornamented this phrase and that. From Evans's smile, Sam supposed the words to the tunes must be cheerful. The music felt to Sam like a strange cross of repulsive and eerie. The wind ripped at the men, pelted them, scooped up shovelfuls of snow and flung it in their faces. All the while Evans's whistle piped a merry protest.

Sam snapped, "Don't you think this is the dumbest thing you could think of—playing music during the storm that's going to ice you to a corpse?"

Before Jedediah could call Sam down, Gobel said in his big voice, "I like the music."

Evans added, "Perhaps even death likes to dance in on a melody."

Sam rolled over in his blankets, putting his back to both his companions and the fire. He stared into the whiteness. He peered toward the big pine trees that surrounded them. Beyond these, he knew, were great rock walls, and a steep canyon. Yet he saw nothing but the snow. He got a thought that gave him the willies: *Whiteness is as blinding as blackness.*

He kept his mouth shut. They all sat awake, and said nothing all night. The wind eased, snow shimmied gracefully down, and Evans piped his nimble tunes. Sam remembered, from time to time, to lead Paladin in a circle. His single other movement was to stroke Coy's head.

The day dawned bright. The morning of May 27 came clear and sparkling, the sun dazzling on the high, sharp peaks of Mount Joseph. But the going was harder now, with an extra fifteen inches of snow for the horses to push through. Gobel forged ahead and made a track for everyone else. Sam was grateful for his strength, and wondered if he could have kept going without the big blacksmith. Coy could have, and that made Sam feel a little better.

After twelve miles Jedediah walked to a high point and came back to report a plain ahead, a flat of grass free of snow.

The captain's word picture of the grassy plain inspired all four of them. Sinking into the soft white stuff up to their crotches, they stumbled and staggered another thirteen miles, the most exhausting walk of Sam's life. At the end they fell on the ground, too weary to speak, to drink, to eat. The feed for the horses was good. Weary beyond weary, Sam half wanted to weep. But he had not wept since the death of the one he would not name, and no tears would come now.

For some reason Coy licked Sam's face.

The men rolled up in their blankets without even bothering to build a fire or cook. Jedediah complained mildly that some time during the day, somehow, he'd lost his pistol.

"Look back," he said quietly. "We crossed Mount Joseph."

No one spoke.

"I bet we're the first white men ever to achieve that."

Again no one spoke. Cold, drained of all energy, Sam felt no pleasure in the adventure.

The captain fell silent.

They slept without the energy to dream.

The next day they rested on that spot, and the horses grazed. Some Indians threw rocks at them from a nearby bluff, as though to drive them off. Gobel volunteered to heave stones back at them, but Jedediah said no, they weren't worth the bother.

The trappers sprawled on their blankets or sat quietly the whole day, too tired to leave, too tired to put a stop to a petty annoyance.

The following day, as they angled down toward the great desert that stood between them and the rendezvous, came a strange incident. Wrote Jedediah:

> I surprised two squaws and was so close to one of them that she could not well escape such an expression of fear [as] I had never before seen exhibited. She ran toward me screaming and raising the stick with which she had been digging roots, in her whole appearance realizing the idea I had formed of a frantic mother rushing to scare away some beast that would devour her child. Wishing not to hurt her, I avoided her formidable weapon and endeavored to pacify her, but all in vain, for when she went off, her screams were still heard until lost in the distance.

That night Diah sank into a strange mood. The man who was always steady, always positive, fell to brooding. Sam could hardly believe it. They were down into the foothills, beyond the terrible mountain crest. The horses now could rest and recuperate. The four hunters would be able to find deer or antelope to shoot. The captain always kept the spirits of his men up, but not tonight.

Gobel tried to interest the captain in a tomahawk-throwing contest. The blacksmith could split an aspen tree with the blade, but Jedediah might have been the most accurate thrower in the entire outfit. Tonight he shrugged off Gobel's invitation.

"What you need," said Evans, "is a good wrestling match."

Diah twisted an eyebrow at him and said nothing.

"As you say." Evans shrugged. "Then why don't I play some songs?"

He seemed to take on Jedediah's mood, for during this long May evening, in the shadow of the great mountain to the west, he played not dance tunes but old Irish and Scottish ballads, slow and mournful.

Coy, who picked up on every atmosphere of the camp, howled along with Evans, out of tune but in the spirit.

"Sam," said Evans genially. He reached another whistle toward Sam. "Give it a try. I have two whistles, one in the key of G and another in the key of D." Sam had no idea what that meant. "We can play along together. I'd be glad to teach you."

Sam shook his head. "Nah."

"It's a long journey," said Evans, the whistle still extended. "Evenings last forever this time of year—many hours to while away. Give it a try."

From mere politeness Sam took the whistle. He put the mouthpiece to his lips the way he'd seen Evans do, and blew a little sound. It was a nice sound, cheerful in the wilderness.

Unexpectedly, he felt something poignant inside, and with it came a small discovery. Yes, he did want to make music on this instrument. He had no idea why—it was madness, as hopeless and wretched as he felt—but he wanted to. And that was enough.

"I'll try it," he told Evans.

Evans contributed the next hour or so to teaching Sam fingerings. Soon he could tweet out "Twinkle, Twinkle, Little Star," with Evans playing harmony. That pleased Sam. He put the whistle in his possible sack feeling as chipper as he had since . . . since the day he wouldn't permit himself to remember.

Evans was thinking of something closer to home.

"Diah, what ails you? You look like you've been jilted." Evans tossed a smile at Gobel, for the captain certainly had never had a sweetheart, not in the years those three had known him.

Jedediah just looked at his three friends for long moments. Finally he said, "She was scared of me. Scared nearly to death. Scared enough to attack. Me."

The squaw, they realized. There had once been a Paiute girl too. When the brigade rode into her village, she looked up at the strangers, who had faces of a color she'd never seen, some of the visages thick with hair, and all the horses huge. The child fainted dead away.

"It is a puzzle," said Evans.

Jedediah stared at the ground. When he raised his eyes, they boiled with self-doubt.

"Why? We are well disposed toward them."

Sam smiled. He could never quite get over Diah's fancy way of talking.

"We come in fact to help them," the captain went on, "to trade them products our people know how to create, and in that way show them the benefits of civilization, the path to a higher life."

He stared blankly into the last of the twilight. "But first she attacked me and then she ran from me as from a demon."

Coy yipped several times.

"Imagine, a decent Christian gentleman like yourself," said Evans. Sam saw amusement in Evans's eyes but heard only sympathy in his voice.

Jedediah nodded yes, but his eyes looked far away. They said mutely, "Why? Why?"

He turned his gaze straight into Sam's. Jedediah's face spoke unbearable intensity. "What have I become? Here in the wilds, have I turned into a beast?"

Coy gave forth a full-throated howl now. Sam wondered whether the coyote was protesting the insult to beasts.

Then Sam's mind was transported back to the night he met Coy and the two of them shielded themselves against the prairie fire in the belly of a buffalo. Soon after Sam had a dream in which he went further—he actually became a buffalo, a man buffalo.

Sam whispered his own name. "He Who Joins with Buffalo."

He didn't think Jedediah was right, believing the beasts were below him.

Eighteen

Journey into Night

THE FOUR MEN and the coyote now set off into a country they dreaded more than the mountain. They didn't know the Indians, who were elusive as ghosts. Jedediah noticed that they went about naked, or the same as naked, and got only the most meager living by hunting, fishing, gathering seeds, and digging roots. Jedediah commented in his journal, "They are more akin to one of the higher orders of beasts than any other Indians we've met."

Still, the dread of the travelers was not of the Indians but the desert. After they passed a big, handsome lake not far from the mountains, the country was arid. It wasn't the red-rock desert, nor the Mojave, but a new kind of parched landscape. There were still dry lake beds, but no ghostly yucca trees or greasy brush. Instead uniform plains of shad scale reaching off to infinity in every direction. The spines of hills bristled with sagebrush and some cedars, trees with bare, dry trunks that seemed to twist in pain.

"Parch not only the skin and the tongue," said Evans, "but even the soul."

As they made camp, Sam looked out into those vast regions, hazy lavender in the twilight, and thought they might stretch forever. He wondered whether he might want to start walking into one of them and never come back.

The captain spotted a high hill with snow on top. Here in early summer, snowpack would mean snowmelt, which would mean drinkable water. So on the morning of June 3 they set out in that direction and rode twenty-eight miles. Along the way a horse collapsed, exhausted. The next morning Jedediah sent the strong Gobel back with water for the horse. After Gobel came in with the horse, they traveled only three more miles, to a range of high hills stretching north-south, and made camp.

So it went. Fifteen miles over the range of hills the next day. Then twelve miles and camp on a creek running east, the way they wanted to go. Twenty-five miles the following day, spotting one Indian along the way, to a camp with good water and grass. Then a day of rest.

On June 10, the horses could no longer carry the men. From now on all would walk, man and beast alike.

Sam's existence shortened itself to trudge, trudge, trudge. Only on the rest days did life offer something more. He doodled on his tin whistle, or played duets with Evans. The music felt good.

After dark one night they steered toward a distant fire and came on a squaw and two children. Once the Indians overcame their fright, the children played with Coy, fascinated by a tame coyote.

Sam got Coy to sit, lie down, shake hands, roll over, and fetch for them. The adults shared their water with the white men, and cooked scorpions for their own supper.

The captain camped three miles away from the Indians, and that night a rain refreshed the horses.

Nothing, not even his new hobby of music, could refresh Sam's spirit. As he made a physical journey with three friends, he made an emotional journey alone, through a darkness whose depth he could not plumb. He talked little and smiled less. He was indifferent to his own physical suffering. The fatigue of the numberless miles, the blast of the noonday sun, the scorch of thirst, and the pangs of hunger—he barely noticed any of them.

Neither did he take pleasure in the travel. The delightful cool of the dawns, the amethyst air in the evenings, the dark, jagged lines of the mountains against the salmon-colored horizons, the immeasurable depth of skies as perfect a blue as the planet had ever made—all were lost on Sam.

Few other pleasure, either. Except for tootling with Evans. He took no solace from the thought of his infant daughter, who in the care of his closest family was probably now learning to crawl. He did not look forward to rendezvous, to the taste of coffee or whiskey, to the fun of card games or the exhilaration of wrestling matches or shooting competitions. He didn't look forward to the sight of old friends, to trading tales of a year's doings with his friends. His life now was only one tale, a tragedy his tongue would never tell.

He kept some connection with his animals, playing with Coy, taking care of Paladin.

His only tie to his human companions, really, was that tin whistle. He found energy to learn the tricky ways of the little instrument from Evans, and even to get a few tunes under his fingers. He passed over the cheerful dance tunes and learned the mournful ballads. Even the fun of playing, though, was mostly solitary. Each night in camp he would meander away from camp, sit in the shade of a rock, and then wander through melodies. Some were the ones Evans had taught him, and some he remembered from his childhood, the Welsh songs his father Lew sang.

Soon Sam began to play his own melodies. He couldn't have said what they were or where they came from. His fingers made them up, not his head. They were mostly in a minor key, slow and desolate. Playing them was not a pleasure, just something he needed to do, an imperative of the heart.

Coy always kept him company while he played.

SLOWLY, THE FOUR trappers forged a way onward across the great desert. Three of them hoped one day to come in sight of the Rocky Mountains, and one trapper didn't hope for anything. From June 10 forward they were on an allowance of four ounces of dried meat per man per day. Though the Indians might have known how to take plant food in this barren country, the trappers didn't. Four ounces for miles and miles of trudging—that didn't add up.

They walked anyway, twenty miles on the eleventh, twenty-five on the twelfth, thirty on the thirteenth. Twice they saw antelopes but couldn't get close enough for a shot, not nearly close enough.

On June 14 they came upon ground made wet by trickles from low hills ahead. Since the horses were exhausted, they stopped after a day's travel of only eight miles and rested. The next day they walked up to the head of the waters in those hills, ten miles, and again the next day they rested at the springs.

If Jedediah suffered from doubts, he didn't express them. Gobel seemed too downhearted to speak. Evans played his whistle in his usual sprightly way, if only for his own ears. The captain left to walk to a high point and scout for the next water, beyond these hills.

Sam sought solitude at a distance from the camp. Tonight he just stared out over the desert. Mount Joseph was far behind them now, beyond the horizon. He might have used the thought of it—all that water, all those deer, even the cold—for comfort. But he sought no comfort. He had heard starving to death was a peaceful way to go. You just got weaker and weaker. After a while you turned fey in the mind, and drifted away.

Very different from thirsting to death, where men went out raving.

Coy barked sharply, his threatening bark. The pup was off somewhere, probably hunting mice or rats or the like. Again and again. Coy was plenty damn mad at something.

Then Sam saw. He levered himself to his feet and ran.

Gobel dived at Coy and missed. Coy snarled and skittered away.

The huge Gobel sprinted with amazing speed. For an instant Coy froze. Gobel flopped that enormous body toward the pup. As Coy dodged, Gobel caught a hind leg. With the other hand he swung his knife.

Coy bit the knife hand, but squealed in pain. Gobel let go and bellowed.

Coy dashed off a few steps and launched a torrent of barks at the blacksmith.

Gobel got to his feet and ran at Coy again.

At that instant Sam blind-sided Gobel with a body block.

Both men rolled and skidded over cactuses and stones.

"You son of a bitch!" Sam jabbed the heel of his hand hard at Gobel's nose.

The blacksmith swatted it away.

Sam rolled away and crouched. *Careful*, he told himself. Sam didn't care about the hundred pounds the smith outweighed him. He was worried about the knife.

Gobel lunged with the blade.

Sam dodged and kicked him in the head.

Evans gave a war cry and bowled into Gobel. They went a-tumble, and Sam could hardly tell which leg and arm belonged to which man. They rolled a dozen steps downhill.

Coy ran toward them, barking.

They fell apart and faced each other.

"Throw down the knife," rasped Evans. "A fair fight. This will be a good sport. Just sport."

Coy circled behind them, barking at Gobel.

Suddenly Gobel dived at the coyote and slashed with his blade.

Coy yipped and ran off. Sam spotted blood on his fur.

Sam charged Gobel.

Evans tripped Sam.

Sam's head hit a rock that knocked him silly.

" 'A fair fight,' I said. Put down the knife."

"I don't give a damn about any pub brawl," said Gobel, snarling, "and I don't give a damn about you. I'm gonna kill that damned coyote and eat it."

"Ah, so that's it. Well, the coyote steak awaits you, but it's right beyond me." Evans could get charm and menace into his voice at once.

"And me," said Sam.

The three of them formed a triangle, all watching the others.

"I'll shoot the first man who strikes another," said the captain.

He stood on a boulder just uphill from them, his rifle leveled.

"We're starving!" yelled Gobel. "Let's eat the damned coyote."

"Drop the knife, or I'll shoot you," said the captain.

Gobel reached the knife high and slammed it point first into the ground. The handle quivered. "We're starving!" he yelled.

Everyone relaxed.

"You're right," said Jedediah, voice steady, firm. "Pick up your knife now and use it. Kill the weakest horse, the bay."

THE MEN FELT uneasy eating horse meat in the middle of the night. The meat was stringy and tough. They watched each other.

Sam had found a long gash along Coy's hind leg. The pup wouldn't hold still long enough to get it salved.

They butchered the horse out and cut the meat into strips to dry. The best parts they were broiling on sticks over an open fire.

If Sam was distrustful of Gobel now, Coy was even more wary. The men had to throw pieces of horse meat, what they wouldn't eat themselves, well out into the darkness for Coy.

"Mr. Gobel," said Evans, "I still want to meet you in a wrestling match."

"I'll beat hell out of you." Gobel was twice the poundage of Evans, and at least twice the muscle.

"Probably. But it will be good fun, and I might surprise you with a trick or two."

"Enough of this," said Jedediah.

They ate in silence a long while.

"I don't like having the coyote along," said Gobel. "He scares game away."

"We haven't seen any sign of game in days," said Jedediah.

Sam added unnecessarily, "There's none to scare away."

"Well, there might be," Gobel said sullenly.

"However hungry we get," said Diah, "we will not kill the coyote."

"Or Paladin," said Sam.

"Or Paladin," Diah agreed. "We're men. We have to be better than the beasts."

There it was again. Sam didn't think much of that idea.

"Before I'd starve," said Gobel, his eyes hard at Sam, "I'd even eat you."

THE NEXT MORNING, though, Gobel apologized to them all.

"It's forgotten," said Sam. He meant it. The blacksmith wasn't basically mean. He just got to simmering sometimes.

That day, June 17, was horrific. Over two ranges of hills they staggered, finding not a drop of water. They camped in the third range, which was bone dry.

In the middle of the next day, contouring along a side hill, Silas Gobel sank to the ground like a deflated balloon.

They hovered over him.

"I'm done," he said. "No farther. I ain't going no farther. Unless God himself picks me up and carries me, I'm done."

Sam, Evans, and Diah looked at each other.

"You have to get up," said the captain.

Gobel gave them a look Sam would never forget. It said, *How dumb can you get? No farther means no farther.* He didn't even bother to shake his head no. He just stared. A look Sam had never seen was on his face—Gobel had given up.

"Let's get him over there," Jedediah said, nodding toward the shade of a cedar.

The three took Gobel's arms and legs and dragged the great body twenty feet into the shade. When they got there, Sam sagged onto the ground. Then, although exhausted, he sat back up. He didn't want the captain to think he was going like Gobel.

They sat beside their friend for a few minutes, not speaking. They all looked at each other, over and over, almost as lovers commune with their eyes.

All acknowledged silently the same reality. Their horns had been dry now for a full day, so they had no water to leave with their friend. Jedediah found some dried meat and set it beside him. Gobel handed it back. Jedediah set it next to him again.

"If we find water," he said quietly, "we'll send a kettle back to you."

They left him his weapons and all his belongings, what mountain men called their possibles. Sam wanted to say, "We'll do whatever . . ." But words were senseless. The three turned away, put their hands on the leads of the remaining horses, and walked off.

Coy growled and snapped once more in Gobel's direction and followed.

In less than an hour all three felt their first flicker of hope. Fourteen Indian men walked along the base of the hills. They didn't run away from the calls of the trappers, but waited to talk. Yes, they were headed toward a spring. Yes, the Americans were welcome to come along.

From the spring Jedediah went back himself. By late afternoon Gobel stood with his friends among the Indians.

And the Indians had two other gifts for the white men. The first was some ground squirrels, which the trappers found better-tasting than dried horse meat. The second was to show them something. A certain water reed was quite edible.

Sam ate it fiercely. Even if he still didn't care about his life, he was damn tired of being hungry. "Not bad," he said.

"A help," said Jedediah, "where there's water to grow it."

The four men nearly managed a chuckle.

On June 19 they walked fifteen miles and crossed another line of hills. Though they found no water, some wild onions made their dried horse meat more palatable that evening.

The next night—eureka!—they found water.

Their salvation now, their only hope, was the snow left on the mountaintops. The ravines that carried the snowmelt down gave the only possibility of water or grass. Later in the summer, when the snows had melted away, the country would be utterly impassable.

Days of walking, days of water, days of no water, days of a dwindling supply of meat. Evenings of silence, from men too tired to talk. Sometimes Sam found the energy to play his tin whistle.

On June 25 they walked along with some friendly Indians, who showed great curiosity about all the white men's belongings and insisted on handling everything, especially the guns. Jedediah wrote in his journal,

I fired off my gun as one of them was fingering about the double triggers. At the sound some fell flat on the ground, and some sought safety in flight. The Indian who had hold of the gun alone stood still, although he appeared at first thunderstruck. Yet on finding that he was not hurt, he called out to his companions to return.

Jedediah tried, over and over, using signs, to find out from these Indians where the Salt Lake was. But instead of answering, they merely repeated his signs back to him.

Frustrated, he led his party off on its own way. As luck had it, they found water several times that day, and replenished their horns and kettles.

That evening, as he doodled out some music, Sam watched Coy hunt pack rats. The creatures lived around the roots of the sagebrush. Coy would wait with infinite patience until one came out and then pounce. However hungry the men got, Coy always found food. Sam thought, *If we men die of thirst out here, at least you'll survive. But Paladin won't.* That bothered Sam.

That night they camped on the bank of a soda lake. Just before they got to camp, one of their horses wandered into a bog, and the four trappers couldn't pull him out. Finally, they killed him and dried about a quarter of his flesh. They'd finished every shred of dried meat from the previous horse.

All four men had the same unspoken questions. How long will this meat last? When will we come to mountains, where we can shoot game? How many days to the Salt Lake?

None had any answers.

In that camp, and others to come, the tin whistles spoke when tongues could not.

June 22 brought twenty-five miles of walking, the discovery of a creek, and no meat. The next day, they walked down the creek until it disappeared into the bed of a dry lake, filled their horns with brackish water, walked on, and made a dry camp. Jedediah recorded that they'd walked thirty-five miles. Sam marveled at how bouncy Coy looked, when Sam was wretchedly tired.

Very early on the morning of June 24, as his men plodded forward, Jedediah Smith climbed a nearby hill to scout for water. Even with his telescope he saw no hopeful signs except for a snow-topped mountain fifty or sixty miles to the northeast. The captain dared not think of their prospects of walking fifty or sixty miles without water.

When I came down, I durst not tell my men of the desolate prospect ahead, but framed my story so as to discourage them as little as possible. I told them I saw something black at a distance, near which no doubt we would find water. While I had been up on [the rise], one of the horses gave out and had been left a short distance behind. I sent the men back to take the best of his flesh, for our supply was again nearly exhausted. . . .

[When] they came up [with the flesh], they were much discouraged with the gloomy prospect, but I said all I could to enliven their hopes and told them in all probability we would soon find water. But the view ahead was almost hopeless.

With no other choice, the four trappers forced themselves forward through the midday heat. Their feet sank in, for the sand was soft, almost sucking at each moccasin sole on every step. Jedediah called for a rest in the shade of a cedar. They drooped to the ground and hung their heads.

"You know," said Diah, "a man can live without water. The Indians don't drink for days during their vision quests and their sun dances. It's the heat that's getting us."

"We Irish, we're not used to this sun."

"Water would cool us off," said Sam.

"Well," Jedediah said, "this heat would be terrible even if we had enough to eat and drink. Under these circumstances, you boys are heroes."

Sam laughed out loud. The last thing he felt like was a hero. Closer to a moron.

Coy yipped. Sam stopped laughing and frowned at the pup. *You better not be mocking me.*

The four gazed at each other, and thought each other ridiculous-looking. All day long the sun whacked their faces and hands, raising blisters. The temperature, they knew, was well over a hundred degrees.

"It makes me yearn," Evans mused, "for the cool earth of a country churchyard."

Death. Yes, cool and restful.

Jedediah's sudden thought was different. "The earth is cool." He pondered it. "Even a foot down," he said, his voice rising, "the sand is cooler. Let's bury ourselves in the sand. It will cool our bodies off."

Sam cackled.

"The linchpin word here," said Evans, "does seem to be 'bury.'"

But the captain was determined. He fetched the only shovel and started digging. "Just a little down, and it will be far different."

He pitched sand out of the hole vigorously. The man bristled with energy, thought Sam, and his capacity for work was endless. *He's the damn hero.*

Even a foot down, they could all see the sand was darker, more moist.

Before long Jedediah got the first hole deep enough. "Squat in it," he told Evans, the smallest.

The four studied each other. This was worth laughing about, or crying, they didn't know which.

Evans climbed into the hole. He squirmed around and got comfortable. "Not really half bad," he said.

Jedediah started pitching sand on top of him. Soon nothing of Evans showed but his arms, shoulders, and head. "By the breath of God himself," said Evans, "it's a miracle. All of you go ahead and do the same."

Gobel took the task of digging the second hole.

"Get in," he ordered Sam.

Sam didn't care whether he was in or out, but the temperature of the earth did feel good. *Mother Earth*, he thought, remembering that he was a Crow.

Gobel then dug a monster hole for himself and climbed in. His grin would have lit a dark cellar.

Jedediah dug the last hole and pulled the sand on himself with his hands. *Damned hero,* Sam thought again.

They laughed at themselves. A damned funny sight, four heads and four pairs of arms sticking out of sand that stretched for miles upon miles in every direction.

Sometimes Coy lay peacefully behind Sam. Sometimes he sniffed at Sam's arms, or Evans's or Smith's, as though to make sure they were still alive. He went nowhere near Gobel. The big man had cooed several apologies to the pup, but Coy didn't care.

As the earth cooled their overheated bodies, they gabbed. They spoke of nothing in particular. First Evans told of going with his father to catch a salmon each spring. The fish made their return to the fresh streams of Ireland every May, and the first one caught was pure joy. Gobel spoke of gardening for the first time. (Funny to think of the huge man tending small plants with delicate fingers.) Strawberries, he'd planted. He'd never tasted anything as good, even to this day, as the first strawberries he grew himself. Sam spoke of the Sunday afternoons when his father used to take him and brother Owen down to the river to swim. They had a good eddy that made a nice, deep hole. Dad tied a heavy rope to the branch of a thick tree, and the boys swung out over the water, bare skin shining, let go, and made a huge splash in the river.

From time to time Coy sniffed a hand or face and lay back down.

After a while, Jedediah observed, "Seems like our talk goes around two things, water and food." They all grinned at that. The grins faded as they thought of the country they were stranded in, without either food or water. And sitting up to their necks in sand wasn't going to fill their bellies or quench their thirst.

"Time to move on," said Jedediah.

That night he wrote in his journal,

After resting about an hour [covered with sand], we resumed our wearisome journey and traveled until 10 o'clock at night, when we laid down to take a little repose. . . .

A short time after sundown I saw several turtledoves, and as I did not recollect of ever having seen them more than two or three miles from water, I spent more than an hour looking for water, but it was in vain.

Our sleep was not repose, for tormented nature made us dream of things we had not, and for the want of which it then seemed possible, and even probable, that we might perish in the desert, unheard of and unpitied.

In those moments how trifling were all those things that hold such an absolute sway over the busy and the prosperous world. My dreams were not of gold or ambitious honors, but of my distant, quiet home, of murmuring brooks, of cooling cascades.

After a short rest we continued our march and traveled all night. The murmur of falling waters still sounded in our ears, and the apprehension that we might never live to hear that sound in reality weighed heavily upon us.

The next night, as they lay in their blankets, Sam Morgan could bear it no longer. Bear what? He didn't know. Being hungry all the time? Getting weaker and weaker? Dwindling to skin and bones? Feeling his throat ache, his tongue and lips cracked from the dry air?

Every night now he dreamed of banquets passing before his eyes—a Christmas goose cooked by his mother surrounded by potatoes and carrots from the root cellar, followed by pies hot from the oven. He woke to delusions of hearing—it felt like true hearing—the delightful sounds of running water, there in a land of dry lake beds.

Or was it something else? *The death I left in California.* Yes, he actually used the word "death" to himself. *The child I abandoned in California? The woman I will never touch again, whose eyes I will never gaze into?*

Lava boiled inside him, an anger huge and corrosive—it was a new, outlandish blast of feeling. The magma ran molten through his veins. It scourged his soul.

Yes, he said to himself in some terrible way. *Yes*, in the face of the unknowable. *Yes*, in the face of a well-earned hell.

Suddenly he was furious. He sat up and peered into the darkness. *All right, death, who are you?*

No answer.

Where are you? The words sounded savage in his mind.

The answer came sweet and seductive—*My spirit lies in Meadowlark's grave.*

He used the name of his beloved freely now. He had nothing left to protect. He lay back down.

Meadowlark is dead, he said in his mind.

Meadowlark is dead.

The lava that boiled up was a kind of courage.

"Meadowlark is dead," he said out loud.

His voice quavered, so he said it again, more firmly. "Meadowlark is dead.

"There is no hope.

"I have no hope.

"I am dead.

"I have no hope."

Over and over he repeated these words, loudly and softly, sometimes with a stinging lash, sometimes with a seductive drawl, often with a stony flatness. Sometimes for the word "hope" he substituted the name of his daughter, which in Spanish meant "hope." "I have no Esperanza."

He fell into a trance of repetition. Time evaporated, and the heavenly bodies ceased to move. He twisted in his blankets. "Meadowlark is dead. I have no hope. I abandoned Esperanza. I am dead."

A torturous sleep mercifully took him away. He pitched all night, and murmured incoherently. Among the words were "Esperanza, me, dead . . ."

When he woke up, the world was fully light. His companions were on their feet. Sam was angry.

What should he do now? His friends stood ready to go, to live. He looked at them, they at him. He stood up, took Paladin's reins, and trod along behind Jedediah.

Hell, why not?

The dead man walks on.

THE MORNING OF June 25 dawned brilliant and desolate. They moved out before the sun topped the eastern line of hills and tramped steadily, mindlessly on. Within an hour the heat was more oppressive than the previous day's. On they trudged. No one spoke—even Evans's merry wit was stilled.

The landscape close before them was either sagebrush flats or salt wastes. Far in front gleamed the ridges and the lofty summit of the mountain, a cool, snowy height they would never reach.

Four men stumbled toward it. Sam wondered exactly where, around what rocky spur, beneath what sagebrush, he would die.

He wondered what Coy would do when his human brother was gone. Would he find a mate among the beasts? Would he always miss his human companion?

Sam looked at Paladin and his heart poinged. Out here, some while after Sam and the other men died, she would simply drop. The coyotes and buzzards would reduce her to a skeleton, and the winds would dry even that.

About midmorning Evans collapsed.

With no idea why, Sam fell down beside him. *Maybe this is it. Probably this is it.*

Evans's face was very flushed, his skin hot and dry. No question he couldn't get up. Diah and Gobel slid Evans into shade. Sam crawled over and joined them.

"You're overheated. We're going to bury you in sand," the captain told Evans.

Gobel did the digging this time.

Sam dropped into the darkness inside himself. *Maybe I could get up.* He looked around at the desert. *If I did, I might walk another half mile, a mile at the most.*

He gazed at the foot of the mountain. Several miles away, it might as well have been on the far shore of an ocean.

This is the time. This place is as good as any.

Evans slid into his sandy hole. His face was empty, spiritless.

The captain looked questioningly at Sam.

"Bury me too," said Sam.

Without a question, Jedediah dug the hole.

Sam crawled in.

Shovel by shovel, now, the end of his life fell on him, the weight of his misdeeds and his stupidity.

He drifted away—where didn't matter. When he came back, he had an additional thought. *Amazing how good the cool sand feels.* Then, *My grave welcomes me.*

It was done. Sam and Evans were buried to their armpits.

Sam looked into the face of the Irishman who would be his companion in crossing the big river. He gave Evans a weird grin. *I'm glad death is a chuckle.*

Diah knelt between the two of them. "Gobel and I will walk on to the mountain. If we find water, I'll bring some back to you."

If. Diah, that if, it's as far as ever a far can be . . .

The four men rested their eyes on each other. Since they were men, they didn't speak of love.

"Leave my rifle close at hand," said Sam. Diah was doing that anyway. Sam wanted the Celt with him, his lasting bond with his father.

Sam reached out and patted Coy. "Bring Paladin to me," he said.

Diah did. Sam nuzzled her nose. They traded breath.

"Promise me you'll never kill her," said Sam.

"I won't," said Jedediah. "For any reason."

They both knew better.

Sam smiled. His possible sack was at hand, Evans's next to him. Their pistols and rifles were within reach. *We wouldn't want to go undefended against Indians, would we?*

Sam thought that was a hoot. *Dying is a hoot.*

Sam faced another way while Jedediah and Gobel trundled off. He looked any other direction.

A splash of shade kept the sun off. It was big enough for a few hours, until midafternoon, when the sun circled well to the west. Sam hoped his spirit would be somewhere else then. He didn't want to get slapped by the sun even one more time. The air was calm, the desert quiet. *A perfect place.*

Sam reached into his possible sack and got out his pipe. Sacred pipe, Hannibal said he should call it. He gently laid it on its wrapping of deer hide, pipe and bowl separate. If he joined the pipe and bowl, the pipe would be a living being, an object of power.

"You gonna smoke and say words to the directions?" asked Evans. Nothing the Irishman ever said sounded quite serious.

"Later, maybe," said Sam. He hadn't smoked the pipe since . . . *The pipe has failed me.*

"Then how about a little conversation to ease the way?"

Sam was cooling off, feeling better. *That won't last long, not weakened by near starvation and deprived utterly of water.* Sam knew the stories of how thirsting men died. Unlike starving men, who went out meekly, thirsting men screamed their way out, raving lunatics.

But it's not the thirst, Diah said, it's the heat.

Fear pinged him. *Death, come, and come quickly.*

"Conversation?" repeated Evans.

"Maybe later."

Sam felt of his medicine bag, which lay on the sand in front of him. He opened it up and got out his two pieces of guidance, the buffalo fur and the piece of paper with Hannibal's words. Picking up one piece with each hand, he let his mind drift, he didn't know where. He remembered the night Hannibal said those words, and

Sam lit out for the West. He remembered Christmas dinner that day, when the woman he thought was his announced her betrothal to his older brother. He remembered the day before, when he and that woman became lovers, first lovers.

"You know," said Evans suddenly, maybe a long time later, "I didn't expect it to come this way. I thought I'd get me brains scrambled with a chair broke over me head, or an Injun arrow through the lights. I never thought on easing out slow. But this way of dying, it feels not half bad. I'm cool, I'm restful, I'm not hurting. I have a good friend. And we're buried up to our necks. Damn near our necks. Two grown men, sitting in the sand, just their heads sticking out, having a bit of a talk. Isn't that a tickle?"

Sam smiled in spite of himself. "Evans, you're two bricks shy of a hodful."

They looked at each other, three-quarters buried.

"What if some Indians were to come along right now?" asked Evans.

"We could wave at them," said Sam.

They cackled.

"Bad luck, we've left our scalps exposed!" said Evans.

They hooted and whooped until tears ran down their cheeks.

They fell silent and sat, conscious of being entombed. From time to time they rotated their heads this way and that. Sam noticed that, though the shade was sliding eastward, they wouldn't be in the sun for a long time yet. He craned his head back and inspected the high sky. At that moment it was perfect, blue from east to west and north to south, without a hint of cloud, or even a dark bird to mar it.

"This business of dying," said Sam, "is slow and tedious."

When Evans didn't answer, Sam got the two pieces of guidance out of the bag again. He rubbed the fur between his fingers. *Sorry,* he thought, *but I am quitting.*

He opened the piece of paper and looked at the words. Though he couldn't read, he knew these words by heart.

"What does it say?" asked Evans.

"My friend Hannibal McKye gave me this advice on the night I ran away from home and started west. 'Everything worthwhile is crazy, and everyone on the planet who's not following his wild-hair, middle-of-the-night notions should lay down his burden, right now, in the middle of the row he's hoeing, and follow the direction his wild hair points.'"

They both contemplated the thought in silence.

"Those are wondrous and eloquent words," said Evans. He thumped his chest, what little of it was showing. "Look where they brought us."

They laughed loud enough to make the needles of the cedar shake.

"You did get good things out of it, though."

Sam nodded. "Adventures galore. My Crow name, Joins with Buffalo. Coy and Paladin. And a great woman."

"A great woman," Evans echoed.

"And a daughter."

"You know," said Evans, "words, they're not strong enough to speak the big truths, are they? It takes music, don't it?"

"Yes," Sam said, "it takes music."

The men looked at each other, dying, content.

"Let's make a song of your life, why don't we?" said Evans.

That sounded to Sam like the strangest idea he'd ever heard. It was exactly what he wanted to do.

They started with some ideas for the chorus.

"What's the main idea?" said Evans. "Follow your wild hair?"

"Yes."

"We'll start with that. 'Friend' . . . 'bend.' Yes. And who was this Sam Morgan, the hero of our song?"

"A trapper. A beaver man."

"And an explorer," said Evans.

"To the sea. We explored all the way to the sea."

Evans hummed a tune, a big one with a sort of grandeur, but

with some bounce in a 6/8 rhythm, not taking itself a bit seriously. Then he made it work with the first line, and raced through the second line.

Sam pitched in, repeating the tune of the first line with new words for a third line, and reached a climax with line four.

"Good," said Evans, "good. But it needs something." Evans pondered. "A half line at the end, spoken—that's always a good trick. 'That buffalo man.'"

In a few minutes they had a chorus:

> *Sam Morgan, a woodsman, a trapper was he*
> *Explored from the Rockies clear out to the sea*
> *His strength was a secret, the word of a friend*
> *He followed his wild hair all the way 'round the bend*
> *(spoken) That buffalo man.*

Now they began to rig the verses. They had nothing to distract or interrupt them, and it was fun, so the song came together in no time at all.

They both got their tin whistles out of their possible sacks. Evans sang the words, Sam piping along in unison. Every once in a while they tossed in a purely instrumental verse, Evans harmonizing above Sam's melody.

THE SONG OF THE BUFFALO MAN
> *The fire, it got started he didn't know where*
> *It woke him, he smelled it and then spied its glare*
> *It lit up the night like a dawn in the west*
> *He knew right away, 'twas his bitterest test.*

(chorus)
> *Sam Morgan, a woodsman, a trapper was he*
> *Explored from the Rockies clear out to the sea*
> *His strength was a secret, the word of a friend*

He followed his wild hair all the way 'round the bend
That buffalo man.

The flames raged downwind, the animals fled
Sam's pulse it ran wild, but he kept a cool head
A small coyote pup, it was yipping and yelling—
The pup led the way to the buffalo's belly.

That buffalo cow, Sam shot her at noon
He gutted her out and left her to cool
Now her gut was a cave or hell's hottest pit
As the two crawled inside, the fire it did hit.

(chorus)

The trees 'round the camp exploded to torches
Limbs fell, trunks popped, even rock walls got scorch-ed
Hid deep in the belly of the buffalo cow
Sam prayed for a miracle—death, miss us for now.

The miracle found them, there in the dark
The buffalo cave was Sam Morgan's ark
He stepped out alive, the pup by his side
The world gray and ashen—only two hadn't died.

(chorus)

But Sam wasn't free from the pup or the cow
The pup wanted friendship, the buffalo a vow
In dream she did come—I saved you from death
Now you join my blood, melt into my breath.

The muscles, the fiber, the belly, the loins
The trapper and beast were miracle-joined.

Sam breathed through her nostrils, he saw through her eyes
Both melted, both merged, one heartbeat, one I.

(chorus)

Now they gave him a name, those people called Crow
They saluted him with it, 'twas Joins Buffalo
The wisdom it carried, if you follow that hair
You're one with the grasses, the waters, the air.

Sam Morgan, a woodsman, a trapper was he
He explored from the Rockies clear out to the sea
His strength was a secret, the word of a friend
He followed his wild hair all the way 'round the bend
That buffalo man.

Evans whistled out the last couple of bars of melody, and the song was done. He burst into applause. "That was the world premiere!" he cried.

Sam clapped as loud as he could. "To an audience of millions," he said. "Millions of grains of sand."

"Let's take a bow," said Evans.

They looked over the sands with the hauteur of true artists and, buried to the shoulders, gravely inclined their heads.

"Encore!" called Evans. "They want an encore."

"Give us a jig," Sam said. He got his tin whistle out of the possible sack.

"A jig it is."

Evans launched into some song Sam didn't know, taking it daredevil fast.

He and Evans both bobbed their heads to the music, and their arms. Sam could feel his heart speed up and his blood rush. Even his legs, far down in the earth, tried to dance along, jiggling against the sands. *Yes,* he thought, *in their own way they are danc-*

ing. My feet are nimble, and my toes are twinkling. I dance as I die!

That was how Jedediah Smith found them, piping and grinning, joyously playing the fool.

Nineteen

Holy Water

"THEY DRANK EVERY bit and cussed me that I didn't have more!" Smith told Gobel with a laugh, "and then cussed me again that there was meat in it—why wasn't it all water!"

Sam slid his head back under the liquid surface. He came up and looked at his friends. He couldn't imagine ever being happier than he felt right now.

"Do you know how much those kettles held?" Jedediah went on. "Four quarts each! And they complained!"

"We had just discovered the pleasure of acting like madmen," said Evans, "and were loath to give it up."

"No danger," said Gobel.

"Holy water, it was. I dare say we liked it ever more than Flat Dog liked the priest's." Evans dipped his horn into the creek and poured the sacred fluid down his gullet.

Eyes met across the small stream. Each man felt how good life was, how good comradeship was.

It was a fine little camp in some trees at the base of the unreachable mountain, with a pool big enough to sit in and some grass for the mounts.

While Jedediah went back to Sam and Evans, Gobel had killed another horse. Now he put more wood on the low fire while Jedediah sliced the meat and laid it on the racks high above the coals.

Sam climbed from the pool and stretched out on the grass naked. He might want to roll back in at any moment.

He looked around. "I almost went to hell, and this feels near to heaven," said Sam. "Why don't we just stay here forever?"

Jedediah looked seriously at Sam. "I thought you wanted to die."

Sam looked into himself, and then looked some more. Finally he said, "I can't explain it, but right now things are different. I'm different."

Jedediah nodded, accepting.

" 'Twas the saving grace of music changed his mind," said Evans.

"Maybe so," said Sam. He had no need to think about it. His heart was light.

"Or of foolery."

They let it go.

THAT NIGHT IN his blankets Sam realized he was different in another way. When Jedediah Smith showed up with those two kettles of water, he felt a freshet of emotion that astonished him. He looked into the man's face. It was weary. It had seen and suffered more than it should. Behind the eyes lived ideas Sam didn't share, and a hardness that put him off. But right now bubbled up a well-spring of emotion, and he knew what it was. Love.

Yes, he loved Jedediah Smith. Not as a comrade or brother—Diah made too much distance for that—but like a father.

Love, a reality, a blessing, a truth, a challenge.

THE NEXT DAY they needed to move on.

"We still don't know where the hell we are," said Gobel. He'd held back from last night's spirit of elation.

"We don't," agreed Jedediah.

"Diah and I could be buried to our necks by this afternoon," warned the blacksmith.

"We don't know where we'll find water," Smith confirmed.

Though Gobel seemed determined to keep them down, spirits were up. Sam and Evans felt like they could whip a pack of wildcats, or leap from the beaches of the Pacific to the summits of the Rockies.

The four marched north, along the west side of the snowcapped mountain that had saved their lives. The earth now was dust as much as sand, and it puffed up into their eyes at every step. Several times during the day they passed springs, but all were too alkaline to drink from. And then they saw in the distance a solitary Indian lodge.

These Indians didn't run. The father walked right out with his son and made introductions in the Shoshone language, which Diah spoke a little. Beak and Rockchuck, their names were.

Sam thought he saw strange gleams in their eyes and wondered what was funny.

"Will you come to our lodge?" said Beak. "Eat? Drink?"

This was beyond belief. Instead of shielding his women, this Indian was leading the strangers right to them. Sam thought, *What's up with you?*

All walked slowly toward the lodge.

When they sat, a woman and a girl of nine or ten came out. They offered the white men water in gourd dippers. Sweet, no alkali—Sam had never tasted anything better. Then in different dippers the wife and daughter brought meat in broth. The stew was lukewarm, and Sam thought it had been thinned with water just now, the way people do for the sick.

"You have no weapons?" asked Beak.

Sam and Diah looked at each other. "He means bows and arrows," said Sam. "He doesn't get it that we have rifles in our hands."

"These Indians have never seen white men," said Diah, in a tone of surprise.

The captain invited Beak to look closely at his rifle, to examine the hammer, flint, fire hole, and triggers. Soon he got to the crucial part, explaining how the rifle fired.

While Diah taught, Sam glanced at his friends, trying not to be obvious, and began to catch on.

Diah told Beak the flint made a spark, the powder burned, and the rifle made a huge bang. When it did, you could kill a deer standing a hundred steps away.

Beak nodded with the tolerance of a mature adult for a child or a madman. Sam could see it in his face. How, exactly, is a bang going to kill a deer?

Sam thought it was too bad the captain couldn't fire it and prove his point. They didn't have powder and lead to waste.

Sam spoke up. "Diah, it won't work."

"I know," said the captain, and went back to thanking their hosts for the wonderful food and drink.

Sam watched the mother and girl eyeing the whites and trying not to giggle. Now he was sure.

"Cap'n, they feel sorry for us."

This stopped conversation. Indians living poor in this miserable desert feeling sorry for white men?

"They do. Look at us. All four of us are near indecent. Some of our skin is pink, some of it's white, and our clothes are tattered and stained with alkali. We're wearing the salt wastes we've walked across.

"All in all, we're crazy, they're sure of that, because we were dumb enough to walk across those places, and do it without any bows and arrows to get even a bite to eat. We don't have hardly enough skin to stretch over our bones, and we look starved as something that died last winter and been shriveling ever since. We've worn out our horses worse than ourselves."

Jedediah coughed, but Sam started laughing and kept talking.

"We're pathetic. We're out of our minds. Indians are considerate of those who are tetched." Now Sam emphasized each word separately. "They think."

All four white men laughed. This was a first. The rueful thing was, it made sense.

THE NEXT DAY Captain Smith and his ghost crew tramped ten more miles north through a valley of alkali dust and alkali springs, and came finally to the north end of the mountain that had given them the saving grace of water. That evening, after men and animals drank liquid that was barely tolerable, the four eagerly climbed the ridge to the east and there, in Jedediah's words:

> I saw an expanse of water extending far to the north and east. The Salt Lake, a joyful sight, was spread before us. "Is it possible," said the companions of my sufferings, "that we are so near the end of our troubles?"
>
> For myself I durst scarcely believe that it was the Big Salt Lake that I saw. It was indeed a most cheering view, for although we were some distance from the depot, yet we knew we would soon be in a country where we would find game and water, which were to us objects of the greatest impor-

tance and those which would contribute more than any others to our comfort and happiness.

Those who may chance to read this at a distance from the scene may perhaps be surprised that the sight of this lake surrounded by a wilderness of more than two thousand miles diameter excited in me these feelings known to the traveler, who, after long and perilous journeying, comes again in view of his home. But so it was with me, for I had traveled so much in the vicinity of the Salt Lake that it had become my home of the wilderness.

Energized, they turned east the next morning, parallel to the south shore of the lake, and walked twenty-five miles. After passing several salt springs, they found sweet water to camp next to.

The next day, twenty more miles east, and now—hell to heaven and back again—they got nearly inundated in what they had sought so desperately, water.

This was the river that ran from Utah Lake into the Salt Lake, and it was in June flood stage. This stream divided the hostile deserts from the mountains that the men knew well and loved, mountains that would be full of deer and elk and busting out with creeks. But they couldn't figure out how to get across it.

They waded through cane and rushes toward the main channel, which was out of sight. Even this far from the river, or what was normally the river, the water was almost waist deep. Already weakened, Paladin seemed to hate fighting through the rushes, but Sam kept her on a tight lead.

When they got to it, the river was a disheartening sight—sixty yards wide, turbulent, and swift.

They decided to build a raft of the cane. The few belongings they had, weapons, powder horns, and possible sacks, needed a ride. They made a few bundles, lashed them into one big unit, and were ready.

"We have to take the horses over first," said Jedediah.

Sam and Diah looked at each other. Evans and Gobel didn't swim worth a damn. From the company's six horses and two mules they'd started with, they were down to one horse, one mule, and Paladin.

"I'll lead two," said Diah. "Let's go."

Like most hard jobs, it was best done without thinking.

PALADIN WAS A pain in the ass. She pulled back hard. Evans and Gobel shoved her from behind and got her off her feet and swimming.

Right off Sam got slammed by the current. He had never felt anything like it. It pummeled him, it rocked him, it turned him half upside down. He had no idea how he could swim it, and he sure as hell didn't see how he could keep hold of Paladin.

He wrapped the lead three times around his left hand, turned onto his side, where he thought he'd have the most stamina, and kicked like the devil for the far side.

It was like being in a barrel rolling downhill. You didn't know what was going to whack you or what direction you were going to bounce. A lot of the whacks came up the rope from Paladin, who was downstream of Sam and fighting the lead like hell.

Sam didn't think they would make it. *Not both of us anyway.*

He thought of letting go of the lead. Maybe they'd both have a better chance if they weren't tugging on each other.

He held on even tighter and swam harder. *We live or die together.*

The river charged into Sam's mouth and up his nostrils. His spirits dipped. Before long his arms were so weak they flailed, limp. He put his mind in his legs, which had some strength left, and told them to kick like never before.

Sometimes his head was buried in water. He kept swimming. When air came, he snatched it. He swam and swam and swam— until he realized Paladin was walking.

He stood up, and fell over.

Paladin charged for higher ground. Sam let the lead go and followed her. Even crotch-deep water felt good. After fifty yards they were onto dry land.

"I'm going back for the raft," said Diah.

Sam flopped onto the ground. *How does Diah do it?*

A tongue lapped his ear.

Coy! Sam had left Coy in Evans's arms, but the pup had gotten loose and made the swim.

Sam laughed. Diah disappeared into the rushes. Sam was too tired to move.

SAM DREAMED, MAYBE. Or maybe not. In seconds, it seemed, he heard an awful thrashing. The captain was fighting the river.

Sam ran through the thigh-deep water.

The raft had drifted about fifty yards downstream. Evans and Gobel pushed from behind. Jedediah swam in front, the rope in his mouth and, Sam saw, around his neck.

Sam dived flat and swam for the captain.

Halfway there he had to laugh at himself. Hell, his arms and legs could barely make it.

He floated up to Jedediah and grabbed the rope with both hands.

Jedediah let go with his teeth, wound his neck out of the rope, and grabbed with his hands. In only a dozen strokes they could stand up again.

Jedediah muttered and mumbled. Sam listened for a cuss word but didn't hear any.

"Get the horses," the captain told Sam.

That meant the single company horse that was left and the company mule. Sam splashed them through the rushes to the raft, and Jedediah, Sam, Gobel, and Evans hitched their belongings onto their mounts, except for their rifles, which they carried themselves. Sam was glad to have The Celt back in his hand.

Now, though, the horses were mired. They'd sunk almost to their bellies in the mud and couldn't get out. No amount of tugging would budge them.

The four men waded to dry land, leaving the animals. They made a little fire, gnawed on the dried horse meat, which was almost gone, and went to sleep.

Overnight the river dropped. The horses were only knee-deep now, and desperate to get the hell onto land. Rested, the men heaved them out. Then they had to spend nearly half a day drying out their possibles.

All four were impatient. They were no more than four days, they figured, from rendezvous. More urgent, soon someone would get a shot at an animal, and they would have fresh meat.

Just before they camped that night, Diah shot at a bear, wounded him, but did not kill him. Across the fire they ate the last of their horse meat. They sat in moody silence and barely exchanged a word, because each man wanted only to complain, and complaining made things worse.

The next morning Diah went alone ahead of the party and got a shot at a buck. Jedediah saw the deer stagger, but it ran off, back toward the party.

Jedediah followed on the run. Seeing lots of blood, he told the men to wait. Sam came to help.

The blood led to a thicket, and there lay the buck.

Jedediah walked around and grabbed him by the antlers.

The buck jumped up and wrenched free of Jedediah's grip. Sam dived for its hind legs. The buck ran off.

This time Sam did hear cuss words, and added plenty of his own.

They followed the blood, Coy trailing, and soon found the buck again.

Jedediah pounced on him and cut his ham strings.

"A fat, good-looking buck," said Sam.

They built a fire on the spot and roasted meat.

Jedediah wrote later:

We then employed ourselves most pleasantly in eating for about two hours and for the time being forgot that we were not the happiest people in the world, or at least thought but of our feast. It was eaten with a relish unknown to a palace.

So much do we make our estimation of happiness by a contract with our situation that we were as much pleased and as well satisfied with our fat venison on the bank of the Salt Lake as we would have been in the possession of all the luxuries and enjoyments of civilized life in other circumstances.

These things may perhaps appear trifling to most readers, but let any one of them travel over the same plain as I did, and they will consider the killing of a buck a great achievement, and certainly a very useful one.

The next afternoon they fell in with a band of Shoshones on the way to rendezvous, and camped with them that night.

The day after that, which the captain said was the third of July, they walked into the big camp their fellow travelers had made on the shores of Bear Lake. They took their time coming down that last hill, still leading their horses. Sam felt like they were making a parade.

Bill Sublette was the first man to come running toward them.

"Diah," he yelled. "Diah!"

He turned and hollered back to the camp.

"They're alive! Captain Smith is alive!"

The travelers got flooded with friends at the edge of camp. One man after another clapped them on the back, until Sam thought he would fall down.

No one asked yet, *Where's the others? You started with two dozen.* Or, *Where's the plews?*

Jedediah saw on every man's face, though, what the fear was. "The men are alive," he said.

Men. Alive. Sam felt that split in his heart again, the one that would never heal.

"Time for that story later," Diah went on.

They could see in the faces of their friends how woebegone they looked. Evans and Sam looked at each other and laughed. *We made it.*

"The news is better than we look," said Diah.

"We gave you up for dead," Sublette told the captain, looking happily into his eyes.

Dead. That split again. Sam would have to tell his story, and he didn't see how he could.

"Before anything else," said Sublette, "you look like you got about a month's worth of eating to do."

David Jackson had an idea. A small cannon had been brought out from St. Louis to rendezvous this year. All the men in camp stood at attention, and Jackson had it fired, as a salute.

They stumbled toward food, water, friends, campfires.

Rest, probably for all of July, thought Sam. *Water, a whole lake full of it. Food, all I can eat. Grass, all Paladin wants. Rest. Talk. Friends. Comradeship.*

Sam was happy.

He hobbled Paladin near the edge of the lake on some good grass. As he stood back up, a familiar voice said, "Yes, you are a hero."

Sam whirled.

Hannibal McKye.

Sam bear-hugged him.

Part Five

RENDEZVOUS

Twenty
Friendship

"I'm in Sublette's camp," said Hannibal. "Let's get you settled." He did a double take on Sam's face. "Your face isn't so pretty now that you broke your nose," he said, "but it's more interesting."

Four big camps spread out along the lakeshore, Utahs on one end, Shoshones on the other, and in the middle the trappers—David Jackson's outfit and Bill Sublette's, a big caravan of horses, mules, and men, many of them new to the mountains.

The camps were chaos. Tipis, tents, brush huts, cook fires,

sweat lodges, maybe a couple of hundred trappers (who were white Americans, black Americans, Mexicans, Indians, French-Canadian half bloods, Irishmen, Englishmen, Frenchmen . . .), and maybe twice that many Utahs and Shoshones.

Here and there along the lakeshore, in separate bands, grazed over a thousand horses and mules.

Hannibal led Sam, Coy, and Paladin through these camps as though through a series of alleys.

"Here," he said at last, "this is our place."

Sam saw the horse flesh first. Hobbled and rope-corraled on good grass among some cottonwoods was Ellie, the fine grulla stallion Hannibal rode. Her name was short for elephant, a reminder of circus days. He had another horse too, a good-looking black mare. "I'll show her off for you later," said Hannibal. They put Paladin in with the other mounts and hobbled her.

Sam's friend had built a fine brush hut, of the supple limbs of willows and other trees. It gave Sam a pang. He hadn't seen Hannibal since the rendezvous of 1825, when Sam went off to steal the horses that might get him a wife. He looked abruptly into his friend's eyes.

"I wasn't assuming you failed to win Meadowlark," Hannibal said gently, "just making room in case."

Sam said nothing. The story was far worse than "failed to win."

He threw his blanket down and stretched out, just for a trial. He hadn't had a shelter over his head since he left California. It seemed good. The leaves were fragrant and the shade delicious. If rain came up—what a glorious thought, rain!—they could throw a couple of blankets on top and stay dry.

Sam peered toward the westering sun through the back of the brush hut, but the leaves nearly filtered it out. "You can't imagine how good green looks," said Sam.

Hannibal crawled in, sat with legs crossed, lit up his white clay pipe, and handed it to Sam.

"Two years' doings to tell," said Hannibal with a big grin. "Get started."

Sam's throat swelled. He felt like he couldn't talk. He took a long draw on the pipe and sent the smoke up to Father Sky. He decided what to say, but the first time he tried the words wouldn't come out.

Finally he squeaked, "Let's just smoke."

SAM MET HANNIBAL McKye on the pivot-point day of his life. On Christmas Eve, 1822, he made love to a woman for the first time, the family's neighboring teenager, Katherine. The next day, at Christmas dinner and in front of both families, she announced her betrothal to his older brother, Owen.

Sam reeled out of that house, berserk with confusion, grief, anger—and ran into Hannibal. They took supper at a campfire on the riverbank, just the two of them. Across that fire Sam told his sad story to this man, an Indian and a near stranger.

Hannibal was the most unusual man Sam had ever met. He was the son of a Dartmouth professor of classics and a Delaware woman who had come to Dartmouth as a student. Hannibal had been raised speaking both English and Delaware; reading English, Latin, and Greek; and reading with equal ease the sign deer and bear left in the woods. He left home early—bored, he said—and joined the first American circus, which was then in Philadelphia. There he became a circus rider, performing tricks on the backs of liberty horses, mounts trained to respond to signals of voice and hand. On the night they met Sam didn't know a smidgeon of that, and didn't care.

The man-boy Sam spoke of was abandoned by Katherine, and was scorned for years by his own brother. He spoke of his love of wild places, his desire to wander where the world still felt like Eden. He spoke of his yearning to go west, to go to the Rocky Mountains. But all that, the boy-man admitted, was crazy.

Hannibal responded with the words Sam now carried in his medicine pouch. "Everything worthwhile is crazy, and everyone on the planet who's not following his wild-hair, middle-of-the-night notions should lay down his burden, right now, in the middle of the row he's hoeing, and follow the direction his wild hair points."

Sam went west that night, and everything he had become, as a human being, came from following that wild hair. *Everything good,* he thought, *and everything bad. Everything.*

Now Sam looked at his friend across an aching gulf. In 1825 at the rendezvous on Henry's Fork, above the Siskadee . . .

His memories were pictures. Hannibal trained Paladin and Sam in their first circus riders' tricks, though Paladin was little more than a filly. Sam left rendezvous to steal horses to win Meadowlark. Instead, he got Blue Medicine Horse killed, his best friend and her brother. He gave a sun dance—he could hardly believe it yet—and in that sacrifice he saw something. He won Meadowlark, lost her, and got her again, forever. Now she was lost forever.

The memories of her, which washed over him now as warm waves fizz up a sand beach, these came in sensations, touches, breaths. If his mind resisted remembering, his fingers, mouth, eyes, the flesh of his chest—these recalled all too intimately. For a moment she was there with him, living inside him, breathing with him.

The two friends sat together for a long while like that. Hannibal refilled the pipe more than once. They drew on it and breathed out. The smoke wafted around them, real but insubstantial, like Sam's memories. Finally, after more time than he could count, Sam said, "Later I'll be able to talk. Later. Let's go sit with the others."

THESE OTHERS WERE friends, many of them.

A handclasp from Tom Fitzpatrick, the Irishman who made the same walk down the Platte River Sam did, seven hundred starving miles, arriving just a few days later. Tom was busy clerking right now, signing plews in and supplies out.

"It's good to see your scalp on your head." This drawled from James Clyman. No evening Sam remembered with this Virginian was finer than the one when James spun Sam the story of Romeo and Juliet, written by one Shakespeare, and reworded to a mountain man's understanding.

A quick rassle from Jim Beckwourth, the big mulatto, and a promise to share some whiskey later. Beckwourth also rolled around for a moment with Coy. Beckwourth knew Coy well—the pup pranced and yipped softly.

"How you, coon?" from Jim Bridger. After being looked down on after the Hugh Glass episode, Bridger had risen amazingly in everyone's estimation. The Blanket Chief, they called him now.

Hannibal and Sam wandered through the camp, greeting man after man, sitting a bit here, taking a swig there, and yonder settling in to listen to a story.

Dan Potts, a trapper Sam seemed to see only at rendezvous, had a tale of unbelievable country. He told it over and over at this rendezvous, and wrote it down and sent it back to civilization with the baggage train, where it got printed in a Philadelphia newspaper that fall. It seemed that, as a member of Bill Sublette's outfit, he had seen an amazing lake:

On the south border of the lake is a number of hot and boiling springs, some of water and others of most beautiful fine clay, resembling a mush pot, and throwing particles to the immense height of from twenty to thirty feet. The clay is of a white, and of a pink color, and the water appears fathomless, as it appears to be entirely hollow underneath. There is also a number of places where pure sulphur is sent forth in abundance.

Certainly his Philadelphia readers were only the first to disbelieve outlandish tales of sulphurous springs and geysers in the Yellowstone country. Potts went on,

One of our men visited one of these whilst taking his recreation—there at an instant the earth began a tremendous trembling, and he with difficulty made his escape when an explosion took place resembling that of thunder. During our stay in that quarter I heard it every day.

The rest of Potts's story was how he made his way to the Yellowstone country through a beautiful hole, Jackson's Hole, they called it, and of being harassed by Blackfeet all the way up north and all the way back to the depot, the trappers' usual wintering place.

Sam and Hannibal wandered on from fire to fire, taking meat and whiskey sociably, and listening to the tales of a year's doings. Every trapper had a story, and many of them were spine-tingling or funny or beautiful or amazing.

Sam's favorite story of that evening was told by Black Harris, a veteran trapper Sam knew only by reputation, a very considerable reputation for desperate adventures and an inclination to tell them even bigger than they were. This one sounded like it had some fact about it, and was vouched for by Bill Sublette. Sam gnawed on hump ribs as he listened, and gave the bones to Coy, who was greedy.

In camp this past winter, according to Harris, as January 1 approached, Sublette began to talk of walking to St. Louis. It seemed that the company's contract with General Ashley required the general to bring another year's supplies to the mountains, but only if a messenger appeared in St. Louis no later than March 1. Since St. Louis was about fifteen hundred miles from the valley of the Great Salt Lake, it was time to get going.

He asked Black Harris to go with him.

"This child thought on it, fifteen hundred miles, just the two of us with thousands of Indians betwixt here and there, on foot, in winter weather. It was a hellacious idea, so naturally this beaver says, 'Let's give it a go.' "

Harris looked a likely enough candidate to Sam. He was lean as moccasin soles, with a face of leather and whip cord. Sam judged him to be violent in his feelings, whether the feelings were celestial or devilish.

"We started on snowshoes, with a pack dog to carry our possibles."

Coy squealed, perhaps in protest of canine slavery.

"In our possible sacks we stuffed all the dried buffler meat we could carry, which was enough to stagger hosses, and we was only men.

"Over to the valley of the Siskadee we saw no sign of buffler. Saw plenty of sign of Blackfeet, howsomever, and it made this child uncomfortable—made his scalp itch, for a truth. Hightailed it on up South Pass—you know how ice-bit that place is, of a winter. Had to melt snow for water all the way."

Sam had nearly frozen to death on South Pass with Sublette and Clyman in the winter of 1824, when they couldn't keep a fire going. A nice contrast to dying in the desert, he thought.

Harris rolled on. "The Sweetwater, she was a sweet sight, and for a while we could carry them snowshoes. On the east side of the Rockies, the clouds shed a plenty of snow, but the winds sweep it right up and blow it on to the Missoura.

"Just more'n two weeks it took for us to get to Independence Rock and the Platte River. Some un you hosses knows them plains, and hungry ones they are."

The plains of the Platte River were Coy's birthplace. It was among Sam's ambitions never to walk down them again. The first time he did that, he fainted from starvation, and was lucky to be found by Hannibal.

"Now and again we seed buffler at a long distance, and we got an antelope now and then, but it was starvin' times. Worse, and you uns might not know this, was the snowdrifts. On them plains the snow piles so deep you can get lost in it. If'n a hoss ain't careful, he comes out'n the drift headed back the way he headed in.

"Also, them plains don't have hardly no wood. Some nights we had to walk straight on through to keep from freezin' to death.

"Now along about Ash Hollow we come on Pawnee sign. Them Injuns, a coon as would trust 'em don't know what way the stick floats. We swerved away from the river and didn't swerve back for three days.

"Some'at further 'long we come on Omaha sign. Now them is good redskins, and we was starvin' sure—we walked right into their camp. Trouble was, they was half starvin' too, and couldn't trade us meat. They did let us have one buffler tongue—Sublette, he had to give 'em his butchering knife for it—and we wolfed it down right in front of them. We was downright impolite.

"On we walked, getting slower every day. Even slower than us was that damn dog. It was gaunted up wors'n us, and weaker. It dragged fu'ther and fu'ther behind."

Sam scratched Coy's head sympathetically.

"One night we made camp in some elm trees. Bill rolled up in his blankets right off. I took time to get some branches and build a little fire. That dog was still out there in the night somewhere, straggling along.

"Finally in it comes, looks so pitiful . . ." Harris shook his head, remembering.

"That was too much for this coon. I says, 'Bill, let's make meat of that damn dog.'

"Sublette, he wouldn't hear of it. Over and over he said no and dozed off again. But I kept after him until finally he give in."

Coy yowled.

"I grabbed the ax and clubbed the dog in the head. Damned if the old thing didn't get back up, though. I uz so weak from starvin' I could hardly swing a second time, and when I did, I missed.

"One more blow—this had to be it. Wagh! What happens, but the blade flies off the ax handle, and the dog flies into the darkness, howling like a maniac."

Coy perked up his head and quivered.

"I yelled at Sublette to help me, and finally we found the dog in the dark, whimpering. Bill, he holds it, and I sticks my butchering knife in, clear to the handle.

"Back to camp we went, and I threw the dog right onto the flames. Singe it, I'm thinking. But that damned old dog, it gives a big shake—don't know whether it was alive or dead—and pops right out of the fire.

"Old Bill, he could stand no more. He grabbed the ax and bashed its skull in."

Coy's expression now was pure disdain.

"I stayed up and cooked her and et her, being keerful to leave Bill some. In the morning he et a little, but he didn't seem none too happy about it. His taste don't run to dog.

"Now we left the Platte angling toward the Kaw, you know the cutoff. Two days we tramped along. We was getting as weak as we was before, and the snow gave under our weight, making the going hard. We managed to shoot a rabbit, though, and that got us along till we come on the trail of a Kaw village. That trail they'd scraped, it was a big help, the snow was tramped down good. Afore long we shot four turkeys and guzzled that meat down, damn near et the feathers with it.

"It was on the Old Vermilion we finally come to the Kaw village, and they fed us. This hoss had twisted his ankle bad and couldn't walk and wanted to rest, but Bill says we have to be in St. Louie real quick, so he trades his pistol for a horse for this coon to ride.

"It was March 4 when we got to St. Louie. Three days late, but a purt'n good job, says this 'un. And food, why you could get eatin's anywhere, just for coins. Shinin' times. This child don't take to no cities, but a place with food set on tables anytime you want . . ."

THE NEXT MORNING Hannibal proposed they work with the horses. Sam knew his friend was backing off and giving him time. Where was Meadowlark? Where were Blue Medicine Horse, Flat Dog, and Gideon? Where was the brigade?

Everyone knew by now that Captain Smith had left the brigade in California and was headed back to get them. But that left out all the parts of the story that were Sam's to tell.

Working with the horses, in Hannibal's way of speaking, meant building that forty-two-foot ring and training both mounts and men. They worked with Paladin first.

Sam put her through her paces proudly. She responded nicely to his hand signals, trotting around the ring each way and then changing to a canter, rearing, and standing still. He got her to repeat all those exercises to whistles. Finally, he mounted, stood on her back, and rode her around the ring at both a walk and a canter.

When he jumped down, Sam was exhilarated. Horse and rider had been perfect.

"You made good use of the two years, for sure," said Hannibal.

They watered Paladin and washed her down and put her back in the rope corral.

The work with Ellie was for Sam's training, not the horse's. Ellie could do anything, as far as Sam could figure. He'd seen Hannibal do forward somersaults from his hindquarter and back to his hindquarter as Ellie circled the ring. He'd never imagined people did such stunts with horses. Or without.

"Let's try something new," said Hannibal, and switched to the black mare, which was named Virginia.

He vaulted to a handstand on her back. Immediately, she started walking, and at his cluck went to a canter. Sam could hardly believe what he was seeing.

Now Hannibal began to turn slowly 'round and 'round on Virginia's back as she ran.

Sam broke into applause.

Hannibal dropped to the ground. "Now you," he said.

"Oh, no," said Sam. He had decided he'd never be able to do somersaults from a horse's back, and handstands were in the same category.

Hannibal put an arm around his shoulder and cajoled him to Virginia's side. "Did you ever do handstands?"

Sam nodded. He and his brother Coy had done them as kids.

"No different," said Hannibal, "except your hands aren't side to side, they're one behind the other." He demonstrated.

Somehow Hannibal got Sam onto Virginia's back, and into handstand position while being held. In no more than ten minutes the horse was walking around the ring while Sam stood on his hands on her back.

Half scared, half elated, he pushed up and off and took the long drop to the ground.

"In a couple of days you'll be doing it at a canter," said Hannibal, "and in a couple more you'll be doing it on Paladin."

Sam made a face. The maturing man wanted to say no, but the ten-year-old brother of Coy Morgan said yes.

S AM SPENT THAT evening doing what, in his eyes, rendezvous was all about. He sat by a campfire and listened to the doings of his friends, and some men he didn't know, over the last year or two. A jug of whiskey circulated. A French-Canadian was making boudins for everyone, and no man knew better eating.

The Frenchy had several feet of well-washed buffalo gut laid out on a hide. This section of entrails had a soft, lacy fat on the outside. Next to the gut was a pile of chopped meat. The cook would roll a handful of the meat in dried seasonings. (Sam didn't know what all the seasonings were, but he could see wild onion and could smell sage.) Then the Frenchy would stuff the meat into the gut, turning it inside out, so that the lacy fat would melt into the chopped flesh as it cooked. When he had a serving of boudin ready, he would hand it to any man around the fire, and that fellow would broil it on a stick.

Sam could think of no better way to regain the weight the desert had stripped from his body.

No man would let Coy have this food—it was too good. But the pup fed on small pieces of chopped meat the cook dropped.

Sam knew three of his companions around this fire better than well—Tom Fitzpatrick, one very smart Irishman; James Clyman, the droll and savvy Virginian, and Jim Beckwourth, the black full of bravado. These were Ashley men, trappers Sam had fought beside, had frozen or starved with, had known shining times with.

Mixed in with them close to the fire, cross-legged and broiling sticks in hand, were Antoine, the French-Canadian cook, two of his fellow mixed-bloods, and Antonio, a Spaniard up from Taos. (True, Mexico had broken free of Spain, but to the trappers Mexicans were still Spaniards.) Sam smiled inside at two men having the same name in different languages. Standing behind these eight men, stepping to and from the fire for boudins, were four or five Delawares, tribesmen who were always seen in clusters. Hannibal stood among them, talking quietly in his mother's language, which he otherwise had little opportunity to speak.

Sam had heard the story of this tribe from Hannibal, a tale of loss that had made them into a kind of ghost band. Once they were a numerous vigorous people known as the Leni-Lenape. They lived in what was now the state of Delaware and parts of surrounding states. A couple of generations ago, the Iroquois had decided to stomp them into the ground, and did. (The Iroquois were like that, explained Hannibal, lording it over everybody and always hunting for a fight, just like the Blackfeet.) So thoroughly did the Iroquois humiliate the Delaware that they granted peace by laying down the biggest insult anyone could think of—"From now on, you are not allowed to call yourselves men."

That weakened the tribe, and the incursion of white people finished the job. Parcel by parcel the Leni-Lenape got pushed out of Delaware and their corners of New York, New Jersey, and Pennsylvania. William Penn's son swindled them out of a big piece of Pennsylvania land in a treaty known as the Walking Purchase. Forced to wander westward in search of a patch of earth to live on, the Leni-Lenape found themselves split into small, ragtag groups trying to hold on in Ohio and points west, land the Shawnees held and the whites were already encroaching on.

At length the Delawares parceled themselves out until they

were no longer one people. They existed in bands of large families, no more, usually attached to another, larger tribe.

But in the last few years something remarkable had happened. Small bands of Leni-Lenape men had joined the fur trappers on the plains and in the mountains. No one knew why—maybe because of the adventure, or because they had something to prove. At any rate, they had earned their way to full membership in the roster of fur men, and were fully trusted. A Delaware, the trappers knew, would fight anywhere and anytime, with a courage that left you drop-mouthed. Any brigade in the mountains was more than glad to have a bunch of Delawares join them.

What struck Sam as funniest about that evening, as they devoured boudins and whiskey around the campfire, was the talk. The native languages among these men were English, Spanish, French, Cree, Ojibwa, and Delaware. The conversation, mainly, was in the single language they had in common, English.

However, since those raised with another language spoke primitive English, and the English speakers had picked up a little French or Spanish and bits of Indian tongues along the way, Hannibal labeled the language of the fireside conversation Mishmash. Sam was tickled that it sounded like an Indian name.

Antoine, for instance, grew up speaking French and Cree at home, married into the Blackfeet tribe, and now had a mate from Taos. The man sometimes studded one English sentence with words of four other languages.

Likewise the white Americans didn't think of words like "plew," "boudins," and "malpais" as foreign—to these backwoodsmen those were just commonplace words.

In another few years, Hannibal had told Sam, no trapper of the Rocky Mountain beaver would be able to go home and be easily understood, no matter where he came from.

Lots of the talk was news about the places they'd been.

"Where Lewis's Fork heads up there's plews a-plenty, and the prettiest country you ever did see."

"That Jackson's Hole is a skeery place, mountains on all four sides and too many Blackfeet around. Best way to *vamos* is the Gros Ventre River, straight east from the hole."

"Damned river's even named for Blackfeet."

"Old Jacques, he got bit by a rabid wolf and went under."

Sam gave Coy a pat. If there were rabid wolves around, he'd have to keep the pup close and make sure he didn't get bitten.

"Them Crows, you think you can trust 'em but you can't."

Sam threw a sharp look at this speaker, a coon he didn't know.

"We was hardly out'n their village, two or mebbe three nights, and them damn young bucks run ever' one of our horses off. Patrick, he had to talk hard at Rotten Belly to get 'em back, and make a lot of presents besides."

"This beaver wintered at Taos and means to do the same next winter."

Sam took note that more and more men were free trappers. Though they might travel with a brigade, they were independent and made their own decisions, including wintering in warmer weather.

One piece of news was big. Clyman said to Sam, "You know we paddled all the way around the Salt Lake?"

"What?"

"Circumnavigated it, as they say." Clyman savored that first word on his tongue, because he could read and write and knew such words and amused himself by dropping them here.

"Well?"

The mountain men had wondered since its discovery where the outlet of the Salt Lake was. Despite considerable marching around, they hadn't found it. Lots of them supposed the river that came out of the Salt Lake would provide the good route to California. In two crossings of those deserts, Sam hadn't found anything close to a good route.

"Diah, come here."

The captain was just a few steps away talking to Evans, and they both came quick.

Clyman looked at his old friend the captain. "Me and Black

Harris and Vasquez and Fraeb, we paddled all the way around the Salt Lake."

"And?"

"No outlet. Rivers flow into the lake, but none flows out."

The men held smoke in their lungs and looked at each other. Such a lake was hardly heard of.

"Why don't she overflow?" This came from a Delaware.

Diah could guess that one. "Evaporates. In the desert the heat just lifts the water up into the air. Or it sinks into the sands."

Sam and all of Diah's men had seen that out in the Mojave Desert.

Thus died the last glimmer of a dream.

Clyman gave a wry grin. "That Buenaventura was one pretty piece of imagining."

"We'd already puzzled that much out," said Diah.

Still, it was a blow.

"There's something else about the lake," said Clyman.

Everyone looked at him.

"You all know where this river goes into Salt Lake, and that big river comes in from Utah Lake in the southeast. But on the west side there are no rivers at all, nor creeks, nor fresh water of any kind. We damn near died out there."

Sam looked at Evans, and they both laughed. No one had come nearer to thirsting to death than they did, buried in sand up to their necks. But that story would hold for another night or two.

The most ominous campfire tale that night was a tale of a big battle with the Blackfeet. It took place just a week ago and only five miles north along the lakeshore, where the Shoshones were camped on the way to rendezvous.

One man after another took up the story. The Blackfeet happened on a Shoshone man and his squaw and killed them.

The Shoshones sounded the alarm—rifle fire and hoofbeats.

The Utes, camped not far away, heard the ruckus and came running. Some trappers who happened to be in the camp rode with them.

"When I got there," Beckwourth said, "them Blackfeet was taken up against the mountain in some trees, a thick grove. Not a war party—squaws, kids, everything. The women was piling up whatever they could for breastworks. The ground all the way around was open, so it was hard to get at 'em."

"Them Utes and Snakes, though," said a man Sam didn't know, "they was hot to fight." Snakes was the common trapper name for the Shoshone.

"I was next to old Bill Sublette," said Jim, "and he was hot too. We crept up within pistol range, and we made them come. An arrow ain't a flea compared to flying lead, or I don't know what way the stick floats."

Now Sublette walked up.

"This man," said Jim, nodding at Sublette, "run up on 'em to close range and shot two, one with pistol, one with rifle. Arrows flew all around him, but he come back untouched, like he had some big medicine. Cap'n Bill has got the hair of the bear in him."

Sublette grinned. "We gave them Blackfeet a licking."

Silence. Someone said, "So how'd it come out?"

"They had cover and we didn't," said Jim. "We shot at each other until it got dark. During the night they slipped away."

"Casualties?" asked Jedediah.

"One trapper wounded," said Sublette, "though I believe a couple of others thought they were about to go under. Three Snakes killed and three wounded. No Utahs killed at all."

"And you should have seen them fight," said Jim.

"What about the Blackfeet?" asked Diah.

"We found six bodies, and they carried off a good many others," said Sublette. "Not bad, when you consider who had the cover."

Sam was thinking, when Beckwourth's an old man, he'll recollect taking a hundred scalps that day.

*   *   *

WHEN SAM AND Hannibal stretched out in their blankets, Coy on the earth between them, Sam found that his tongue was loosened by whiskey, or his feelings were rattled, or something. He started with Gideon.

"I had to cut Gideon's leg off," he blurted out. He didn't know why he started here.

Hannibal turned on his side and gave Sam that look he had, all his attention on you. The fire, down to coals, pulsed out a yellow glow.

"He came to help when I got into trouble. Blackfeet were chasing me. He got a little wound, an arrow in the foot. It turned black and went bad. He thought about letting it carry him over, but . . ."

Sam told how he had taken the leg off at the knee, with many sharp knives, the help of Clyman, and great dread. Told how Gideon afterward wanted to die and dived into gloominess. How he finally got a better attitude when Flat Dog and Beckwourth made him a peg leg. There was more to the story, but there were also more stories to tell.

"And I got Blue Medicine Horse killed." Sam related how they ran off a whole Sioux village's horses, himself, Blue Horse, Flat Dog, and Gideon. How, during their getaway, they rode smack into another Sioux band. How he saw an arrow go into Blue Horse's chest and the tip stick out the other side. "Meadowlark's brother, and it's me that got him killed."

He told, too, briefly, underplaying it, how he escaped the torture of those same Sioux and got back to Meadowlark's village. "That hair ornament you gave me saved my life."

With some wonder he told how he gave a sun dance and got strength from it, and went against the Sioux with just Flat Dog and avenged Blue Horse's death.

How Meadowlark's parents wouldn't let them marry, but they ran off together.

How her relatives stole her back.

How she left her village and rode into the last rendezvous with her brother and made herself Sam's wife.

Then, for a long while, he couldn't speak.

He could still feel Hannibal's attention, open, piercing.

"She died in California," Sam said.

Then he shot out of his blankets and walked away. He couldn't be in that spot, couldn't breathe the air where those words hung. He walked down to the shore of the lake, Coy trailing. He didn't think anything, especially not words. He looked at the waters, and watched the half-moon rise, its face jostled by the waves.

Finally, Sam went back to the brush hut and laid down. Hannibal was asleep. As Sam was going to the same place, a thought came to him: *What did I forget to tell?*

He'd said nothing of his misery in the desert, and how he let himself be buried nearly to the neck, and waited for death. Nor anything of how water came like manna and saved him.

But something else . . .

His last conscious thought was, *Esperanza. Oh, my God, I forgot Esperanza.*

Twenty-one
A Battle

THE NEXT MORNING, and every morning during the rendezvous, they worked with Ellie, Virginia, and Paladin. Hannibal said that it wasn't quite fair, what they were asking of the animals. Normally, liberty horses were trained to respond to signals without a rider, and different mounts trained to lope while a rider did what Hannibal called acrobat routines on their backs.

"Since we don't have a stable of talented horses, though . . ."

They worked on the liberty part first, training Paladin to do more tricks to signals of hand and voice.

Hannibal said that these tricks were actually useful. His business, when he was working, was trading with the Indians who lived near the Missouri. The unusual part of it was that he traveled alone, always, and somehow over a decade of trading had befriended all the tribes of the area. Sam didn't know another man who could ride the entire lower Missouri country alone in safety.

While they worked, Hannibal told the story of the first time he'd ever run into the Pawnees. They were far east of their usual country, and Hannibal stumbled onto them. While they were considering what to do with him, he said he would show them his powerful medicine with horses.

The Indians stood in a circle and Hannibal put Ellie through his paces. The Pawnees gasped in awe. Hannibal made a deal with them. If they would trade with him, he would spend half a moon teaching a few young men his medicine, and would come back the next summer and do it again.

He'd been welcome in Pawnee camps ever since.

After an hour or so of liberty work, they switched to what Sam thought of as stunt riding. He was catching on to that handstand. The bare back of the horse was slick, and the balance was tricky, but he could get in the air on his hands and stay for a while.

Hannibal spoke, Paladin moved, and Sam slammed into the dust on his face.

Paladin cantered nicely around the ring, and reversed direction when instructed. Hannibal was laughing.

Sam glared at him.

"That's what we work on tomorrow," said Hannibal. "Doing it on a moving horse."

COY LED SAM and Hannibal through the ring of men. The coyote always liked to sit and listen to music and watch the dancers.

Fiddlin' Red was perched on a low boulder, tuning up. He

would twist a peg, play a couple of notes, twist a peg, scrape out a fragment of a tune, and twist a peg again.

In a big, open space several trappers had paired up with other men and stood, waiting to start dancing. Shoshone and Utah women mingled with the crowd, and when asked, they would swing into the dance arena for a couple of tunes and then slip away with their partners for another kind of sport.

Just then Robert Evans burst through the circle, leading Silas Gobel by the arm. Sam grinned, supposing they were going to make a mismatched dancing pair. But why were both naked to the waist?

"Hear ye, hear ye!" cried Evans. "Hold the music!"

Fiddlin' Red scraped out a phrase.

"I say, *hold* the music!"

Out in the middle, still holding Gobel's arm, Evans turned the two of them around and around to show themselves to the crowd. Gobel made two of Evans. "Silas Gobel and I," Evans called, "have agreed to provide for this splendid audience a fine demonstration of the refined art of fisticuffs."

The crowd laughed.

"Brawling, you might better call it," shouted Evans.

One man cackled loudly.

Evans advanced upon him. "Laugh if you will, young man, but let me warn you, never bet against an Irishman in a brawl."

More people cackled.

Evans backed up to Gobel. As he walked, he weaved a little. Sam recognized that gait—Evans had been applying himself to the whiskey, or vice versa. And Gobel had stayed drunk since he got to rendezvous.

"The contest is best two out of three falls. If a man is knocked down, 'tis one fall, and one more to his doom."

"Keep your eyes sharp," roared Gobel, "I'll throw the little bastard in less time than it takes to blink."

"Who will volunteer to referee our fine exhibition?" asked Evans. "Who?"

Tom Fitzpatrick stepped forward. "I will," he said quietly.

"They're both stewed," said Hannibal, "and Gobel is mad."

"All the worse for Evans."

Hannibal shrugged.

"Now," cried Evans, circling the crowd, "I will not wager on meself. It is not fitting. My code is that a man should fight for the beauty of the thing, and not take advantage of his own prowess."

A nearby trapper fell down laughing.

Plenty of men in the crowd took the hint, giving and taking odds. Near Sam and Hannibal two men reached a quick agreement, an entire twist of tobacco against a pipeful. The man who put a pipeful on Evans did it jauntily, like it was too little to matter.

After Evans and Gobel had huddled with Fitzpatrick, Evans announced, "We have agreed upon certain rules. No weapons, no eye-gouging. All else goes. Best two out of three falls."

Now Gobel appealed to the crowd. "Let every man know that I ain't huntin' for this fight. The runt here done goaded me into it."

Sam hadn't seen Gobel drunk enough to issue that many words all in a row before.

Gobel swaggered a few steps, leapt into the air, spun around, landed facing backward, and let out a huge roar.

"He's agile," said Hannibal.

"He's a warrior," said Sam. "I'm scared for Evans."

"Howsomever," continued Gobel, "I promise to go easy on Runt and return him to his friends in such condition that he can be put back together."

"Bravo!" cried Evans. "A generous spirit."

Then, with a sudden darkening of tone, he said, "Ready, Mr. Gobel?"

Silas nodded. Gobel took an ape position, letting his arms swing, looking for an opening.

Evans charged.

A couple of steps away from Gobel, who looked bewildered, Evans launched himself into the air feet first. He kicked both feet into Gobel's chest, as hard as a horse kicks.

Evans fell on his back in the dust.

Gobel rocked only one step backward. Then the big man laughed, looked down at Evans. "The first fall is mine!" he shouted.

Evans gathered himself up and backed away.

"It must be you, Gobel, that throws him down," said Fitzpatrick, "not himself. No fall."

Gobel grumbled.

Now the two men circled. Evans did an exaggerated ape hunch, mocking Gobel. A few men laughed.

The brawlers sidestepped almost halfway around the circle. "Get to it," someone yelled.

Gobel let out an enormous roar and charged, head down.

At the last instant Evans threw himself onto the ground sideways and shot his feet toward Gobel's legs.

One foot jammed between the knees. Gobel tripped and plunged forward. He hit the ground on his great belly and bounced.

The crowd roared with laughter.

Tom Fitzpatrick stepped up and stood between the fighters. When the crowd had quieted and both men were on their feet, Fitz declared, "First fall to Robert Evans."

Cheers and boos from the crowd.

"He's on the ground too," complained Gobel.

"But you didn't put him there," said Fitzpatrick. "First round to Evans."

Again in his ape hunch Gobel started stalking Evans. Evans backed away, but Gobel followed until Evans was up against the crowd. They circled.

Gobel's charge came so fast Sam didn't see the start. He came head down, bawling out a war cry.

Evans dodged to the side, but Gobel just as nimbly changed direction.

On Evans's second hop Gobel caught his calf and jerked it ferociously into the air.

Evans whumped to the ground and lay there gasping for breath.

Fitzpatrick stepped between the two. Otherwise, Sam thought, Gobel might have flopped full weight on Evans and pummeled him.

"Second fall," Fitzpatrick called, "to blacksmith Gobel."

"They're both athletes," said Hannibal.

"If Gobel gets his hands on him," said Sam, "it's over."

As the brawlers began to circle once more, the murmur of the crowd grew agitated, boiling.

Circling, circling, circling.

Evans jumped onto the boulder where Fiddlin' Red was sitting. Red leapt into the crowd.

Gobel approached suspiciously, arms out like a lobster.

Evans feinted a kick at Gobel's head.

Gobel nearly caught the foot with a hand.

Gobel crept closer, still circling.

Sam thought, *What the hell does Evans think he can do from the top of that boulder?*

Gobel lunged and got both of Evans's ankles in his fierce grip.

Evans launched himself forward in a somersault down the big man's back. His legs bent Gobel's arms back severely until Evans tore loose, landing on his feet.

The crowd gasped.

"Nothing either way," called Fitzpatrick.

"The smarter man will win," said Hannibal.

When Gobel got past astonishment, he ran at Evans bellowing. He sounded like a thousand barbaric Scots charging.

Evans ran. Ran all the way around the circle, tantalizing Gobel by staying just ahead. Finally Evans jumped back up onto the boulder.

Gobel approached warily this time, a look of cunning on his face. He crept closer.

Evans feinted with a foot.

Gobel jerked back, then resumed his position, arms open and ready. Sam thought he was about to dive at Evans's legs.

Evans hurled himself at Gobel headfirst.

His skull bashed Gobel square in the face.

Blood gushed from the big man's nose.

Evans landed on his feet, staggered forward, and kept his balance.

Gobel wobbled. He let go of Evans. His eyes rolled back in his head.

With one delicate finger Evans pushed him over.

Gobel shook the earth when he hit.

Pandemonium!

The crowd cheered. Men slapped each other's backs until some fell down. The Utah and Shoshone women trilled their tongues for the winner. The losers, paying off, were almost as happy as the winners.

Fitzpatrick held up Evans's hand. Fiddlin' Red sounded out a victory call.

"Evans can have his choice of squaws tonight," said Hannibal. "Maybe we'd best check on Gobel."

"Yeah, I got my nose broke, so I know how to fix one."

As they bent over the fallen man, they were still chuckling.

LIKE EVERY OTHER trapper, Sam had to do some trading. This time Hannibal had no trade goods. Sublette had insisted, in return for giving him an escort from St. Louis to rendezvous, that Hannibal sell Sublette his trade goods and work for wages. Hannibal thought that deal was fair enough, for the moment.

Since he could read and write, Fitzpatrick was running the trade blanket. He checked the company ledger. Sam's wages had been paid by Jedediah in California, but he had some credit for the plews he'd trapped. Even though they were all back on the other side of Mount Joseph, Jedediah had listed them as received by the company. Sam started picking up things he needed.

Clyman walked up and studied the list of prices that Fitz had posted. He read it out loud to Sam, and both men twisted their mouths. Prices were a lot higher than they'd been at the first rendezvous two years ago.

A comparison of items sold at both rendezvous:

1827	1825
powder $2.50 per lb.	$2.00 per lb.
lead $1.50 per lb.	$1.00 per lb.
coffee $2.00	$1.50
beads $5.00	$5.00
pepper $5.00	$1.75
blankets (three-point) $15.00	$9.00
scarlet cloth, $10.00	$6.00
blue cloth, $10.00	$6.00
ribbon, per yard, $0.75	$0.50

"A beaver's not gonna get rich on beaver," said Clyman in his soft Virginia drawl.

"Fitz, why's everything so high?"

"The company isn't making anything on the beaver. Only profit at all is selling the trade goods."

Fitz didn't yet know the total value of the fur brought in. It would be nearly $23,000.

Sam had picked out a bunch of merchandise. Powder and lead were essential. A fellow needed tobacco as gifts for any Indians he came on, and beads and cloth and ribbon to trade. Coffee felt essential. Sam looked at what he had and raised a questioning eyebrow at Fitzpatrick.

"Don't worry," said Fitz, "Diah said to carry you on credit."

Credit? Hell, he'd just started buying, and he was already in the hole? Well, Sam supposed credit was a good thing.

When he was finished, he was in debt to Smith, Jackson & Sublette for $12.15. It didn't seem too bad. If the brigade had gotten a fall hunt, he would have done better than break even.

Sam was keeping some coin to buy whiskey at this rendezvous. Not that he felt all that riotous.

Clyman bought surprisingly little. Well, he'd said a coon couldn't get rich on beaver. Looked like he'd been right.

Trading done for the moment, they sat down next to Fitz. "What's the news?" asked Sam. "Where's everybody trapping this year?"

"Diah is going back to California," Fitz said, "has to, and from what I hear, you need to go with him."

Sam nodded.

"Sublette is going way north to the Nez Perces, Flatheads, and Blackfeet."

"Blackfeet?"

Fitz nodded. "Strange. They sent a man to Jackson's camp about a month ago, asked us to come trade with them."

"I wish Sublette good luck," said Sam.

"Jackson will trap the Uintys. Good beaver country."

Clyman said, "That's where I'd go."

"Where are you gonna go, James?"

"Back to the States. I've had enough."

Sam looked at his friend with surprise. Clyman just shrugged.

"What about you, Fitz?"

"I'll be Sublette's clerk."

"Who's going with you?"

"Bridger, Beckwourth, Harris. We're taking top men."

"Watch your hair."

"You watch yours in California."

EVANS ASKED SAM to join him and Fiddlin' Red playing music later that evening.

Sam did an aw-shucks act, "I'm not good enough."

"Lad," said Evans, "I have in mind something special."

They spent the afternoon working it out.

Sam ate with Hannibal, Evans, Clyman, Fitz, and Beckwourth, as usual, thinking about his strange life with these friends. In a couple of weeks he would go to California, Hannibal and Evans to

wherever they pleased—neither had told Sam their intentions—
Fitz and Beckwourth to Blackfeet country, and Clyman back to the
U.S. Maybe they'd see each other this time next year, maybe not.

"It's time," said Evans.

Sam was nervous.

Evenings were long on Bear Lake. Because of the mountain
on the west, twilight came early. Now, only a couple of weeks
past the summer solstice, dark came late. Whiskey flowed freely,
the men were woman-hungry, and they danced from dusk to
dawn.

Fiddlin' Red customarily started the dancing off with a Virginia reel, which he insisted was an ancient Irish dance called the
rinnce fadha (sounded like ring-kuh fah-duh). As he fiddled out
the first go-round and called the turns, half a dozen partners faced
each other, one line of men and one of women. (Some Indian
women were now practiced enough to follow along.)

"Forward and back," Red called, "honor your partner."

One couple at a time did what Red called.

When it came his turn to jump in on the melody, Sam didn't
know if his fingers would find the right notes.

"Forward and turn with the right hand 'round," called Red.

Now Sam fingered silently along with Red, trying to hear the
tones.

"Forward again with the left hand 'round."

Sam thought maybe he was finding some right notes.

"Do-si-do."

So progressed the evening in a spirit of fun. Within an hour
Sam was having a grand time, proposing and playing tunes he
knew and following along on those he didn't.

Fiddlin' Red introduced a very old Irish tune called "Bridget
O'Malley," calling it "a sad tale of lost love." It began,

Oh, Bridget O'Malley you left me heart shaken
With a hopeless desolation, I'll have you to know

It's the wonders of admiration, your quiet face has taken
And your beauty will haunt me, wherever I go.

Evans declared, "It's time, Sam. It's time. Now."

Sam nodded.

"Ladies and gentleman," called Evans, "we have a special song tonight, one made up by Sam and meself and some of our companions who now languish far away across the mountains and deserts, in California. The hero of our song is one of our companions, for 'tis called"—he lifted his voice now—" 'The Never-Ending Song of Jedediah Smith.' "

A general huzzah went up. Men clapped Diah on the back. The poor captain looked sheepish.

Sam sang and Evans piped. Sam's main virtue as a singer was being loud enough to make the words understood.

THE NEVER-ENDING SONG OF JEDEDIAH SMITH
We set out from Salt Lake, not knowing the track
Whites, Spanyards and Injuns, and even a black
Our captain was Diah, a man of great vision
Our dream Californy, and beaver our mission.

(chorus)
Captain Smith was a wayfarin' man
A wanderin' man was he
He led us 'cross the desert sands
And on to the sweet blue sea.

Red had caught onto the tune and joined in vigorously, giving it a new bounce.

Now Sam told in music of the red-rock desert, which was so dry (one of his favorite lines) they got to drink mud. He mentioned eating fleas, then told how the brigade got lost, and Diah looked in the Good Book for a map.

Every few verses they came around to the chorus naturally, and all sang together—

Captain Smith was a wayfarin' man
A wanderin' man was he
He led us 'cross the desert sands
And on to the sweet blue sea.

Now Sam sang of the getting to Californy, and how the Spaniards threw a big jamboree for them. The captain, however, proved too moral ever to lift a skirt. This brought lots of laughter and more claps on Diah's back.

The only trouble was, Sam sang, the brigade couldn't get home. There were mountains chock-full of snow in the way, and beyond the mountains the driest desert any man ever saw.

That brought Sam to the verses they'd written only this afternoon. He hoped desperately that he could remember all the words.

Diah, he stared at the mountains and snow
How to get over, I think I may know
A few men I'll take, and hay for the mounts
We'll fight and we'll claw and come through when it counts.

His words gave no hint of the desert beyond
The fierce sun, the hot winds—mirages, not ponds
They wandered but found only dry watercourses
And finally, half starved, they ate up their horses.

Singer, piper, and fiddler now pitched into the chorus. Sam was hugely relieved at remembering the words so far.

One terrible noon, a man fell to his knees
No more, he cried, just leave me—please

They shoveled the sand clear up to his chin
We'll be back, they promised, don't never give in.

After three stumbling miles, they came to a spring
They drank deep, they splashed—oh, water was king
Diah took back a kettle, good as his word
They knew then they'd make it—Die? That's absurd.

Captain Smith was a wayfarin' man
A wanderin' man was he
He led us 'cross the desert sands
And on to the sweet blue sea.

They spied out the Salt Lake, and thought journey's end
Their hearts were for meat and whiskey and friends
When the camp saw them coming, they gave out a hoot
Got out the cannon and fired a salute.

So the story went 'round, from white men to red,
Jed Smith may be pious, but living or dead
He's a captain to ride with, a partner to side with
A leader with art, and a friend of big heart.

Captain Smith was a wayfarin' man
A wanderin' man was he
He led us 'cross the desert sands
And on to the sweet blue sea.

As the song swung to its final cadence, the audience yelled and applauded.

Evans held up his hands for quiet. "Don't you think it's finished yet. This song can ne'er be finished. As long as Jedediah Smith lives and leads, there will be more verses to sing his praises, and maybe to twit him a bit." Evans paused and then yelled, "Hurrah for the captain!"

Everyone hurrahed.

Jedediah actually grinned.

Late that night Sam went to the brush hut happy. Music made him happy. But loneliness, here in the blankets, made him miserable. He reflected that out of nearly two hundred men, probably the only ones without the comfort of a woman's love tonight were Jedediah Smith and himself.

Twenty-two

Laughing

HANNIBAL GUIDED HIS friend to a fire with lots of meat for the midday meal. Sam needed all the eating he could get. He didn't know how bad he looked, his fair skin piebald with sunburn and peeling, his body gaunt, and his eyes haunted. That was the worst of it, the eyes.

Hannibal wanted to help. That was simple, and it was his way. Not that he made gestures to save the world. No, to help those he came across and liked, that was challenge enough.

In Sam's case he felt responsible: "Follow your wild hair." Truth, but sometimes truth led to deep and searing pain.

Hannibal was patient. He knew that part of the grief, the blackness Sam brought back from California, kept him from speaking.

After gorging themselves, Hannibal suggested a dip—this was a blistering July day. They walked down to the lake, stripped off their clothes, and jumped in. They played a little, the usual tomfoolery, but then they sat on the sandy bottom, up to their chests in the cooling water, and looked around at the mountains and the sky. Hannibal liked skies like this, which you saw only in the West—a dome of perfect deep blue, unscratched by clouds, unblemished by even a slight variation in color from horizon to horizon.

Maybe it was the water, maybe the comradeship, maybe the glory of the sun-struck afternoon, but after a while Sam talked. Halting, true talk.

"Meadowlark died birthing our child."

Hannibal waited, openhearted.

As Sam told the whole story, Hannibal could tell he was keeping it as short as he could, striving to stay on an even keel. He heard how Meadowlark and everyone lost weight and got weakened on the crossing of the deserts, how Sam worried about her, because she should have been eating for two. How they recuperated at San Gabriel Mission. How she got swollen hands and feet as the baby's time approached, and her shortness of breath. How Sam took her to the mission at Monterey to get the best doctoring that could be found.

Then Hannibal heard the true words of darkness: convulsions, cesarean section, and finally the fatal childbed fever.

He knew them well. Hannibal was a man acquainted with death. As a young man he had struggled with cynicism and anger at the world. Now, knowing how full of pain the world was, he simply tried to live happily each day. It was a resolution notably difficult to keep, but he practiced resolutely.

Sam surprised him. "Esperanza, my daughter," he said, and fell silent.

A girl child, left in California. That's why Sam would be going back to California with Jedediah. Hannibal considered this. To his way of thinking, Jedediah Smith walked far from Hannibal's path—he filled life with duties and struggles. A man like Jedediah could never do well enough to be satisfied with himself, and would make others feel the same.

In a lurch of haunted words Sam went on with his story. It was water scrapes, starvation, and other troubles, bigger ones than even other mountain men had lived. What Hannibal was paying attention to, though, was the listlessness in the way Sam told it. When emotion did come through, it was self-castigation.

I am truly, truly sorry, my friend.

At the end of the story Hannibal studied his companion's face. Sam sat next to Hannibal, chest-deep in precious water, on a glorious summer day, yet his spirit was mired in a black swamp.

Hannibal understood, and could think of nothing to say.

"Why don't we swim across the lake and back?" It was a big lake.

"Why?" said Sam.

"Why not?" said Hannibal, with tease in his voice.

Afterward, as they slipped into their clothes, Sam seemed not as weighted down. Not until he spoke the next words: "I'll be going to get Esperanza."

Hannibal nodded. He wasn't much on have-to's, but Sam was right about this one.

They sat on the bank of the lake, turned around now, watching the sun slide behind the western mountain, saying little, and speaking idly when they did. Mostly they just soaked up the colors and the company. Hannibal thought, *These are the times that make life good.*

SAM FELT THE days dribbling away from him. The rendezvous was good. Right now everything else felt hard. The deserts between here and California. The thirsting and starving. Seeing Flat Dog, Julia, and Esperanza, and what they would remind him of.

Jedediah said the brigade would leave in a couple of days.

Sam told Hannibal how gloomy he felt about leaving. Hannibal said the solution was to play hard and learn to laugh again, really laugh.

This morning Sam was putting the finishing touches on another horseback trick, a cartwheel from his handstand on Paladin's back to standing up on her rump, then back to the handstand. It was fun. Work was fun, play was fun, anything that wasn't remembering was fun.

Soon Hannibal applauded. Sam had the cartwheel down.

"Now let me show you," Hannibal said, "what comes next."

He led Paladin out of the ring and Ellie in, then jumped onto his stallion's back in a sitting position. To his cluck Ellie started loping.

Up Hannibal went onto his handstand. Then, with astonishing ease, a somersault in the air onto Ellie's rump.

Over and over Hannibal flipped, grinning, playing.

At last he jumped down.

Sam was bedazzled. "God, I want to do that."

"You will, you will."

They watered the horses and splashed them off in the lake.

On the way back to their rope corral Sam said, "Why don't you come to California with our outfit?"

Hannibal walked a few steps musing. Finally, he said, "Sure. Why not? Sure."

A quick conversation with Jedediah and it was set. He was glad to have a man as reliable as Hannibal along. The brigade would be a dozen and a half men, and they'd leave day after tomorrow.

WHEN THEY WOKE up on their last full day of rendezvous, after a late night of music and dancing, Sam and Hannibal built a small fire, ate, drank strong coffee, and looked into the coals. The air was cool—mountain mornings were chill, even in July.

Hannibal could see something was on Sam's mind. He'd been mulling, quiet, all yesterday. Now it finally came out.

"All that reading you did, all those classics you learned . . . Anything there to help me . . . square up to death?"

Hannibal was taken by surprise. After a moment he thought it was a good surprise.

"Maybe." He reached to a pile of kindling and picked up a twig. He held it up to Sam and then tossed it on the fire.

"It was a twig. Now watch it become something else."

The twig burst into flame, then slowly subsided to coals and then to white, papery flakes. Sam watched the spurts of light, the pulses of darkness, the shift from wood to ash.

"It was a piece of wood. Fire changed it into something else, heat and light."

He sorted his thoughts. "You can see this in all the old religions. Fire creates and destroys. Everything in the world is being created and destroyed, all the time."

The expression on Sam's face hadn't improved much.

Hannibal tossed on another twig. "Look at it burn. This is what happens to every one of our days. We burn it up. By night it's gone, behind us for good. And the next day we burn another twenty-four hours.

"Here's the way of it. Life is change. Everything changes every day. You're somewhere else. You bend down for a last drink at night, a first drink in the morning, but the water in the creek isn't the same. What you drank from yesterday is way downstream. The wind is gone on, haunting someone else. The friend you rode with yesterday has taken another trail."

He sat waiting, looking straight at Sam. "You had a dad, and lost him. You had a best friend, Blue Medicine Horse, and he got killed. You got Meadowlark, lost her, got her back, lost her for good. Tomorrow you will gain, and lose, who knows what." He paused. "Never-ending, ever going on . . ."

He sighed. "If it matters, I don't think we go away for good.

Nothing goes away. Like the stick, we change. Into what? I don't know. Maybe energy."

He thought. "You can look at this one of two ways. You can grieve the loss of what you had yesterday. You can welcome what comes today."

He couldn't tell what effect this was having on Sam.

"Love it or hate it—that's your choice, pure choice.

"Me? I embrace it. I bear-hug it."

Hannibal waited a long time, sneaking an occasional sideways glance at Sam. "Any of this help?"

Sam didn't answer.

FOR TODAY THEY'D made two decisions: First, they would train all day, because tomorrow they'd be on the trail. Second, they'd see if Paladin would do her tricks to music.

"I've never been quite sure," said Hannibal, "whether the horse follows the musicians, the musicians follow the horse, or some of both."

First they did liberty work with Ellie. Sam piped a four-square tune, "Old Zip Coon." Hannibal gave the stallion hand signals, and the horse's hooves seemed to make drumbeats in time with the whistle.

"Actually," said Sam, "I think we're both following your hand signals."

"Now let's try Paladin doing it along with Ellie. Maybe the example will help."

It worked great. Sam whistled, Hannibal waved signals, sort of the way a band conductor would, and Paladin kept perfect time—forward four beats, stop on the fifth, backward three beats, prance to the side in rhythm, stop on the fifth beat, curvet in rhythm.

It felt like a miracle to Sam.

They worked and worked. Sam did his handstands, and before noon he managed to stay up for two full circles while Paladin cantered around the ring.

They were so happy they took a short lunch break.

After lunch they worked first with Coy. Now he was good at doing somersaults while Paladin walked. They signaled the horse to a lope. Coy had caught on to staying on during a lope, and even to sitting up. When he tried to somersault, though, he fell off every time.

After a while, Hannibal said, "Let's quit before he gets discouraged."

Toward the end of the afternoon Sam piped while Hannibal did somersaults on Ellie—bounce off the rump, spin in the air in a tuck, and land back on her rump when she was about a horse length forward.

The stunt amazed Sam. Hannibal did it exuberantly. They even began to draw a crowd. Robert Evans came up and started piping with Sam.

Hannibal somersaulted as if he were in a trance.

"Come on," said Evans. "You get up there, Sam. I'll pipe, and we'll get a regular circus going."

Sam ran for Paladin. He got her into the ring and in position behind Ellie.

"I'll give the signals," said Hannibal. It would have to be by voice.

Hannibal called out, Evans whistled the tune up to the sky, both horses started cantering in a circle, and both men launched into their tricks.

Hannibal bounced into the air, flipped, and came down with perfect grace. Sam rose to his handstands, cartwheeled back to the hindquarters, and jumped forward into another handstand.

'Round and around they went. Evans picked up the tempo, and the horses followed his rhythm. Faster and faster they cantered, 'round and 'round, faster and faster each man soared into the air, came back to his horse, and soared again into the air.

Sam was laughing from the center of his belly, rich and real.

Author's Note

THIS IS THE third novel in my Rendezvous series, which tells the grand story of the Rocky Mountain fur trade at its height, 1822–38.

All the novels follow closely the actual doings of the mountain men. The first volume, *So Wild a Dream,* told of the trappers in the employ of General Ashley in 1822–23, from their first land crossing to the Rockies to their return, in fragments, to Fort Atkinson. The second novel, *Beauty for Ashes,* mirrored the adventures of the same outfit in 1824–26, through the first two rendezvous. This book tracks the expedition led by Jedediah Smith to California in 1826–27.

The curious reader can find excellent historical accounts of this important journey, the first crossing of the continent to California. I recommend Dale Morgan's *Jedediah Smith and the Opening of the West* and *The Southwest Expedition of Jedediah Smith: His Personal Account of the Journey to California, 1826–1827,* edited by George R. Brooks.

These trappers endured great hardships, wandering through the deserts of the Southwest without knowing where their next water might be, or food, even without knowing where they were going, or why. Luckily, they left two journals that tell the story of the expedition almost day by day, in such detail that history buffs have been able to retrace the outfit's route through central and southern Utah, and across California's Mojave Desert on the way to the West Coast, then across the Sierra Nevada and the high deserts of Nevada and Utah on the way back to the Great Salt Lake.

These journals, written independently by brigade leader Jedediah Smith and his clerk Harrison Rogers, do more than give us a full picture of the details of daily living, even to where they camped. They voice eloquently the interior life of the young explorers, especially Smith's, their hopes and fears along the way.

Dancing with the Golden Bear is a personal story woven carefully around the hard framework of the brigade's adventure. I have stuck closely to the journeys in describing how the trappers traveled from Cache Valley through southern Utah and crossed the Mojave Desert to the pueblo called Los Angeles; how they spent weeks there, under threat of detention; how they trapped their way north along the Sierra Nevada, and how Jedediah Smith led a small party across the mountains and back to rendezvous. Even the episodes of being buried in sand are taken from Smith's journal.

Sam Morgan, his wife Meadowlark, her brother Flat Dog, Gideon Poor Boy, Grumble, Abby, and most of the Californios in this book are fictional characters. I hope that through them the reader can not only know what happened, but see, hear, taste, and feel it.

Smith, Robert Evans, Silas Gobel, John (the black slave who takes the name Sumner), and others are drawn from history. Though I have changed nothing about them that is known, I have filled out their characters and interior lives considerably.

My view of Smith has changed over the years and now departs from tradition, even from my own earlier account of him. Now I see complexities in his character (some will call them faults) that escaped me as a younger writer. Debate is welcome.

I've made one particular speculation: Smith said that his purpose in heading south and west from the Salt Lake was only to find new country for hunting beaver. I believe (as other writers have) that in fact what drove him was a half-acknowledged yearning to see new country, to venture ever into the unknown, simply for the joy of exploring. So in this novel I have supposed that he knew, when he set out, that he was bound for California.

My crucial job here, though, was to paint the picture of a crisis of the soul of Sam Morgan, the young hero of the Rendezvous series. In this book he matures by journeying through a great darkness and into light.

In telling this personal story, within the strict limits of what is known about the expedition of 1826–27, I've sought to put the flesh of living men on the bones of history.